CRIS MAZZA

Charlatan

NEW AND SELECTED STORIES

Edited by GINA FRANGELLO

Foreword by RICK MOODY

CURBSIDE SPLENDOR PUBLISHING

Published by Curbside Splendor Publishing, Inc., Chicago, Illinois in 2017.

First Edition
Copyright © 2017 by Cris Mazza
Library of Congress Control Number: 2017952300

ISBN 978-1-945883-06-4
Cover and author photo © Cris Mazza
Designed by Alban Fischer

Manufactured in the United States of America.

www.curbsidesplendor.com

PRAISE FOR CRIS MAZZA

"Mazza's newest work stands first and foremost as a supremely accomplished body of individual artistry. Again and again, what this collection showcases is Mazza's rarest of talents: the ability to leave judgment out of exploration, to create characters whose desires may enact violence (both emotional and physical) but whose existence is not an examination of how society "should" react to that violence... An impressive compendium of an important career—Mazza's work shines."

—*KIRKUS REVIEWS* (starred review)

"The genius of Cris Mazza is to overturn every applecart she can reach."

—LUIS ALBERTO URREA

"Cris Mazza takes no prisoners — and we wouldn't want it any other way."

—RILLA ASKEW

"And now may you find way into the complexities, and convolutions, the deeply moving investigations at the heart of the work of Cris Mazza."

—RICK MOODY, author of *Hotels of America*

"Startling, candid, revelatory and revealing, but most of all brilliant — the collected stories of Cris Mazza are essential reading."

—CHRISTINE SNEED, author of *The Virginity of Famous Men*

"Bold readers, brace yourselves [for] high-energy prose and pitch-black compassion... dense, relentless, tender, savage and strange as moment-by-moment life itself."

—ELIZABETH SEARLE

"This book is a must read for anyone interested in experimental prose, literary fiction, or the depiction of women in contemporary culture."

—AIMEE PARKISON, author of *Refrigerated Music for a Gleaming Woman*

"[These stories] are remarkable for the force and freedom of their imaginative style. Ms. Mazza's characterizations often have the stark quality of black-and-white sketches. And her portraits of suffering are tempered with a fey humor."

—*NEW YORK TIMES BOOK REVIEW* on *Animal Acts* (1989)

"Literary sitcoms from hell . . . Ms. Mazza is a subversive, anarchistic writer . . . hardly forgettable."

—*WALL STREET JOURNAL* on *Is It Sexual Harassment Yet?* (1991)

" . . . similar to watching a porno flick and a game show simultaneously."

—*COLUMBUS DISPATCH* on *Revelation Countdown* (1993)

"[L]anguage in this short story collection cuts right to the bone . . . With delicious satire, Mazza . . . illustrates our human frailties and oddities, showing us that keeping our eyes and hearts open is the best defense."

—*LIBRARY JOURNAL* on *Former Virgin* (1998)

" . . . pivotal moments in the lives of . . . emotionally fragile and isolated characters . . . stifled and stymied, repressed, suppressed, hung-up and damaged, lacking the imagination and courage for adult relationships. [T]hese stories reflect those complicated and divisive years with humor and insight."

—*THE SHORT REVIEW* on *Trickle-Down Timeline* (2009)

After long fearing I'd slipped into this profession with fake credentials, I've now realized my charlatan-complex was sustained for the wrong reason. My original assumption: that I'd been published and continued to be published only by luck or fluke, that soon the literary world would realize I had no talent and nothing to say. But my disguise, the role I played, the imposter that I am, has not been that I am a writer.

—CRIS MAZZA,
"I Write as a Charlatan"
from *Something Wrong With Her*

CONTENTS

INTRODUCTION

Cris Mazza, novelist, essayist, professor, dog trainer, and now even star of a fictionalized film of her memoir, *Something Wrong With Her*, has worn many hats since the 1980s, when her novel *How to Leave a Country* was a PEN/Algren award winner and launched her onto the literary landscape. Since, Mazza has published seventeen books, including *Is It Sexual Harassment Yet?*, *Your Name Here _____*, *Dog People*, *Indigenous: Growing Up Californian*, and *Various Men Who Knew Us as Girls*. Her work has garnered attention from the *New York Times* and even, oddly, from Congress, when her controversial FC2-edited Chick-Lit anthologies were the subject of NEA "obscenity" hearings. Amidst such acclaim and even notoriety, Cris has remained stridently loyal to the world of independent publishing, and remains, despite the raw candor of her work, essentially a shy and private figure, eschewing many of the self-promotional practices in which the publishing industry now pushes authors to engage. Through the decades, Mazza has instead become something of a cult figure, known for her bluntness and refusal to pull a punch, from interrogating the overuse of first person point of view, to her writings on sexual harassment, her explorations of gender politics, and — in a sexually saturated world — most recently her breaking the taboos around anorgasmia. Mazza's fans have come to expect a no-holds-barred truth telling, and an intense adherence to the general principle that "art should comfort the disturbed and disturb the comfortable" — a quote attributed to everyone from Cesar A. Cruz to Banksy to David Foster Wallace, and ideology that has found champions among the indie publishers that have put out Mazza's work, from Coffee House to FC2 to City Lights to Red Hen to Emergency Press to Soft Skull.

One of the "disturbing" aspects of Mazza's work is her continual exploration of the lines between victimhood, personal accountability, and provocation. Generally thought of as part of the "postfeminist" literary movement of the 1990s, Mazza's fiction often explored sexual politics and acts of violence with a more complex and messy lens than the dominant, politically correct zeitgeist encouraged. Though it is my opinion that Mazza is clearly a feminist writer (the "post," in my own view, being a now-passé categorization of a certain branch of feminism, which is not, of course, homogeneous, though the label itself was problematic in that it implied the "conclusion" of a thing far from concluded), her feminism resists easy roles and, especially, binaries of Victim and Perpetrator, bucking against both the infantilization of women (including teenage girls, whom Mazza has sometimes depicted as willfully seductive and conniving, though also vulnerable), and the reduction of male desire and aggression, often exploring male psyches and demons with a depth and empathy often not found in Second Wave feminist literature or, frankly, even so-called "postfeminist" literature of the postmodern period. When one considers other complex interrogators of gender politics, such as Margaret Atwood, Mazza's male characters are less likely to ultimately serve as a case study in how the oppression of women occurs, and more, like Mary Gaitskill's, likely to sometimes be more sympathetic than the women they "oppress." Although the majority of her protagonists are female, Mazza clearly empathizes — to the point of identification — with her male protagonists too, making her work a study in moral ambiguity and the eternally unsolvable "he said/she said." What is clear in almost all Cris Mazza's fiction is that there is more than one "truth" in any story, and that the past is never done.

In keeping with both of these guiding principles, Mazza herself has expressed incredulity about her reputation as a sexual writer. She writes:

> From the very beginning, when my first book earned words like *lasciviousness* in its first pre-publication trade review, I was marked as a new writer unflinchingly exploring female sexuality, following in the footsteps of Erica Jong and Judith Rossner... I was a frank, brash, even assertive surveyor of sex and sexuality. In fact, my sex-life, for over 30 years since losing my virginity, could be described with other adjectives — painful, desperate, dysfunctional, uninspired, unresponsive, perfunctory... This voice of female sexuality and postfeminist sexual politics actually knew diddley-squat about sexuality.

It is this topic that Mazza at last explored in full in *Something Wrong with Her*, a groundbreaking memoir about lifelong anorgasmia, lack of physical desire, and possible transgendered and asexual leanings. With the addition of this autobiographical work to her ouvre, it would now be possible to go back and "reread" Mazza's 30+ years worth of fiction as though in the possession of a decoder ring, reassigning the "real" significance to everything in her stories and novels, based on events and truths of Mazza's own life. To read her work this way might indeed be fascinating, but it would also be the very sort of reduction Mazza's fiction itself has always so stridently bucked against. It is for this reason that the release of Mazza's selected stories is timed in ways that compellingly reflect the themes of her work: her long publication history, presented here in the chronological order in which stories were written, not published, is both informed by what readers may now know of Mazza's life, and yet at the same time, Mazza's own life is irrelevant, as the stories contain their own truths, their own world building, their own self-contained realities. For the fan of independent press fiction and alternative culture, these stories reflect changes in the ways certain political issues were processed over the decades; for the Gender Studies student, they reflect different ways female sexuality have been presented since the 1980s, but also, of course, a deeper and layered story of the way one writer's sexual and gender identity shaped her fiction. In other words, to say that Mazza's revelations about her own sexual life "shaped her fiction" is on the one hand, of course, true, yet on the other hand, it might be just as pertinent to say that the reading of her fiction shapes how we understand her nonfiction.

Although gender politics are under-recognized as a part of "political literature," Mazza's politics don't stop at gender. She is a fierce investigator of class and of the way economics impact psychology. She is also, of course, an avid student of animal behavior, unflinching in her presentation of (usually highly self-aware, analytical) humans as fundamentally animalistic in their urges and motivations. Though not usually classified as a psychoanalytic writer (and I suspect she herself would highly resist the term), Mazza's work is also as concerned with the way the past impacts the present as any writer I can name. A Mazza character is a "haunted" character, and the ghosts of the past are never far from the mistakes of the present day. Her characters, locked in their own games of Eternal Return or repetition compulsion, rarely "exist" in only one time frame. Time, in Mazza's psychological world, is fluid, and what happened Then inevitably comes to bear on the Now.

It is a given in our publishing climate that many powerful and compelling writers never reach the wider audience their work deserves. Although Mazza has certainly garnered more notoriety than "most writers" achieve, it is simultaneously true that she is under-read, under-recognized, underappreciated as a chronicler of our times. Her career, which began with the potential for a meteoric rise, was likely impacted, later, by the publishing industry's group think that "short stories don't sell," that fiction about women needed to be "inspiring" and about plucky heroines who "overcome," and, most recently, that writers need to be young, with massive social media platforms, in order to be relevant to a wide commercial audience. Editor after editor (Alan Kornblum, Richard Nash, Kate Gale, to name a few) has fancied that s/he will publish the book that finally "breaks Mazza out" to the masses, and among writers — such as Rick Moody — it has always been a given that Mazza's work was deserving of such a breakthrough. With these Selected Stories, it is exciting to imagine Mazza's work reaching, if not that "mainstream" audience it could long have discomforted and challenged, then a new generation of readers who will be enriched by her complicated, disquieting, deeply internal world. Long known for her generosity to her students and other writers, it is my pleasure — as such a former student, then colleague, and ultimately friend, of Mazza's — to have curated this important body of work from a writer who both embodies and yet defies categorizations, and whose work is as timely now — sometimes eerily so — as when it was first written decades ago.

Gina Frangello
July, 2016

A CATALOGUE OF POSSIBLE FOREWORDS TO THE SELECTED STORIES OF CRIS MAZZA

by RICK MOODY

1. CRIS MAZZA, SHINOBI WARRIOR

Cris Mazza, estimable polymath, trombonist, teacher, dog enthusiast, memoirist, novelist, and unparalleled master of the short story form, is also skilled in the martial arts, *though this is not widely known*. The training began when Mazza was an undergraduate, but accelerated significantly during her early adulthood, when she had reason, for a brief period to travel to the kingdom of Bhutan, in which nation certain Shinobi warriors from an earlier epoch had kept bright the flames of secrecy and bedazzlement over generations, maintaining a small elite training facility in Himalayan caves. Mazza's instructor in the arcane Shinobi arts, whose name does not come down to us from the source material, was especially interested in *nunchaku* (ヌンチャク), and in the venerated *ahimsa* interpretation of nunchaku in which the one stick is breath and the other is the giver of breath. Mazza's use of the nunchaku, according to this tradition, does not involve bodily harm in the foe, but rather stuns the foe into *reflection*, through the illusionary appearance of such unseemly amounts of force that any foe would come to know in a paroxysm that resistance is foolhardy. Mazza, though not of outsized physical stature, has adopted, with only minor alterations, the dazzling of *ahimsa*, and on one occasion used nunchaku in a dispute with a minor experimental writer, at a certain celebrated writing conference which was held that year in Chicago. During a tedious cocktail party, the experimental writer disparaged (in a fashion he believed witty) writing by women, and Mazza calmly exhumed the nunchaku from her attaché case, tore off her modest and unprepossessing pea coat, and dazzled the fuck out of the experimental writer, who retreated underneath a coffee table, after which he left the conference, that very night, claiming migraine, for his assistant professorship at Eastern Kentucky State, where he wrote a minor prose poem sequence entitled *Ahimsa*.

2. CRIS MAZZA AND LACAN'S *FEMININE SEXUALITY*

The wry simplicity of the prose style in question, the Mazza style, is especially winning, as is her tragicomedy, as is the way that irony tucks itself into the lines again and again (an irony that comes from knowing well both narrator and antagonist and the ways that power might be transmitted dialectically between them). And because of the sometimes devious openness of the language, it is surprising to note that Cris Mazza has taken a keen interest in Lacan's seminars, and has even translated a passage from "Intervention Against Transference." Yet this *is* one of the unlikely twists and turns of her excellent career. In her published diaries, which are every bit as electrifying as is this wonderful compendium of her short fiction you hold in your hands, she notes that this particular sentence from Lacan has long transfixed her:

> *A second development of truth*: namely, that it is not only on the basis of her silence, but through the complicity of Dora herself, and, what is more, even under her vigilant protection,

that the fiction had been able to continue which allowed the relationship of the two lovers to carry on.

(Italics in original.) Mazza's conception of truth in this fine translation recalls Derrida's argument about Lacan in "Le Facteur de la Verité," from *Cartes Postales*, in which the idea of possession of truth is revealed as an anthological compendium of delusions. Truth, in Mazza's translation of Lacan, as in her own work, is a thing of context. It is the truth about which we should be worried, truth as implacable construct, empiricism as the ultimate conveyance system of the simulacrum. Mazza's preoccupation with "fiction" in the lines above concerns fiction as a constitutive and original modality of consciousness, an autonomic function, in which, as in *the mirror phase*, the oscillations of imagination, the commitment to the unveiling of the imagination *create* the self. The true self, which is a false self, and for which there is no other.

3. *41 MAZZARIA*

The recently identified comet known as 41 Mazzaria, possibly originating in the Ooalt cloud out beyond Neptune, is in fact a *twin* comet, of a kind not normally seen among icy planetisimals of our own solar system. Initially it was called Heliotrope 13, but recent observations by the team at the very large array operated by the University of Nevada, using radio wave transmission against measurements by the Hubble Space Telescope, have noted that Heliotrope's wobbly progress is indeed that of *two* comets, whose gravitational influences upon one another perturb their progress through the heavens. Sharif Qazi, PhD, took the lead on the paper in *Scientific American* that heralded this fascinating discovery. Even stranger than the fact of the twin comets, however, is the fact that Qazi is an obsessive reader of American literature of the independent press variety, and, when the naming commission came to him to rename the comet known as Heliotrope, now revealed as *two*, he referred to the consistently inventive short fictions of Cris Mazza, in particular the truly electrifying story known as "Is It Sexual Harassment Yet?," which appears in two columns, two different versions of the same sad tale, bound together like tropic and temperate, like sweet and savory, like Apollonian and Dionysian. Qazi proposed naming the twin comet, that icy planetesimal, in honor of Cris Mazza and her short story, remarking in the *Las Vegas Review-Journal* that "Mazza's career is no less striking for being conducted with the espionage aforethought with which it has been conducted, our admiration must be acute, for the variety and scale of the work, for its intrepid qualities, for its commitment to the unflinching, and the naming of a comet seems fit celebration."

As you know: if the statistical modeling is correct, 41 Mazzaria will, alas, collide with the planet Mercury in the year 3047.

4. CRIS MAZZA AND THE MASCULINE SHAME PHEROMONE

Have you heard? The theory of the masculine shame pheromone has been all the rage in the peer-reviewed psychiatric journals lately. The idea is this: certain pheromones *rectify* a sense of masculine privilege in the male of the species. Snediker, et al., in *Journal of the Proceedings of the American Psychoanalytic Society*, refer to the cultural productions that can cause a flooding of these pheromones as *reality enhancers*. According to Snediker, et al., the first *reality enhancer*, statistically measured by Eastman and his team at Yale in the late nineties, was the novel entitled *Nightwood*, by Djuna Barnes. *Horses*, the album by Patti Smith, is also often referred to. Recently, volunteers dragooned at a local World Gym in the San Diego area, many of them habitual users of anabolic steroids, were plied with *reality enhancers* and were then asked to assess films of road rage incidents, noting their own limbic activity. Among the *reality enhancers* employed in this particular double-blind survey (some control-group respondents were given novels of Anne Tyler) was the story "Former Virgin," by Cris Mazza, from the collection of the same title, a story that deals with the ramifications of an exceedingly painful teacher-student relationship. Indeed, "Former Virgin" is among the few such stories to entrap the grim complex of feelings of those relationships effectively, where all the acute nuances and transferential moments are correctly rooted out, where remorse and chagrin are evenly distributed. Using galvanic skin response monitoring and E.E.G.'s, the aforementioned users of anabolic steroids were plied with copies of "Former Virgin," or at least those who were sufficiently able to read were given the story, and then measured in regards to their reactions to films of road rage events. In a statistically valid seventy-three percent (73%) of cases, "Former Virgin" had the effect of negating the priapic and narcissistic emanations from the sweat glands and the kind of clonus that we associate with masculine self-regard, which, in the aftermath of "Former Virgin," we see mitigated to the point where universal child care and the Family Leave Act suddenly seem like reasonable ideological positions for the men in the study. Further testing, at intervals of three, six, and nine months, after the consumption of "Former Virgin," and the *reality enhancement* that follows on from contact with the work of Cris Mazza, indicate a surge of what clinicians are now referring to as the "masculine shame pheromone," wherein former anabolic steroid juicers eschew some of their previous behaviors, up to and including road rage, binge-drinking, convulsive explaining to women, support for fringe gun rights organizations, etc. While Mazza's work has been swapped out with other *reality enhancers*, the GSR testing has indicated that few other literary artifacts are quite as effective. A collected or selected stories volume by Mazza, such as this one you hold in your hand, would make possible a ten- and twenty-year test horizon, in which results might be duplicated and cross-checked and referenced, assuming funding can be procured.

5. THE IMAGE OF THE FISH IN THE WORK OF CRIS MAZZA

In Cris Mazza's revolutionary memoir, *Something Wrong With Her* [1], Mazza mentions, in passing, her avocational interest in fishing:

> In the Midwest's remote north woods, where I go to *fish* . . .

(Italics mine.) There are photographs of Mazza displaying examples of her fishing prowess to be found online, for those who wish further evidentiary demonstration. As it turns out, excepting exactly one story known to this writer, "Not Here," fish are a decidedly suppressed image in the shorter work of Cris Mazza, and there are moments when her dogged unveiling of

---

[1] There are very, very few memoirs as daring and honest as *Something Wrong With Her*. It mocks, through tenacity, a certain kind of light, triumph-over-adversity memoir that continues to be popular these days. You should throw out all those memoirs and read this one instead.

FISHING EFFECTIVENESS

As Practiced by Cris Mazza

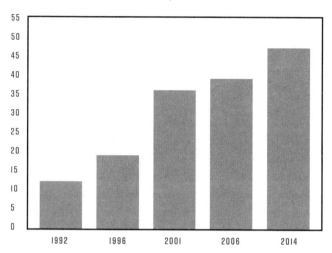

Fig. 1, Fishing Effectiveness of Cris Mazza as measured in number of catch-and-release events.

cross-currents of power in gender and relationships, for example, are simply attempts to distract a reader who is perhaps bent on teasing out a frank discussion of Mazza, the complete angler. Mazza somewhere in Minnesota, in one of those ten thousand lakes, Mazza in hip waders, Mazza bargaining over the price of night crawlers, Mazza tying her own flies. Would Cris Mazza be a catch-and-release type of sportswoman, or one who eats what she catches? Exactly how successful is Mazza with regard to fishing? Does she prefer live bait?

The above chart, constructed with data provided to me by various parties in a position to know, indicates that by concerted effort, Mazza has become one of *the* premier female sport fisherpersons in the American literary landscape. We can probably project annual expenditures in the hundreds if not thousands of dollars spent on fishing trips, and fishing trips that simultaneously involve her other pastime: dog ownership and breeding.

If fishing occupies such an outsized place in Mazza's life, why just the one story?

I asked a Jungian analyst of my acquaintance to speak to the fish image in Mazza's work, and he responded as follows:

"Jung has much to say in the *Liber Novus* (also known as *The Red Book*) about the image of the fish. For example, there was the day in 1916 when an entire day in Jung's life was given over to repeated hauntings by fish.

> That evening, someone showed him a piece of embroidery filled with fish. The next morning, a patient he hadn't seen in ten years, described a dream she had the night before about a large fish.

"Later, there were repeated reiterations of the fish image in Jung's researches, including, for example, a fish laboratory, in the 1940s, which appeared in a Jungian dream; his studies of the "fisher king" and the Holy Grail; Christian mythology, with its fishing imagery, all of which prompted his observation that we are living in an 'Aeon of Fishes.' Which is to say in a time of *soul investigations*.

"Mazza eliminates the fish image from her very best stories so that we might analyze an absence of fish as a reification of fish, especially as fish are subliminal in her keenly observed and trenchant investigations of power and gender. The forms of these stories are restlessly rediscovered, and surely in this way, though she very nearly suppresses the entirety of the marine community, especially, in fact, those species that are liable to be caught in a Midwestern lake or stream, she is sketching out a kind of Jungian self-investigation, for which the fish serves as emblem."

I'd put it this way: with *Something Wrong With Her*, her "real-time memoir," Mazza offers us a decoder ring for the psychosexual dynamics that, in her own journey, undergird stories like "The Second Person," "Former Virgin," "The Cram-It-In Method," "Her First Bra," et al. The forms, the differences of structural intent, the tremendous ingenuity, are the sign that a symbolic of fish is being worked out in substratum, which is to say a *soul investigation*.

6. STATEMENT ON QUALITY BY BIEL, KREUTZER, MILLBROOK, AND SANDERS, LLP

To conclude my catalogue, I thought I might secure an external evaluation by a duly certified evaluator from the venerable Chicago firm of Biel, Kreutzer, et al. Jennifer Strout who is a senior cultural evaluator (and a former paramour of mine, but that is another story) was engaged for a tidy sum to speak to the overall effect of the stories in Cris Mazza's *Charlatan*, and Moses's evaluation is herewith:

> As a nationally registered four-star evaluator of cultural products, I have reviewed the selected stories of Cris Mazza, and I have concluded that here is the work of a major American writer, whose fearless and bold investigations of love, sexuality, dogs, music, and the form of contemporary fiction are such as to be admired by writers and readers the world over. Mazza has been doing what she does for more than thirty years now, and her journey is no less urgent now than it was in *Animal Acts*, her very first collection of stories (which, in fact, I read and admired deeply when I was an associate

editor at Farrar, Straus & Giroux, in 1987), and, according-ly, her career looks from this vantage point to be one that has been conducted with great ferocity and purpose, not to mention astounding consistency. This retrospective volume anneals the base materials of Mazza so that they are more apparent, more completely persuasive even than in the orig-inals, which were and remain important, incisive, and inven-tive contributions to the art of the contemporary American short story. By any barometer of literary success, therefore, these stories constitute enduring American art; they speak of things incompletely spoken about in American literature, and therefore they speak where there has long been silence. Cris Mazza is an American original. Hers is a vital, engaged, imaginative presence in American letters, and this volume crystalizes and secures that reputation, which she has long deserved. If you have any questions, please feel free to con-tact the firm on this matter, or for any further evaluations.

Couldn't have said it better myself, and Jennifer Strout has done a great job here, don't you think? And now may you find way into the complexities and convolutions, the deeply moving investigations at the heart of the work of Cris Mazza.

CHARLATAN

SECOND PERSON

I remember the first time I saw you.

BAND DIRECTOR

In the spring, I was an undergraduate working in the band office: sorting photographs, you know — alone because it was hard to work photos when people were around. Too tedious to try to answer them. I was told to expect you — not inspect. But no name was offered: "A well-dressed guy, young-looking and clean cut." They told me to tell you where to go.

"Hello?"

I looked up and saw you and thought, *It must be him, the one expected*: dressed well, yes, and clean. It's always a good word. It's what's clearest, sharpest, most vivid, distinct, and perceivable — in a photograph.

"I'm looking for Mark."

"He's down in the practice rooms."

Oh, I can picture myself with that loose straight hair all around. I had long hair then. Maybe if you had asked, "Why do you have long hair?" I could've said, "Because I'm a girl; because most girls have long hair and are successful with people — get the connection?" Then I would've cut it.

But you didn't ask that. You said, "Where are the practice rooms?"

"I'll show you."

I cut it off in the summer anyway.

I didn't go out of the office. I pointed the way from the doorway. You smiled thanks. A clean smile, and I kicked myself for not having my camera loaded. I looked at the back of your head as the hall door swung open, then shut, the slowest of shutter speeds — what I'd use for a full-moon shot to open the darkness, expose the details, illuminate hotspots. I remember the way you walked — not like a solider, not even like walking. Like sliding on glass. And your hands: sturdy, clean! Again, clean. They'd catch highlights in a photograph, even in a night shot. Then I thought: A new band director. And I knew if the university had consulted me before hiring, they'd not hire anyone else. Already I was planning and practicing the clicking of hundreds of photographs, a whole wall of them, to join the others in my room: A gallery, a hall-of-fame where each photo of someone was a souvenir to keep, where I could look them in the eye while they finally told me why I needed to know them, why I needed to know anyone.

All that was ten seconds, maybe a minute. But for five months I remembered you — a man with a smile like a window flung open. Even among recently washed windows, an open one is the cleanest. The easiest to photograph through, also. And for five months I planned a portrait. I knew how to tone the lights to a moonglow — how they would bounce back from the softest umbrellas, bathing you from two sides. No shadows anywhere. And my lens would cut the real-life haze, the dust that jostles in a light beam. So inside my camera there would be only you.

But it's always in September that everything starts. The hottest weather begins then. The grass on the football field where I marched with my trombone remained green only because someone watered it. Every day was brilliant-hot, everything seemed too sharp, colors too pungent. Every morning was a color photo taken with too many filters, turning a bleached-white sky into deep blue, giving buildings and trees bold contrast against it. Shade was black and sidewalks blinding.

When classes at the university started — and football practice, and band rehearsals — portrait photographs were due at the printers for programs. That was my job. But you had yours done by a professional, then you lost the print after he mailed it to you. I told you I should've done yours — there would've been extra copies. I did the drum-major's photos, and you complained: "There's black across her eye."

"No! Hey, if she looked into the sun she would've squinted."

"You were too far away from her. You didn't need the shot to be from her waist up." You were waving the photo around so much, you couldn't have really been looking at it.

"I had to get the whistle in the shot. I had to keep the uniform and her features *distinct*." I tried to take it away from you, but you held it too high for me, out of my reach, like a boy teasing a puppy. I said, "Hey, how would you like to sit around talking about pictures of *you*."

And then you smiled. I never saw you in the *process* of smiling, and I never saw the sun *coming* up — it's just suddenly there, muscling its way over mountains, around trees, or through cracks in clouds. Your smile was always something waiting inside, on your other side, like where the sun is at night.

"I'd hate it. Don't come at me with a camera. I hate pictures of me. Look at Jo here in your picture of her. She doesn't look this bad."

"Listen, it's never the photographer's fault if someone looks dopey in a picture. Film doesn't lie."

You held the photo in front of your nose, but you looked at me over the top of it. Then you tapped it against my forehead. "Are you explaining or defending?"

"No, wait, I — "

You stopped me with one hand palm up: hold it, whoa, halt. "Are you explaining or defending?"

I looked: your hair colored perfectly for photography under stadium lights, your brow, your eyes looking out from underneath, your cheekbones absorbing the fluorescent lamp's hot highlights, the darkened dents below each cheek, your chin without a beard, your neck, your streamlined arms and conductor's hands holding a photograph I'd taken that wasn't awfully good now in comparison.

"Defending."

I sulked. We both knew it. I could've drowned in it, but you were magic — a photo come to life. You prodded my shoulder with your finger like a blunt nail. And each time you touched me on the outside, something hit hard on the inside: ping! Like that.

"When someone has a bad day, I push more and more and more."

My glasses had slipped, so when I looked up, I looked over, and you were a soft focus. "Why?"

"To make you tough."

There were people in and out of the office, back and forth, between and beside. I didn't want to *be* tough if it meant I would have to give up the singing of my nerves when you strummed them. You had to leave and I couldn't preserve it: keep your smile thumping inside. The vibrations slowed. This was no action shot — the movement frozen in a blur to move forever. Transitory, intangible — unless I had a picture to look at. I sat in your chair with my camera between my legs. And I held tight with both hands, and I squeezed with my knees. Nothing but a light-tight box without you inside it.

You started something. I stared at my hands — yellowed from time spent bathing faces in photographic developer. If you had looked at the drum-major's photo and said 'nice,' I might've just gone home, cleaned my lens, mixed chemicals, picked an old negative, polished a face on glossy paper. Someone else. Anyone else. Not you. But you started something. You had to be my only model.

DARKROOM CHEMICALS

It was a place you never saw, but I took you there with me often. Down in my basement, a wooden workbench and a cement floor, film to soup, negs to print, people to meet.

I had kept my camera in my shako hat while I marched the halftime show. Then in the stands during the game, that perfect light, that perfect sky background were mine. Through the yellow darkroom safelight, I chose a negative. You. Up on a ladder in the bleachers, you leaned forward toward the terraced band members. I cropped them out. So it was only you, a profile, saying something, pointing to your ear. I smiled in the yellow dark. You hated that picture when I showed you the proof sheet. "Destroy it," you said. But I answered, "No. It's a classic."

Blown up, burned into paper, and sunk beneath the calm, amber liquid, it was even better. In the background was the crowd, blurred splotches of blacks and whites. But the lights above were on your other side, so you were cut out, separated from that confusion with an outlined glow. It was also better there in the dark, under chemicals, than it had been on Saturday night. Of course, Saturday night there were five piccolos and three clarinets between my lens and you. I shot over their heads. If I'd called over the noise, you would've said, "What?" or maybe, "Go back to your seat." The chemicals made a difference. I was right there next to you, no clarinets, no piccolos, they were cropped out; no noise except the timer ticking. I jiggled the chemicals and your coat darkened, but your hair remained fair, and I could say anything to you without shouting.

The next negative was shot from the back — your back, the band's front — and you held your arms out straight on either side, bombarded by the last chord. I'd told you, when I gave you the proofs, "Look at this under the magnifying glass. Look at this timing."

You took it. I tried to picture the way you looked at it while I drained the developer off the print before slipping it in the stop-bath. You leaned back on the springs in your chair. I didn't have my camera; you'd said don't ever bring it into the office. Otherwise I'd remember more.

I had another negative loaded in the enlarger. This one from the front, directing the band. Yes, I was right, the hands were made for photographs. And the hair. This one I'd shot upwards, had positioned the stadium lights in a ring around your knees. The glow crept around your cheeks, shone in your hair, but your eyes were lost in blackness. Not the crinkles, though — I rubbed them in with my fingers in the developer, smoothing them outward like a sculptor does on a head of wet clay. The lines slowly darkened, and I could see the cheekbones rise, the dimples lengthen, the neck harden. But the smile was already there, had been there all along. I couldn't create it myself.

"You couldn't hate this one too," I said as the sky finally darkened into a warm-tone true black.

"I hate them all," I heard you say.

I stared at you floating in the tray. There was nothing tickling inside me. You weren't the same down in the basement, in yellow solutions, as you were up in the light, in the office, on the practice field, or in the stadium at night. Maybe I didn't have the perfect shot yet, hadn't zoomed close enough. Others I worked on became and remained real in the chemicals, had smiled shyly when I said, "You know, you're so boring to know outside this darkroom, just telling me what to do, what not to do, what has to be done, what should be done then 'Good job, good job.' I'm not a job." Then, as I smoothed skin-tone into their cheeks and hands, I asked, "Why do I waste my time with you?"

I moved you over to the clear fix solution to make you immune to hard light.

BAND DIRECTOR II

The reason I was standing there talking, instead of in my position to start rehearsal, was bad enough. That guy, the skinny one with bony hands — you didn't know, you couldn't know — he had once told the virgin queen she didn't give him enough, didn't put out. I could tell that day on the field under the sun, under his laughing and jokes, I could tell what he still thought: *Why did you leave me, I told you I'd change, I promised, I changed can't you see, I've changed, I've changed.*

I *wanted* to walk away, to roll in the damp grass and erase all traces, to say, "You see, people are so boring to know, talk talk

talk, they never say anything new, always want something." What could anyone want from anyone else?

Then you, on your ladder, your podium, your pedestal, with the sun making points around your fair hair, called down, "Andy! Leave Toni alone. She's supposed to be on the field."

Leave her alone.

I cursed not because you were rescuing me, but because you didn't know. What if I'd gone up to the ladder and looked into the sun, blank-faced in direct lighting, and said, "He was my boy-friend and attacked me once in my parents' garage." Or what if I'd developed a picture of it for you: He had me backed up against his front, one bony arm a vise around my chest, pressing me flat. And the other hand raking against me like a claw, a crow's foot, a hook trying to pull my insides out.

Then, standing down on the grass with you on the ladder: would you stroke the numbnesss out of me again, make me thump for a second or two? And me without a camera. So instead I said, "Shit," and I went out to my position on the field.

"It was funny," you said in the office afterwards. Lots of people there as usual. "You stared at me with your mouth wide. I had a hard time keeping my own face straight. Then you said 'Shit' with such stomach support that the band thought I said it over the loud speaker. You stalked out onto the field, *wham wham wham wham*. If you were a cartoon there would've been a baritone sax or a tuba to emphasize each step. A final *wham*, trombone on the grass, arms folded, and eyes back to me, black and angry."

Then you touched my shoulder with your fingertips. "Tell you what, when I have no one to pick on, I'll pick on you, okay?" Your fingers tightened, ground into my bones, breaking through my rigid muscles, and you laughed.

I remember the laugh — felt it rub me inside but couldn't photograph it. Damn, I couldn't bring my camera into the office. I don't recall when it was, a week before, two days before. What difference? Three important frames were blurry, and I'd said, "I can't accept money for these prints."

"Let me see them."

"I'm embarrassed. They're blurry, fuzzy, I can't fix them."

"Let me *see* them." You snatched them out of my hands. I sat and looked at my yellow fingers. You sat in your chair, leaning back, unfairly graceful. Then you stood and leaned against a table near me. I watched with a corner of one eye. Without a camera, no need to keep you framed and focused. What could possibly happen? No one in the office looked at us, of course — nothing was happening.

You looked at the photos again. I did too, without my glasses, papers of fuzz, all gray. You touched my knee and said, "You can't be perfect all the time."

"I want to be."

"But no one can. No one is. It's impossible." A smile. I needed my camera.

"Some people are."

"No."

Once you told me you practiced everything you did to make it perfect. Except you never practiced knowing people. "You are."

"Oh . . . !" Your laugh swept over me so it hurt and tingled and soothed and pricked — the same laugh two days or a week later after I said *Shit*.

But it didn't last. And I knew it wouldn't.

NIGHT PHOTO

I think I am out on the football field. I don't remember, after all, I'm asleep. You climb off the podium, down the ladder, out of the clouds. I am waiting with my camera.

"May I lodge a complaint?" I'm joking, of course, to bring an expression onto your face.

"You are a complaint." Your eyes do not crinkle, in fact are almost sullen.

I am impatient: "No, I'm tryna tell you — "

A pause: you take hold of the back of my neck with one powerful conductor's hand, shake me like a kitten with a toy.

Now clearly against the black velvet backdrop you are outlined perfectly. Eyes set deep, looking, laughing from the inside out. The corners crinkle. A smile that stretches dimples into furrows and tightens neck tendons like anger might on others but doesn't on you, eyebrows arching up and out.

My mind begins to click thousands of photographs. I need flash-fill to see your eyes, lost inside unfocused shadows. I want to illuminate details.

"Stop it."

"Stop what?"

"The camera. I hate that camera."

"You don't understand this camera."

I can't stop. Endless film. I want every angle. Your embarrassment won't show in black-and-white.

"Forget I'm here. Forget me." Photographer's chant. I must've heard it somewhere. I don't remember.

"Don't. I hate the way I look."

"But I can make you look good. Hold still. You'll be blurry."

I move faster and faster, trying to keep my lens on you, trying to keep focus, keep exposure; and though you do not wiggle or dodge, together we whirl, parallel circles that never cross, one around the other. Good, a blurred background. Indicates action.

"What did you do!" There, over my shoulder, my house is on fire. It is unrecognizable. I reach for fresh film — color. The flames are pretty, red and yellow and blue and orange all mingled up inside. Dark sky, dark ground. I am fumbling in an empty camera bag. I left it inside, with the fire...? Sun through my upturned lens sparked my film to flames.

"Forget it! Run!"

I don't hear you. Afterwards I remembered you yelled, after the sun came back up. But the fire is louder than you are. My camera is in there. I know you hate that camera. You never understood it.

I dodge flames and get past the door. You don't try to stop me. I thrash from side to side, tangled in my sheets, dousing the blaze. There's no smoke from this fire, but everything's as black as ever.

My camera is black, lens-up on a burning bed, fire in a ring, red, yellow, like sunlight, moonlight, stadium lights. I have to reach through to touch it — hot, blistering, but whole. I clutch it to me, pressing it to my chest, my stomach, a hot lump against my heart. Treasured photos inside. Photos I save but will never see.

BAND DIRECTOR III

We had an important rehearsal. I guess I knew that. But I was warm. Not uncomfortable... *warm*, with just shorts, halter, trombone, sweat that made my skin shine. Why did I feel so set free? There were three boys, brown-muscled, bare-legged, hair streaked with sun. All of us felt it: sun, grass, skin, horns.

I melted. I stood front-and-center below where you directed, and gave in to the sun that made me rubber. They — those boys — pulled me, stretched me, flattened me then rolled me up and bounced me around like a ball. I forgot I owned a camera. I forgot you were up there. Two-hundred people were walking around on a football field, each hitting the ground at the same time with the same foot. We laughed at that, at ourselves, and they teased: "Trombone-Toni knows all the positions." I giggled, squirmed, could've rolled like a puppy on the grass, twisting an upturned belly to be tickled.

I guess we were screwing up the drills. Distantly I think I heard your voice giving instructions. Wasn't the loud speaker working?

One of the boys said, "This is full of shit."

Then I wanted to rush up to you and explain, he meant his squad, me, the others messing up. Too late.

"This is stupid," you said. "It's a *stupid* rehearsal. I'm disappointed in most of you. Some people have worked very hard for this, and they're making it. Some haven't done anything. Hey! What you just said about this show or this rehearsal, that's what I'm saying now. About *you*."

The three boys blinked and stared with owl-eyes. I squinted up there. The sun burned spots in you. I couldn't see, couldn't take a picture anyway, but couldn't see if your mouth was hard, your cheeks shallow, your eyes like black smudges.

You said, "Aw, you're not even listening. I wasted all that, didn't do any good."

I wilted. The three boys wound down then wound back up again. They rode me like merciless riders on a spiritless bronc. When you left, when you climbed down, you left alone. Fast. I couldn't see you through the mob of broken ranks.

What next? I wanted to follow. What to do? I *did* follow. Back to the office.

I keep following.

In the dark I am at the beach. My lenscap is on and I carry my camera not by the body, but with my hand around the lens.

I am alone, and know it, but I hear you breathing. Just like back in the office when I slipped past you, but not unnoticed. Eyes on each other, we moved in circles.

The sand falls away under my feet, and my feet fall away under me, and I'm on my stomach on a dune. I cradle my lens, protecting it from the salt.

I wonder if I had smiled, would you have? I sat and never tried, and looked down at my yellow fingers. I heard you breathing. My eyes were drawn up like by a magnet. You watched my hands also, then slowly, so slowly, raised your eyes and slapped me hard with that look.

And in the dark I am at the ocean on the beach, my eyes pressed shut against the brackish sand. The yellow light, above and on my left, is not my yellow darkroom safelight. I know it for a second. It's the light on the porch of your beach house. But magic in the dark, it lets me see without destroying the photograph on soft white paper.

I hear you breathing.

Ivory figures on the ivory sand rippled in the amber light. The flesh smooth and full and solid — no claws or rakes scraping the other. Nor inside me. Instead the rhythm of the figures is melodic. And I hear you.

Everything was noisy and confusing after rehearsal. I tried to hear what you were thinking. No clue. No sign. No camera. I couldn't bring it into the office, remember? You barred me out.

But both of us had left the office in the afternoon. And my

camera is warm against my chest, pressed there and protected. The waves whisper in the background, caressing our ears, and I still hear you breathing. I cup the lens in my hand on the lip of a sand dune, deftly remove the cap. Is it the yellow light flickering? The chemicals rippling in a tray? Or the muscles of the ivory figures. Contact and relax, back and forth, between and beside.

People were in and out of the office. I never noticed. I stood and backed away from you, ran into a chair, moved it, backed into someone who said, "Watch where you're going." I was not out of reach, and you hooked a finger in my pocket and jerked me forward; my head snapped back.

You said, "I want to tell you something."

Like magic to be watching through my lens and seeing the picture develop and feeling only warm and smooth where the hook-scar is. I hear two people breathing — breathing each other's breaths. A breeze off the water stings my ears. And something rings in my ears: you *had* tried to tell me something. You had your hands in front of your heart, palms in, fingers spread, like an orator before speaking. You shook them, made fists of them, shook again, then pounded the desk with one. You looked at me, and I, looking back through shaggy hair I hadn't combed, watched and shook my head.

I watch through my lens. The sand makes a bed, round hollows for your shoulders and hips. I split the images and put them back together. I cock the advance lever. With one finger I toy with the shuttle release.

"What," I said.

"Tell me what's wrong with me. What went wrong in rehearsal today?"

"Today?" I pretended I didn't remember. Maybe we were talking about it a week later. Or a month. Or somewhere else, outside the office. A stuffy bar? An unsteady boat? The light-flecked beach at night?

"Today was warm," I said.

The night is warm and thick to touch or taste, to hold in a photograph, to keep forever the throb inside.

"Not too hot."

"No, I mean warm. Good warm. Like warm-tone glossies. Comfortable."

Finally!   You hit the desk once more,   the two of you rise together into the air and bounce back on the sand,   your lips tightened,   the ivory muscles flex,   lines deepened, your neck hardened,   you shudder — together — over and under, between and beside. You are dancers with liquid joints, yet quivering tight muscles. You're the looseness of helpless laughter, yet also the pounding of drums, percussive waves, a hugely pulsating heart sobbing for more room to expand. You explode toward each other and collapse to sleep limp in the sand.

And there it was — you smiled. "I hate pictures."

"I know. You hated the rehearsal today also."

"But why?" You took my arm and twisted it behind me, and twisted me around, your knees on the backs of my legs. I fell backwards against your hip — it pushed into a soft space on my side.

"No, wait, I'm tryna — no I can't tell you. I don't know what happened."

You released me, and I collapsed, sagged, but did not sleep.

And the sand makes hollows for my toes and knees, and my heaving ribs. I push the shutter-release with my legs pressed against my stomach. It clicks against me — a thud with no ring.

And at home I souped photo after photo — of you, on the ladder, in the bleachers, even during rehearsals: your clearly focused eyes focused on something else, something else, never quite vivid enough.

CAR SHOW

You wanted to hear the tape of the band's latest halftime show on the finest sound system available. Mark, your assistant, had four speakers with his tape deck in his Volkswagon.

"When am I not gonna have to run my battery down while we hear these tapes?" he said.

"When you buy me a tape deck for my car," you answered.

"You've got money. That thing you drive that looks like a dump truck is a Porsche!"

"That's why I don't have any money."

"I don't even have a single-speaker radio," I said while stacking my books according to size. "Unless I count myself — I have to sing to myself while I drive."

"Plug the tapes into Toni," Mark said. "She'll sing them to you."

You clamped your hand like a vise on the top of my head, then pounded me like a nail with your other fist.

"Come on then, hurry," Mark said. "I've got things to do tonight."

"Like what?"

"Like things. Come on."

"Afterwards, you can buy me a beer."

"You already owe me a six-pack."

"Ho ho."

I went out of the office then, left you complaining or making bets for more beer, to get my camera from my locker and go home. That's why you were past the tennis courts and halfway to the parking lot beside the frat houses when I caught up, by accident. You were walking slowly, but Mark had stopped complaining, and Jo, the drum-major, was there.

We four were walking along behind the frat house. You were like a colt, side-stepping, head tossing. I would have shot some photographs, but I had too many books to carry. I trudged along behind, watching. My camera bag slapped my hip to remind me it was there. Jo was giggling and bubbled over off the sidewalk.

"Watch it!" you pulled her back. But the car there in the alley had been going slowly. I thought it was parking behind one of the fraternities. It pulled up beside us, a shiny green fender, chrome hubcaps. I looked in, you kept walking. The eyes inside were bleak...yes, that's the word.

"Hey, stay outta the road. I'd advise it." You didn't hear him, I don't think.

"Don't you know what life is?" I couldn't see that one — just that he had a beer can. I moved, the green car followed. Close, with those dirty eyes.

"Hey, you wanna stay alive?"

Three more steps. Only half a rotation for the white-ringed tires. You and Jo were shoulder-to-shoulder ahead, up past the headlights. Mark, by the back door, muttered, "Hey, what the hell, what — ?"

The heavy-lidded eyes inside looked out at me. Beer in the back seat. I halted; likewise the car. I think you stopped and turned around, way up by the headlights.

"Hey, stay outta the damn road, I'd advise it. Stay on a side."

The green fender was dirty. The eyes said nothing, only looked. The words came from the back seat darkness. Gravel ground under black rubber as the green pressed closer. "You wanna know about life? Huh? You wanna live? Stay outta the road."

I was in the middle of a circle, the midpoint in a plane. You and Jo watched from beyond the headlights, way up there, how far away? Mark back behind the rear bumper. Way back there.

I see myself step forward, put an obnoxious hip against the green metal. I hear myself say, "Here's life for *you* guys" — extended middle finger — "you assholes, you fuckups, what do you know about living except swilling beer?"

They asked and I told them. What else were they following for? What is there to be so angry about! I hear the car door bang open, bouncing on its hinges. They are piling out, tangle of arms, legs, beer cans, eyes, fists. Whee, now we'll see! Now we're getting somewhere. I dodge and squirm and block their blows with my textbooks, slam my foot into bulging crotches. But I throw my camera bag to you and watch you run — and grin because there's magic inside, and this time *you* rescue it: an epic on film, black-and-white muscle and blood toned ivory without contrast. Trees fall, the earth shakes, the sky breaks stormy black. Shadows of people run, distant screams echo. Cars, lost in the density, collide and flame like far-away sparks, throwing dancing patches of dark and bright across the road. Down I go. I watch from the ground up. I smile victory as I join the dust. I know where my camera is.

Before I did it, before I said anything, you brushed past, crowding me away. I was on the sidewalk next to Jo. She said, "What's going on?"

Mark crossed the road behind the car. Two with faded jeans

tumbled out on that side. I don't think he said anything to them. They had him covered from both angles.

You leaned in the window and talked to the sleepy-eyed one. Not a colt anymore, no switch tail. I wished I knew what you were saying. Slowly, so you wouldn't know, I set my books down and unzipped my camera bag. Then you shifted your position; allowed the sun to slide past your shoulder, trapping a drop of it on your profile, against the opaque blackness of the car's insides.

I watched through the lens, twenty frames untouched by light, waiting for this: The polished glass cut through the dust, the car, the bold light, the street, the fraternities, the beer, and the loudness. Just you remained, pale against a black night, and pale sand all around, miles of it, and a yellow moon, two figures wrapped up, between and beside, the glow of slow motion, soft blurred action — and my heart racing inside. Prepared to take it all.

I lowered my camera and removed the lens cap.

When I next saw those sullen eyes inside, you'd gone around to where Mark was flanked in the road, where they told us not to be. You looked over the green roof once, at Jo and me. She said, "What's going on?"

I was staring, eyes big as that sloping, tinted windshield. Then I raised my camera again, narrowed the field with a 250mm. Your lips moved, then a smile, then moved again. Never both at once. They — the ones in jeans — had clenched fists. The beer waited on the green hood. I got it all in one line: green metal, beer can, the two guys with thick necks and broad shoulders and hard-knuckled fists, taking steps backwards, forward, sideways as you talked. One pumped his fists up and down at his sides, then shook them out into hands. The other rocked, right leg, left leg, right leg. And you — that smile, loose and relaxed, pale palms at your hips open and turned forward: *Hey pardner, I ain't gonna draw.* I wanted to tell you to go ahead, *go ahead*, but I couldn't get close enough. No lens was that strong.

Jo said, "What's going on? What're they doing?"

"I don't know. Nothing, I guess. Nothing, now." Nothing would happen, it would never happen, it would never include me. This shot was no good. I lowered my camera.

You turned to leave, music in your pocket. Looked at us, an all-clear. Jo scampered across the road, daring to step on it now, the turf you won. She bubbled again, relief.

My smile was small and aimed at my shoes. I didn't need to watch my hands as I wound the neck strap around my camera and tucked it into the red plushness of its case. The only picture I ever wanted, I didn't shoot. It wasn't mine to take. You might've even defied the film completely. Yet even if a photo could've held you, it would always just be you, and never me too.

I cut an angle across the road, through the parking lot, around the dusty cars to my own, the dirtiest. I looked back once, but couldn't see you. It was a wonderful show. Thank you. Not boring in the least, even though I missed the beginning and the end, and a few parts in the middle.

FROM HUNGER

Many times he could've said, "You claim you're an artist. What kind of artist is it who never paints anything?" It came to that anyway. Whether he said it against her ear or kissed it into her mouth.

Perhaps she should've said, I could have painted you.

No. Not me. You chose the wrong subject.

Not the wrong subject, the wrong technique is all.

The only time Keith had come to Charmaine's garage-studio, he found her scraping thick wet paint off a canvas with her hands and smearing it on her face, scrubbing it in, filling her nose and ears, wiping it up and down her arms, bawling, her tears skimming over the surface of her face, sliding right off. And she put the next two fistfuls into her mouth, trying to swallow them. From behind, Keith grabbed her hair, gathering the paint-plastered strands from her face and eyes. He wound her hair in his fist, pulled her head back, punched her in the back, and she spit the mouthful up into his face.

"Breathe," he said. He slapped her spine with his palm again.

"It was lousy!" she screamed, her mouth blue and black. She retched and blue dribbled down her chin. "It was lousy, it was such a mean bastard." She put her face against his shirt and bit a button off. She wouldn't take water to clean the paint from her throat, so he had to spit it into her mouth.

Then he supported her while she coughed against his shoulder. He still held her hair tangled in his fist. She bit his collarbone and said, "It was beautiful, so beautiful. I loved it. But it wouldn't love back." He said, "Shut up," and patted her back while she coughed on his shirt collar.

Charmaine still painted in her garage. Three huge canvases stood propped against walls, worked on so long, they'd turned black, almost by themselves. Yet all three were unfinished, practically untouched. They were a poor excuse for art — didn't make her mouth water when she faced them every morning.

Painting was in her blood: so she'd told her mother when — hungry and gaunt — she'd packed her trays and tubes, easels and canvases. She set up shop in a garage, twenty-five dollars a month with one lightbulb in the ceiling and moths that stuck to the wet canvases. She painted over them every morning. She boiled the same tea bag for a week. She popped corn in a soup can over a candle, ate it with paint-smeared fingers, but she was used to the tacky taste of black, acidy red, bitter blue. Sometimes she closed her eyes, dipped her fingers into her paint tray and sucked them, trying to guess the color by the taste. She washed in a bucket. She used the garbage pails out back for a toilet — only at night. The alley had no street lamp, although she could imagine her white butt like a small moon in the dark.

Week nights, Keith sold magazines door-to-door. And on weekends he played folk music with his violin in the park, his empty fiddle case at his feet, open and showing its frayed velvet lining, baited with small change, probably his laundry money. Folk tunes helped fill the case faster than sonatas or concertos could.

After college, Charmaine used to visit Keith once a week, call him, or at least walk through the park and wave. But he got married, got divorced, and spent his time with the violin.

When Charmaine finished painting over moths in the morning, she and the colors (mostly black and blue) stared at each other. She hated them. Once she'd cut her finger and tried to paint with the bright blood seeping out, which had also turned black, crusty, then chipped off. Painting had yet to feed her. It had not satisfied the thumps of hunger.

If Keith wasn't playing, at least the record player would be. Charmaine didn't hear music on the other side of his door. So she knew he was still on his route. She sat in the hall with her legs straight out, bumped her head absently against his wall and tapped the toes of her sneakers together. She noticed black spots on her shoes. Her shirt was smeared with handprints. Keith came out of the elevator with a briefcase. Charmaine didn't get up or say hello. She said, "The elevator? For the second floor?"

"Hello, Charmaine."

"Getting soft?"

He unlocked his door and she followed him inside. She lay on the couch while he changed his clothes. His furniture was rented, plaid sofa and chair, two wood-grained plastic coffee tables which came unassembled — she'd helped him screw the legs in — one in front of the couch for magazines, one against the wall for the stereo and speakers. He had a few postage-stamp-sized pictures on the wall, tacked up. She noticed he'd added a few postcards, also with tacks. She thought she'd given him a few of her early paintings — maybe as a wedding gift. She didn't see them around anywhere. Maybe his wife had won them in the settlement.

The only decent room, she remembered, was the music room.

The others — well, she'd never seen the bedroom, except once caught a glimpse of his unmade bed. The bathroom was too fluorescent and smelled of purple aftershave. But the music room was walled on three sides with wood paneling, the fourth with the music, in alphabetical order. The center of the room was empty. She'd helped him rip the rug up in there before he was married, to help the acoustics.

"So what's up, Charmaine?" He came from the bedroom in pressed jeans and a blue sweatshirt.

"You sending the laundry out now?"

"No."

"Who's doing your ironing?" She kicked her shoes off. One landed on the coffee table, the other fell onto her stomach, so she dropped it over the side of the couch. "I'm getting expelled."

"Evicted."

"Yeah. I guess it's all over. I guess I gotta get a job now, secretary or nurse, phone operator, teacher, waitress, housewife, mother, mistress . . ."

He sat in the chair and crossed his legs, rested one arm on each of the armrests.

"I see you're following the instructions that came with the chair." She looked at him without getting up. "Well, one more painter bites the dust. I'll line the shelves with my art history term papers. Except I don't got shelves. Hey, you do — want some shelf paper? Hey, Keith, you wanna maid? A personal valet? An interior decorator? Expert landscaping?"

Not a crease appeared on his face. She wasn't too worried about what he saw when looking at her: a mop of ordinary brown hair, Italian olive skin, thick eyebrows, substantial features, a gash mouth. But Keith should've been more than ordinary. His skin apricot-colored; his hair dark, so straight, too fine, strands soft and separate as though he combed each by itself. His brow was intense, his eyes not darker than his skin, with only a slight bulge of weariness beneath each. His neck was long, his only flaw a strawberry mark under one sleek jawbone where he cradled his violin.

He got up, went into his music room, and came out with his violin. He held it to his ear, plucking and tuning it, staring vaguely at Charmaine. But his face did become even more colorful next to the instrument, glowing like the varnishing wood, cared for — even loved by the doting violin. Charmaine's stomach growled.

"You're still at it, huh?" she said.

"Yes."

"You really still practice?"

"Of course."

"What for?"

"Auditions." He strummed the strings softly. "I've got one next week, and one a month after that, all winter."

"All planned like a train schedule: practice on your way to an audition, then practice on the way to the next."

"Something like that."

"Well, I quit today." She kicked her legs up and stared at her feet in black socks high above her face, raining grains of sand into her eyes. "That ever occur to you — quitting and trying something more satisfying?"

He resined his bow. "I've got to practice, Charmaine." His eyes were lazy. She recognized the look of drowsy love a musician has for his instrument. She said, "I can't stand the sight of my paints and brushes anymore." Once, long ago, she'd seen him play the instrument like a lover; he made it moan with pleasure and called it music. Musicians were funny, married to their instruments. An artist, though, had to try to create a new lover every time the hunger was great enough — not an artistic tribute to love, nor the expression of love in acrylics, nor an oil-based appreciation of love, nor a watercolor rendition of the sound or look or feel of love — but the lover himself.

She watched Keith rub the violin's wooden body with a soft cloth, poking his fingers under the strings to clean away all the resin powder. He tucked the chin rest under his jaw, the fiddle snug against his neck. "Please, Charmaine."

"I'm hungry, okay, Keith?"

"I'm going to practice."

" . . . A banquet, a small feast . . . "

"You've got to go."

She kneeled on the couch, separated the cushions, looking for lost change. "I always figured it was your wife who gave you that hickey on your neck." She put her shoes on and went home.

At six the next morning she stood in his hallway and kicked on his door.

Keith actually wore pajamas, plain, pale blue, trimmed with white. Charmaine went straight to his music room, deposited her easel and one fresh canvas, went back for her paints and brushes, one last trip for her paper bag of clothes, which she gave to Keith. "Put these in the bedroom, please." Then she took a shower. When she came out, wearing the same clothes, her hair in tight wet curls, she found him drinking coffee in the kitchen, her bag of clothes on the corner of the table.

"Oh, okay. I'll put them away myself."

"Charmaine, wait — "

"You're not going to be able to wear those pajamas, Keith."

"What?"

"Not while I'm doing you into a portrait."

"But — "

"And you won't be allowed into my new studio, either. That's where the canvas is. But you won't need to pose for me. A lot of my work can be accomplished wherever you are."

"I thought you quit painting."

She smiled. "Maybe you've inspired me. The way you coax music out of that thing of yours." But she wouldn't be squeezing art out of herself — out of her wet insides like tubes of paint. She would paint him with her hands in his colors; no brush strokes, just fingerprints.

"I have to practice, Charmaine. That thing and I have an audition in four days."

"That's okay." She leaned down and kissed his cheek. Hesitated, then kissed his mouth, tasting the coffee. "Take another sip." He did, and she sucked it out of his mouth.

Keith said, "I'm not practicing."

"I noticed."

"The audition is in three days."

She lay on the couch, her head in his lap. His stomach buzzed against her ear when he spoke.

"I'm going to have to practice soon."

"Of course." She hooked a hand on the back of his neck, yanked his mouth down to hers.

"I think I'll eat before practicing. You hungry?"

"Yes." She opened her mouth against his throat.

"Wanna eat here or go out?"

"Neither."

"Charmaine, I've never seen you eat."

"Well, I do." She sat up, straddled his legs, chewed on his

mouth. Holding his lower lip in her teeth, she said, "You always were so damn dedicated."

"Because I eat?"

She let his lip snap back. "Remember in the library, we really weren't studying together, it was a contest, to see who lasted the longest."

He checked his watch. "It's getting late. I probably shouldn't eat first."

"And you won. I can look real serious sucking a pencil. But really, you won."

"They have a brutal audition list for this one."

"You probably already have it memorized."

"Not quite."

"You must've practiced that thing half your life."

"I wish."

She pressed her nose against his. "Lemme see your tongue." He stuck it out and she bit it. "I'm painting you, ya know."

"I was wondering what you were doing."

"You're organic. Some paint isn't."

They were talking into each other's mouths. "You know," he said, "there'll probably be fifty people showing up to audition for one opening."

"I remember I missed your senior recital."

"I want to at least make it to the finals."

"I always wondered if you missed me, but Bertha was probably there cheering wildly." She licked the roof of his mouth.

"Her name was Betty. I'm gonna practice soon."

"But you worked so hard for it, and we were buddies."

"I know they'll ask to hear the Tchaikowsky first."

"I admit, Keith, I missed the recital on purpose." She rubbed her front teeth against his.

"Auditions can drive me crazy — I may try to practice the whole time before my turn."

"Engine engine number nine . . . "

"Or I can stand around socializing with the people I'm competing with and worrying about whether the audition room is too hot or too cold."

"Going down the county line . . . "

"I've gotta be able to run through that sonata like pouring honey. So they can't stop me."

"If the train goes off the track . . . "

"They'll do that, you know, wave you aside right in the middle."

"Will you want your money back?"

"Tell me to practice."

Their mouths stuck together. He shuts his eyes; Charmaine watched. With one hand he held her bushy hair behind her head.

While Keith slept for a few hours on the couch, Charmaine went into the studio-music room. She set her paints up, but left the caps on. She put the canvas on the easel. She took a break to look through the closet for the paintings she might've given him. She found a cake of resin in the pocket of every jacket and coat.

Later on, as soon as she heard his bow touch the strings, Charmaine came out of the studio. He had shut himself in the bedroom to practice. When she opened the door, he stopped. "Go on, I need to watch you," she said.

"I thought you were working."

"I am."

He played a note, and she put her hands under his arms. "Go on, Keith, practice, I need to feel how tight your muscles are."

"For a painting?"

"What else would I be doing?"

She put one hand on his shoulder, reached down and clamped the other in his crotch.

"What're you doing?"

"Measuring. Go on — play."

He raised the violin again. Charmaine kneeled at his feet, ran her hands down the outside of his legs from his hips to his knees. "I wish you'd take your pants off. I can't paint you through jeans."

He laid the violin on the bed and stepped out of his pants. "Now will you let me practice?"

"The shirt too."

In underwear and socks, he put the violin back under his chin. He was playing his warm-up: long notes, full bow, plenty of vibrato. He played three of them while Charmaine kneeled quietly behind him. He stopped when she put her hands on the insides of his thighs.

"Keep going, Keith. I have to get it right."

He poised the violin, hesitated.

"Go on, Keith." She kneeled like a spring at his feet, staring at his legs. The bow touched the strings and squawked when she put her face against the back of one leg. "Charmaine, what — "

"I hafta *test* — to see how much of you vibrates when you play."

The phone rang.

"Who would be calling you, Keith? You don't know anyone else."

He went to answer it, so Charmaine went back into the studio. She looked at her canvas — then switched it from vertical to horizontal. His footsteps finally whispered past the door. When she heard him pluck each string on the fiddle, then tune by bowing two strings together, she slunk down the hall, crept into the bedroom, dropped down on all fours and crawled up behind him.

Stopped, crouching there. The floor vibrated. She rose. Barely an inch away, she stood quietly at his back, staring at his shoulder which moved as he bowed. She swayed slightly so his bow arm wouldn't bump her. Then she bit him, a wet phantom kiss, on the tip of his shoulder blade. Keith yelped, the violin squired high in the air and landed on its back on the bed.

"I'm being quiet as I can, Keith. But I gotta know how your back muscles work while you play."

"Paint it from the front."

She shrugged. "If you say so." She dropped to the floor again, sat waiting while he picked up the violin, peered inside, and checked it all over.

"What took ya so long on the phone?"

"I ate an apple."

"Didja leave me the seeds at least?"

"You can have the whole apple if you want."

When he started to play, she kneeled upright, pressed her ear to his stomach. He managed one scale. "Are you stopping again? I'm listening for the apple."

He sat on the bed, the violin and bow beside him. "Charmaine, maybe I'd better tell you the musical facts of life."

Still on her knees, she stumped over to him, put her hands on his legs and leaned forward. "Is this gonna be like *The Little Engine That Could*?" She pushed her hands up his thighs, up to the elastic of his underwear. "I think I can, I think I can, I really think I can." Keith held her shoulders, looking at her. She wiggled her fingers into his underwear, singing, "And you can do most anything, if you just think you can."

Keith fell over sideways on the bed, missing the violin but breaking the bow in half.

At dusk he went into the bathroom, showered, shaved. Clouds

of violet-tinted steam came from under the door. Charmaine was still sitting on the floor. She watched him return.

"You sure have everything, Keith, pajamas *and* a bathrobe."

"I even have another bow. I don't have another Thursday afternoon."

He sat down to dry his feet. He dried between each of the toes on one foot, then began the other. Charmaine licked all his toes, and he dried them again.

"Hungry?" Keith asked.

"Nope." She sucked the stickiness off each of her fingers. "I'm happy about your progress."

"I didn't practice all day."

"The portrait — you're going to be beautiful."

He put the violin away and then dressed. "Can you fry me an egg?"

"I know how to mix paint."

He looked at her. They never spoke of his visit to her garage. "Never mind."

Before dawn she kneeled at his bedroom window, her chin on the sill, naked, shivering. The metallic sky opened up and bled, oozing water. She could not see the drops sparkling as they fell, nor the lines of liquid whips. No thunder and lightning broke. Only a heavy excuse for rain. It was a watercolor wash background, just wet.

The sheets rustled behind her. She didn't turn. She rested her pinched butt on her heels, pressed her knees together. Keith's feet thumped on the floor. "Charmaine . . ." He sat beside her, pressed his hand down her back. "You're all bones."

"We had to learn the skeletal system in anatomy class."

"You're freezing. You've got to drink something warm."

"Okay."

His mouth was wet and slick and hot. He put his bathrobe over her. "The train leaves at eight."

"Engine engine number nine..."

Keith got dressed and put some extra clothes in a small suitcase.

"It's going to be a pretty day," Charmaine said.

"It's raining, isn't it?" Keith folded a pair of underwear.

"There could be a rainbow." She knew dampness changed the mood of a string instrument.

He carried his music folder and violin case. The suitcase hung from Charmaine's arm and bumped against her knee. They sat in red velvet seats. Charmaine's hair was wild from the dampness, and Keith said it tickled his face, so he found a rubber band and fastened it back for her.

Keith was asleep when breakfast was served, his violin case held tightly between his legs, the music folder clutched at his side. Charmaine ignored the breakfast announcement. The window was drippy and cold. She opened it a crack. Kneeling on her seat, she pushed her tongue out the window and caught a few drops of rain. The edge of the window was dirty and she crunched grit in her teeth. Keith slept with his mouth open. The music folder was easy to slide out from under his arm. One by one she slipped the sheets of music out the window. The wind whisked them away. The folder went out last. Keith held her hand and continued to sleep.

There was no rain on the trip home. He was out of the running in the symphony audition within the first hour. They boarded the train at noon on Saturday, after Keith checked the lost-and-found for his music folder. He held the violin case across his lap. "I didn't plan it this way," he said.

"Engine engine number nine..."

"Not that I expected to win the very first one."

"Going down the county line..."

"Stop it," he snapped.

Later on, Keith went to the dining car alone. When he came back, he stood in the aisle a moment, holding onto the luggage rack with both hands, looking down at Charmaine. Then he fell into his seat. "This won't happen again."

"You mean you're finally quitting?" She licked her lips.

"Of course not."

He slept the rest of the way home while Charmaine looked out the window. The sky was clear black. The train raced under a big dumb staring moon.

Keith took the elevator and Charmaine climbed the stairs alone. She was waiting at his door. He carried both the suitcase and the violin. He put his clothes away. The bed was still unmade, sheets trailing onto the floor. Charmaine went into the music room, then came back out. Keith came from the bedroom.

"I want to see the portrait."

"Didn't I give you some paintings once?"

"C'mon, I want to see what you've got so far."

"I can remember those paintings, but I might've forgotten to actually paint them."

Holding her arm, he opened the door and took her into the music room. The easel's back was to the door. The paints were covered. The brushes clean. No dabs of color had dripped on the floor. He walked around the easel, taking her along. She leaned against him.

"Beautiful, Charmaine." He looked at the clean canvas.

"I looked in the closet. I couldn't find those paintings. Did I forget to paint on them — did I give you blank canvases by mistake?"

He hesitated by the door. "You wanna eat before you go home?"

She shook her head. "I have painted with colors, Keith. But so many colors — color on color — it always turned black."

She took her paints and easel and the canvas back to her garage.

On his end, she knew the phone was screaming. She held her breath. His voice was low, unfrightened. "Hello."

"It's me."

"Okay . . ."

"I've been painting, Keith, I really have — really, I'm trying. I've worked all night.

"What time is it?"

"Three. But Keith, there's no color, the paints aren't working, nothing goes on the canvas. Nothing comes off the brushes. I threw the whole jar of black, it hit and splattered all over, but nothing on the canvas."

"I'm very tired. I have to get up early to practice."

"I threw *every* jar, Keith, they all cracked right against the canvas, they're puddles of color all over the floor. Nothing on the canvas. It's still blank."

"Who is this?"

She waited, wiping spittle from her chin.

"I'm sorry I called you. I'm sorry I tried to wake you."

"Okay."

She left the phone booth. Sitting on a box in front of the blank canvas, she pictured the planned portrait: Keith's Night. One train in a dark tunnel, sleeping there, black and glossy, eyes glowing drowsily. And here comes another train, screaming out of the night, fire in the control room, teeth bared as it races head-on into that same tunnel on a single track. Moments before impact. Unwilling art: The collision will never happen.

With a razor blade, she sliced the webbing between her thumb and index finger, on both hands. The blood came in weak trickles. She waited until it filled her cupped palms. Then she pressed her hands against the white canvas and squeezed, kneading it. Blood oozed up her arms, dripped from her elbows. She stopped and looked at her painted skin. The canvas remained untouched.

ANIMAL ACTS

Are you still unadulterated? Can you still ignore the tricks, the sleight-of-hand or juggling, and all the rest of the gala presented for your benefit by the girls in your circle? You need to realize that to gain the attentions of a dedicated man, even for one ceremonious hour, is their sought-for proof of beauty and desirability, a demonstration of their talent.

Setting. A party in Los Angeles: the living room of a patron of the Philharmonic. Minimal props — couch flanked by several chairs, circular arrangement. In the center: a coffee table with party food.

Sunday evening following the Philharmonic's matinee. Several guests are dressed in tails and white tie or floor-length black dresses, indicating they are musicians. Some of the other guests are in glittering gold or silver tuxedos or gowns: the patrons. There is one ordinary red-nosed clown and one costumed pink cow who has to hold her wine glass between papier-mâché hooves. The guests, as they enter, will stand or sit in a casual arrangement.

Low conversation; specific words inaudible. An occasional moo.

Stage directions. Enter the NARRATOR, *female dressed in workman's coveralls. Nondescript plain brown hair in no particular style. Empty-handed. She spots* ANTONIO, *standing slightly behind the couch, listening to the conversation of a few musicians, but not participating nor contributing. He is a blond Italian, wearing off-white slacks and jacket, a light-blue pin-striped shirt. A large man, but trim.*

VOICE OVER

Antonio is a conductor of small orchestras. Several years earlier the narrator played third trumpet under his direction in San Bernardino, and hasn't seen him since. To tell the truth, he doesn't remember her.

Stage directions. The NARRATOR *cuts through the party, and people step aside for her, even the two musicians* ANTONIO *has been listening to. She steps right between them.* ANTONIO *takes one step back. The* NARRATOR *is between him and the rest of the party. Toe-to-toe.*

NARRATOR

I have to warn you about Randi.

ANTONIO

Excuse me?

NARRATOR

Just listen, it's very important. A matter of honor or degradation.

ANTONIO

I'm not sure I know —

NARRATOR

Yes, that's why I need to warn you.

VOICE OVER

He was older. He'd thickened. Not so much in girth, but in the skin on his face, like leather swollen with rain then stiffened in the sun. He'd conducted one small-time symphony after another, from San Bernardino to Albuquerque to Little Rock. Always the same lean sweeping style, power in his arms which made the brass respond, believing they were in Cleveland or Chicago, but their clams and pitch told otherwise. And also the same — the fleeting look he would give with one bold eye to the musicians who missed entrances or cracked notes. Except for the few times someone earned his smile, for quality performances, or courageous ones. Never for the cheap ones. Like Randi's.

He'd come to Southern California again for his new position in Riverside, but without a girl on his arm tonight — that striking wife who is a doctor and beautiful, and therefore seems to make him all the more desirable.

NARRATOR

I've known I had to tell you this since I first saw her, during those years I lived in New York playing the shows. Now I record jingles for commercials, you know.

But you just listen, because so far you've only known the silly amateurs, their props and costumes. They practice for hours alone in closets. But Randi's act can't be done alone, can't be rehearsed, is always live and has never yet failed because she's the one who gets the volunteer from the audience, and you could be next. Just imagine the marquee: The Great Antonio, featuring *Randi*. Is that what you call success? She will.

ANTONIO

You mean someone who's here tonight?

NARRATOR

Just listen —

VOICE OVER

It's been hard, he must've had years of coquettish pageantry, yet remained untouched. His age sits well with him. Yes, still those good looks, which gave him charm and happiness and every personal perfection including fidelity like a diamond, hard so it would never crack, yet clear, so the whole world could look in at him. He had some talent too, and perhaps some heartbreaks, which never stopped him.

Stage directions. A few of the people on the close end of the couch turn toward the NARRATOR *and* ANTONIO, *watching and listening. A few of the standing guests also come closer, quietly waiting and listening. The volume of the other buzzing conversations lessens considerably.*

The NARRATOR *reaches offstage and is handed a microphone.*

She addresses ANTONIO:

NARRATOR

You just listen and perhaps you'll always be thankful you never made it to New York, where you would've come across Randi, the girl I'm going to tell you about. Maybe once, long ago, she did start as a starry-eyed young thing dreaming of the stage. She managed to catch on in a few choruses, way off Broadway, but she was always around, at the parties and in the circle, because she let Clarence think he was catching on with her, and he knew everyone one way or another, from freelancing, I guess. He played electric guitar — what else — and he called himself a musician because an amplifier made him loud and the part said "improvise."

Well, Randi'd already had a kid, who she'd given up for adoption sometime before I ever saw her, and an abortion, which I never knew about until afterwards, when she told us all about it at a fondue party on the Upper West Side. I guess if it weren't for Randi, I'd never know how an abortion can hurt like hell, sometimes worse than giving birth, but doesn't stink as bad.

VOICE OVER

During the concert that afternoon, he may've been deciding whether or not to try that Mahler symphony with his new group. He would have to consider personnel — the second bassoon he didn't have or the horn player he knew couldn't cut the part. Important thoughts, accompanied by the Philharmonic, about his upcoming season, how to make it his biggest yet, and yet do it all with the local talent — school music teachers and housewife musicians — he would be given to work with.

Mostly his age showed in and around his mouth and the corners of his eyes. He used to seem almost giddy backstage before a performance in San Bernardino. But in those days, New York, Cleveland, Philly, Chicago — they were all in front of him.

NARRATOR

The gathering, the circle, was usually pit musicians and a few people from the chorus seated around a platter of crackers and cheese or chips and dip. Randi always arrived starving and immediately began to load clam dip on wheat crackers, or she dipped her hand right into the bowl of avocado and sucked the lumpy green blobs from the tips of her fingers. Sometimes saliva ran down her chin, tinted white or green or even red, if there was chili sauce. And in between mouthfuls she would talk, and belch, and spit into ashtrays, and hiccup, and spray mouthfuls when she laughed, and fart then fan the air behind her ass — to share it, she said. And she would talk about shit and piss and snot and puddles of puke her cat left around her apartment; and cum, or spunk, as she called it — she talked about the texture of it when rubbed between her fingers or swished around her mouth. She demonstrated how to "chew" it once, with a mouthful of onion dip, then she opened her mouth so everyone could see how the creamy dip had liquefied and coated her mouth and made murky bubbles when mixed with saliva. She offered to share it with someone, and no one volunteered, so she made Clarence try it and spit some into his mouth.

Stage directions. Enter a pirate who removes his wig at the door and an elephant who removes his green derby hat. The cow begins doing some soft-shoe alone in a corner.

NARRATOR

Then when the laughs died out, Randi might find the pet of whoever owned the apartment, hopefully a male dog, because, she said, she kept a file in her head of the appearance of their balls. Some were tight and neat and pink; others, she'd noticed, were baggy and/or crusty and blackish. But once — no, more than once — someone had a female cat, and Randi said, "Oh good, we can rub her pussy and make her yowl," then turned to a man — any of the men there, she seemed to know without hesitation which one she would choose — and said, "You do it — I know you know how." The guy would smile but never deny it, and the girl next to him would blush, but when Randi "knew" something like that, you can bet she really, personally, knew.

Stage directions. A peacock enters, a gorilla on his arm. It's a girl gorilla, who takes her head off and has long blond hair. The elephant juggles bowling pins and the clown pulls paper flowers out of his sleeve. Just a few of the original guests still hold private conversations, but most of them, and the cow, who has stopped dancing, press closer to the NARRATOR.

NARRATOR

She had a freckly face and a sharp nose and small eyes set close together. And she got plenty of men to do the act with her. Once one of the guys was talking about the way he would play the lead, if he had it, and Randi told him he might as well daydream about simultaneous orgasm. Wait, this one's even better: A guy was talking about how he'd impressed a certain music director when he was called to sub and learned the whole book in one night, and Randi was listening seriously, attentively, then she said, "Are you still doing it in the missionary position?" Wait a second, I'm not finished —

Stage directions. ANTONIO *has been taking side steps, moving behind the couch toward the other side of the party, but the* NARRATOR *also moves slowly sideways, parallel to him, and they remain face-to-face. The already listening guests continue to watch the* NARRATOR, *although she has moved to the other side of the party with* ANTONIO, *where more guests abandon their own conversations to listen. They shush the peacock, who has started a mating call and dance. He says, "Oh!" and also turns toward the* NARRATOR.

The microphone whistles and the NARRATOR *clutches it to her chest with a sheepish smile. The mic picks up her heartbeat. Slightly rapid and very irregular.*

NARRATOR

Wait, because there are some things about Randi you still need to know. I just told you the background. Men seemed to find her irresistible, so I thought you should know. You who were never jostled in a crowd, even at rush hour. An admirable skill — but not good enough.

Stage directions. Giggling, the NARRATOR *bumps* ANTONIO*'s arm and spills wine on his light-colored jacket.*

NARRATOR

You see, I just want you to be careful and not prize your fidelity too lightly because Randi's tricks always worked. A party was always sort of dull — like this one — until Randi arrived. The circle would just sit and talk about the performance that night, or other performances other nights, or other productions, or why they'd left whichever symphony orchestra they'd come from — except Clarence because he played electric guitar. Maybe once some orchestra somewhere hired him in the summer when they played highlights of rock 'n' roll adapted for strings and winds, and they called in an electric guitar from the union book for flavor, to make it realistic.

Then Randi would come in, dressed as always in faded jeans and a huge man's shirt stained with wall paint, her favorite shirt ever since her own painting party when a gang of guys she knew helped to paint her apartment. And I mean a *gang*. Then the only thing to wait for was someone to say, "How's tricks, Randi?" because she always had an answer.

A lot of times she had a new voice teacher to tell about, and she usually began with what he looked like without clothes, his posture when naked, and how he smelled.

"Which reminds me," she said once in a stage whisper to the girl in the circle next to her. "Every time I pass your husband I smell B.O. — and I like it!"

Stage directions. Several more people enter, most dressed as animals, one a giraffe on stilts. The clown begins to walk on his hands. Someone steps on his knuckles and says, excuse me, to his feet, then quickly turns back to the NARRATOR. *A horse enters in two parts. Each quickly drinks a glass of wine, then the hindquarters bends over and fuses itself to the head section. The horse tap dances. Both pairs of the horse's legs can jump and click heels in the air. Then someone, hurrying across the party toward the* NARRATOR, *goes right through the horse and breaks him in half again.*

NARRATOR

But I thought I'd better describe her entrances and her cues because it all depended on what the setting was at each party, although only she knew how to read the conditions, talentless as she was for musical theater. I saw her audition once, from the pit; her voice was shrill and she minced about on stage like an elf in pointy shoes.

Stage directions. Holding the microphone between her knees, the NARRATOR *puts one hand inside her shirt, across her body, under her armpit, flaps her other elbow up and down creating a fleshy popping sound, which gains the attention of the last of the original guests not already listening. Also of a bear walking on a beach ball, who, because he can't stand still, circles the knot of listeners, pressing close to the* NARRATOR *and* ANTONIO.

When she speaks again to ANTONIO, *she hooks an arm around his neck, bringing him close, only the microphone between her lips and his ear. If* ANTONIO *did not hold onto the* NARRATOR *by her waist, he would surely fall over.*

NARRATOR

Maybe it's even more important now for me to be sure you know about Randi, with you starting your new position. Like I say, someday, after all the acts, you'll see the grand finale: tricks, spoofs, and marvels like you've never seen, and you've got to remember to remain unimpressed, as you always were.

VOICE OVER

In many ways, he was like wine, the finest wine — to someone who knows little about it — expensive, cool in a slender bottle; clear, bright color.

NARRATOR

At one party there was a dog which sniffed each and every person's knee, and I watched him go around the circle, to everyone in turn. No one seemed to notice, or someone may've moved a hand away if it was within reach of the dog's nose. When he got to me, I patted his smooth brow. Each time I stopped, thinking my turn was over, he pushed his nose under my hand, nudging me, and I kept patting. Until Randi came in, and the dog turned toward the opened door, then leaped over the circle to greet her. She let him stand up against her, his front paws on her shoulders, and everyone watched. She said, "Oh — does he do tricks?"

"Ignore him," the owner said. "Get down, Animal. He's just trying to get attention."

"Animal — great name for a dog," Randi said. She stepped into the circle to take some cheese off the platter, stuck her tongue out and slapped the slice of cheese there. She looked around the circle, and there were no empty seats, so she kneeled right there, at the buffet table, in the middle of the ring. "A guy I knew once had this real neat dog," she said. "He was in commercials because of this trained dog of his, and only he could command him, so he acted in commercials. He was going to get me a spot too, but I didn't see him again."

Stage directions. A lion roars through a speaker in his plastic nose. A sword swallower is eating olives from the tip of his sword, pushing them down his throat, then bringing the blade out clean. He has an accident, and the tip of the sword comes out his pants. A big parrot has a little dummy of a man on his shoulder. The gorilla has been blowing up balloons and twisting them into animal shapes. As she finishes each, she tosses it into the crowd clustered around the NARRATOR, *all jockeying for a better view or to be able to hear more easily. The balloons lie underfoot, are kicked occasionally, sometimes stepped on and popped.*

NARRATOR

This is one of the reasons I'm telling you. I always thought fidelity was a talent like that to you. You know, loyal, man's best friend, whatever.

"That dog loved me," Randi said. "The guy said it was weird, because he was such a one-man dog, but he kept sitting up for me and wanting to shake hands. Can you imagine — kissing a man while shaking his dog's hand?" She made a little layer of cheese, salami, and another cheese and put it onto her tongue. She tried to roll her tongue into her mouth, like an elephant bringing in its food. It was an awfully big mouthful, but she went on with the story anyway.

"When we were on the bed," she said, "we couldn't seem to keep the dog off. He wanted to lie right between us, of course, first licking my face and then the guy's. It could've been fun, you know? Maybe I wasn't drunk enough. So the guy told the dog to sit in the bedroom doorway, and he told him to stay. He was a trained dog, so that's what he did." She gestured a lot, when she wasn't picking up more food. Not expressive gestures, necessarily. Sometimes she just picked spilled crumbs out of the rug while telling something. I noticed the wine in Randi's glass was cloudy, crumbs at the bottom from drinking with her mouth full, and I thought of you — glad you weren't there. Yes, glad you never made it to New York.

Stage directions. When the NARRATOR *stops to drain the last drop of wine from* ANTONIO's *glass, he takes this opportunity to wipe his ear with one hand. The clown hands him a dotted handkerchief. Two white doves fly out of it. But when the* NARRATOR *continues speaking,* ANTONIO *drops his hand and has to hold onto her again. The difference in their heights makes this mouth-to-ear position difficult for him, but he doesn't seem to be complaining.*

NARRATOR

Well, Randi changed her position, so she was sitting flat on her ass with her legs in front of her. Whenever I saw Randi at parties, I would think of you and pretend you were with me, as though you were seeing it firsthand, so you would be prepared. But I also always knew I would have to tell you about her myself someday, so I had to watch her for both of us.

"Like an audience," Randi giggled. "That dog watched us on the bed. He never panted either, that dog. Just stared. I wouldn't've minded so much if he would've panted a little, would've been more normal somehow."

The host went into the kitchen to refill the trays, so Randi waited for more food and ate a few crackers while she waited. Crumbs always spilled from the corners of her mouth.

"Anyway," she continued, "I don't know how far along we

were, you know — who keeps track? But the dog, he jumped on the bed again. I think the guy had groaned or something. And the dog jumps up there and bites me! Right on the boob. I could show you the bite mark."

Someone said, "That's okay, Randi." She had already been pulling up her shirt. "No? Okay. Well, some other time." She reached for some carrot sticks and dragged her sleeve through the bean dip. Really, it's hard to imagine her at one of your parties, I know. I used to hear people talking about times at your house after concerts — the spread your wife put out, the music, the view from your picture window.

Randi wasn't finished, though.

Stage directions. The NARRATOR *looks around, spots an empty chair, hooks it with one foot, and drags it over; she sits* ANTONIO *down and mounts his lap, facing him, crosses her ankles around the back of the chair.* ANTONIO *smiles. He takes a dish of peanuts and feeds them to her, popping them into her mouth with his fingers. The elephant exits in a huff. The rest of the party is absolutely silent. Then the* NARRATOR *laughs out loud, into the microphone.*

VOICE OVER

He was never sure who it was, in San Bernardino, who sometimes blared the notes too loud and made him look — and did make him wince, at least.

NARRATOR

Probably this time more than others, I tried to imagine Randi saying this with you in the circle, maybe telling it right to you alone, with the rest of us watching. And I tried to picture the way you would look or answer. Maybe the way your eyebrows rose when the flutes were flat, or the small smile you wore to deceive the audience when you bowed. Or maybe no way I ever saw you before.

"So I told him," Randi went on, "I thought he ought to kill it, you know, to avenge my honor."

Listen to this, are you listening?

Randi said, "We tied the dog's legs with my shirt. I think I put my underwear on him too, but I was drunk, you know, so I'm not sure. And he blindfolded the dog. We had him across the bed, right there with us, and I was getting impatient, you know, but he, the guy, wanted to do it right. I just remember laughing and laughing. He used a letter opener, it was all he had, and I caught the blood in two hands, very warm and smooth, and we used it for extra lubricant."

She popped a pickle slice into her mouth, and I could smell the juice of it.

Action. ANTONIO *stands, lifting the* NARRATOR *with him, her legs still wrapped around his waist. He walks to the couch, looks at the guests still seated there. They rise and back away. The guests begin to exit, by ones and twos, while Antonio lays the* NARRATOR *on the couch and begins to undress her. He does so in such a way that her body is never totally revealed. Strategically placed chairs — moved during the party — block the audience's view. When* ANTONIO *lies on top of her, no part of the* NARRATOR *is visible. The microphone picks up her breathing and her heartbeat, and her stomach growls, but she has disappeared. When all the guests have exited, they gather in two groups in the wings and begin to applaud.*

Finale. A trained dog enters walking on his hind legs. He passes the couch and is handed the microphone, which he then carries away as he exits. The passion on stage is in pantomime.

DEAD DOG

You Lizzie — you're in heat again. Another two weeks of this I suppose. A killer instinct: coupling and running in packs, the romance of being something wild . . . for a few days, at least. You're supposed to be a clean animal, that's what they said when I bought you, much cleaner than a dog. Clean personal habits, they said.

Years ago, when the family dog died in stud service, Lea dropped to her hands and knees on the cement driveway and threw a girlish, hysterical tantrum. But even after her mind resumed routine rationality — when she could think of the old dog and smile — her body continued to mourn. Her periods stopped for a year.

In those days, no law required leashes or fenced yards.

His job was to protect them: Lea and her brother and her two sisters, and the house and parents. But whenever neither of them was busy — Lea with Girl Scouts or tennis practice or violin lessons, Laddy with personal affairs discreetly accomplished away from home — they spent a great deal of time alone together. Especially those evenings in late spring when the sky was still light after supper. Out on Valley View Lane, she batted a stale tennis ball with her old racket and Laddy brought the ball back, damp with his saliva. All too soon the ball would be drenched, so it splatted when she hit it. (Then someone gave him a small, green-plastic football which wouldn't get soggy. It was too big in the middle, so he carried it by one tip, in the side of his mouth, like a fat cigar.)

Soon, his long dripping tongue would hang from the corner of his mouth, wet-red; and he would pant and lap water and fog the evening air with his breath. The sunset put an amber glow in his tri-colored coat, and a firey tint in his eyes.

At the end of every physical education class, Lea gathers the girls around her for a talk. She dresses every day in lean stretch pants, white blouse, and a patterned pinafore. She keeps her uniforms at school, washes them in the school laundry with the towels because of the cat hairs at home. She believes it's a good idea to talk to the girls frankly once a day.

They meet in the dance room. The girls sit or lie on the mats there. After games of basketball or tennis, they fill the small rooms with hot dampness and the smell of socks. The mirrors fog slightly. On warm days the girls sit lifting their hair from their sticky necks.

"Basic hygiene," Lea says, "is so important — especially after exercise when the pores are open." She smiles. "When you wash your face, work away from problem areas. Otherwise, instead of removing the oil, you're distributing it." Lea's own face was never marked by blemishes; she's never needed make-up.

"Work the cloth down the sides of your nose and out across each cheek. Rinse and wash from your chin downward to your neck."

The girls' breathing has regulated, and Lea knows it's not good for them to sit long in damp clothes, so she dismisses them to the showers.

She was never good enough for the first-string tennis team. She never made first-class scout. She didn't ever solo with the school orchestra. She was not abnormal, just average. She didn't date early, and she didn't date much, but she never said no — until her trouble after Laddy died. Laddy was a family dog but she called him hers.

She claps her hands softly. "Calm down, now, girls, take deep breaths. There now." She pauses. This is her favorite part of teaching. "I'm sure you all know how important it is to wear your bras while engaged in physical activities," she says. "It's equally important to exercise those special muscles which are always working to keep your busts from sagging." She puts her heels together. Standing above the girls, she clasps her hands in front of her own trim figure and holds her elbows high. "Like this, you see, each hand pushing against the other tightens those important muscles, keeping them fit to do their duties."

But no one could say she lacked the rhapsody of youth, even though she didn't read pulp nor watch much television. She danced alone to records, or lay down with an arm across Laddy, listening to Brahms, or, her favorite, Mendelssohn's "Songs without Words." Sometimes she held Laddy's front paws and made him stand up in front of her. She led, and he followed on rickety tiptoe, doing a two-step during a waltz.

She took Laddy on a backpack trip and hiked for miles on a wilderness trail. Laddy didn't stay at her heels, in her footsteps. He trotted ahead, stopping to look back every few yards, urging her to hurry, but his feet gave out before hers did. Lea had leather boots. She tried to carry him, but he struggled in her arms and wanted to walk. So she put socks on his pads while Lea hummed tunes from the Berlioz Romeo and Juliet. She offered to walk to the creek and bring him back a bowl of water, but he went with her, barefoot, and drank straight from the running river.

Laddy lived thirteen years, from the time she was six through eighteen. After he died, there was no point going camping alone. Or dancing either.

The girls troop into the dance room and flop onto the mats. Some open their top buttons and fan their sweaty chests.

"Why can't we play co-ed volleyball, Miss Palmquist?"

"Yeah, Miss Palmquist, it would be faster and more exercise."

Lea smiles. They need so much guidance. "Some things, girls, are best done without men." She kneels neatly, legs together, in order to be closer to their level, more intimate.

"The examination of your skin and hair is important, girls, because there are some personal conditions even a daily shower can't combat. For example . . . well, body lice is one." Lea brushes her long, chestnut hair one hundred times twice a day — as soon as she gets to school in the morning, and right before she leaves.

"It's not as old-fashioned as you may think. Although in less civilized times it was more common, and our language was given words like lousy. But the condition is by no means extinct. Fleas which you may pick up from a family pet won't stay with you. But lice will. It'll itch, you might have a rash, but you'll seldom actually be able to see the creatures. You may believe you're moody or irritable, but your body is telling you something."

Lea lets this sink in a moment while some of the girls squirm or look down at their knees until she sends them to the showers.

All the pups born on and around Valley View Lane carried resemblances to Laddy. He was gifted in that way — the bitches never refused, in fact, were glad he came calling when it was their time. Laddy was never one of those dogs caught stuck end-to-end with his bitch, looking sheepishly over their shoulders at each other, sometimes with a ring of people around them throwing stuff, trying to make them run away together or pop apart. Laddy was too smart, too discreet, and loved his bitches in private. So until his end — until they put him up for stud — Lea was only allowed to watch the courtship. He would trot directly to his bitch, panting his dog-smile, swishing his brush-tail. He had long enough hair to hide his privates: they didn't bob around in back under a puckered anus like on naked short-haired dogs. There was one of those on Valley View too; one tooth always showed outside his upper lip, and no one liked him much. Lea had been there when that naked dog had humped a bitch in the middle of the road, not even caring which end of her he mounted, head or tail. And he ran around unsheathed, his pointed tool red and shiny, and he drooled a lot, and wet on everything.

Laddy was more mature. Circling his bitch, he would sniff delicately, never poking his nose right in there under her tail for a taste. But he would lick her face, especially dog-kisses in her ears, and sometimes gently, but firmly wash her closed eyes with his tongue. Lea would sit by the side of the road, poking sticks into the dust, rapt eyes on Laddy's impressive popularity, but she knew she would have to walk home alone because soon Laddy and the bitch would be on their way to his secret lair to enjoy each other. She imagined it to be shady, but warm, down in the weeds, in the canyon below Valley View, a sudden mat of gray hidden in the dry sage and tall, yellow straw. A place she never saw, or may've seen and never knew it.

One time Lea had called to Laddy as he began to lead the bitch away, but instead of looking back, he had trotted faster.

Later, when he would come home, Lea ignored Laddy for a while, secretly watching him from the corner of one eye as he dozed on the porch, but she would always break down and go to him, kneel, and roll him over to rub his belly. She loved it when he licked her ears, and sometimes, but not always, he would.

She calls them early from basketball in the gym. This gives her extra time for a delicate topic.

"The problem of cramps during the menstrual period is one we all have to deal with." Her smile is modest. She wants the girls to have clean thoughts about life.

She waits for them to stop shifting and looking at one another. Finally, everyone is still; most of the girls look at the mats in front of their knees. Not a giggle. Lea is very successful at this.

"Nature's cure for cramps is to have a baby, but she provides no alternative until that time. There are, however, exercises you can do to alleviate the pressure on your womb." She holds onto the word, drawing it out like an endearment. Girls should learn to love their own bodies. Lea has taken excellent care of her own. "Lie thus." Lea reclines on the mats, sideways to the girls, knees bent, feet flat. "Put a book or board under your hips, tilting the angle of the uterus, then place two or three books on top of the abdomen, forcing the natural pressure to defuse and be absorbed. Also walking and lightly strenuous sports are by all means encouraged to relax and stretch the muscles there which otherwise will tend to fight back against the heavier load." Lea sits up, cross-legged.

"Also important during this special time is frequent washing. Not too hot or too cold, and girls — wash the outside of the orifice only, don't allow dangerous suds to enter your body."

Every girl's neck is bent, face turned toward the mat in front of herself, and Lea speaks to the tops of their heads. One girl looks up, squinting. They're listening, all right.

One afternoon after he'd come home from a private outing, Laddy lay on the porch quietly for several minutes and Lea was alone on the other end of the porch, sitting on a lawn chair with her feet tucked underneath herself. They were silent for a while, then Lea hummed a little tune, and Laddy opened his eyes and looked at her. So Lea got out of her chair and came to his end of the porch to kneel beside him. She continued humming and rolled him over to pat his belly, where the long white hair was fairly thin and his pink skin showed beneath it. She rubbed him for a while there, then looked at his genitals. This was the only way she could see them, with Laddy on his back. She looked close. There was a knot, like a walnut, in the middle, halfway down. She thought immediately it must be cancer, some strange tumor. But it hadn't been there last time she'd looked. She touched it. Laddy swallowed and looked away. Then she rubbed it, trying to rub it away or smooth the knot down into the rest of him. His body stiffened. His legs jerked a few times. When she realized it wasn't a cancer at all, she stopped rubbing it. She went away and came back in half an hour. He was sitting. She extended her palm to him, and he gave her a paw, as he'd been taught. So they shook hands. But then she dropped his foot and continued to offer her hand. Laddy put his nose close, reached out, and just touched her palm with his tongue.

Lea blows her silver whistle. Her decision to stop their tennis games, to call them off the courts they shared with the boys and bring them into their own locker room, came when — for the third time that year — the coach asked her for a game of golf and lunch on Saturday. Instead of the usual answer, this time she blew her whistle.

In the dance room, waiting for the girls to check in their rackets, Lea thinks quickly, a fingertip against her lips. An important day for the girls.

"I've often said," she begins quietly, "that if I had a daughter your age and she had a boyfriend, I'd take her to the doctor for birth control pills. Now, I'm not so sure — not due to any puritan reformation on my part, but a rethinking of what's best for a young girl. Birth control is important, and we can deal with it our own way."

At this point she sits, facing the semicircle of girls. "Well, God knows we all have our little itches, but really, who is the one who best knows how to scratch in exactly the right way? And what better birth control is there?" The girls are watching her; she knew they would, their interest is natural. "Above all, be comfortable with yourself and give yourself time. Be kind, gentle, and patient. Clip your fingernails beforehand, all of them on one hand or just one nail, depending on your favorite finger. Afterwards, take a shower and wash. Sometimes it's even advisable to shower beforehand, too, but in any case," Lea raises her index finger into the air, "be sure your hands are clean."

Okay, Lizzie, let me tell you something that might change your tune. When Laddy was an old guy, they tried to breed him with a dancing little bitch in her first heat. But they were afraid to let them go free, to Laddy's place — they actually thought someone else might do her. They said they had to be sure it was Laddy. So he and she had to be locked together in the smelly garage.

Everyone hoped it would be quick, without complications. Lea wasn't the last to talk to Laddy before he went into the garage. She had to watch through the window. He did try to nuzzle against the bitch, to calm her giddy anxiety. After all, it was her first time, and he understood. But she put her chest to the floor and wagged her little ass in the air, looking up at him, laughing. A few times he put just one paw on her back, but she slipped away, wanting to play; she was so young. Lea could barely see, everyone was jostling for window space. Then someone bumped against the door, and Laddy looked up and saw the faces pressed against the window. He looked around the garage with its dust-filled air and cloud of flies and open rafters, and he turned to the bitch and mounted her and humped, all business, and everyone watched, but the little bitch dropped her hips and wiggled away.

The stupid little bitch. So silly. Everyone decided to leave them alone, give them an hour. When I came back, there was Laddy: he'd crashed to the floor of the garage. I thought he was asleep. And she was still doing her dance all around him: such a tiny, silly, teasing, stupid, taunting, cruel, wretched creature.

She's on her way home, on the bus, exhausted, but pleased with the day's work. The girls didn't even look at each other and smile today. Their school year is almost completed. The bus is crowded, but Lea has managed to get a seat, wedged between a couple of thickset older women, one with a newspaper, the other studying a romance novel. She doesn't read over their shoulders. In front of her, holding on to a strap, there is a middle-aged man with a briefcase and a suit box. One of his legs is shorter than the other and he wears a shoe with three inches of wood attached to the bottom to even him up. She catches him staring at her, but he doesn't quit staring just because he was caught. Lea looks away quickly; looks straight ahead again. His hand in his pocket is right in front of her eyes. She can see his wrist between the end of his coat sleeve and the edge of his pocket. His suit box and briefcase are held upright between his legs. His hand moves in his pocket. Becomes a fist. The pocket material is tight around it. She can see all four knuckles. The bus shakes and rumbles. The man holds his strap. Lea catches him staring and looks away. He rattles coins in his pocket, then removes his hand and straightens the suit box and briefcase slightly, so their edges line up evenly. His wood-bottomed shoe keeps slipping on the floor. The sound gives her chills. The bus lurches and the standing passengers fall toward the sides. The man braces himself with one hand on the window above Lea's head. She looks straight forward, her head tipped back slightly to avoid touching the front of his pants. His breath hits her scalp. Short, hard, quick breaths. She closes her eyes, putting herself back in the warm, damp dance room, telling the girls, *The best course of action, in this case, is to use your teeth*, hearing their guileless laughter amid lockers banging, the scream of her whistle in the empty gym. Then everyone readjusts, shaking out crushed newspapers, straightening hairs and clothing. One of the fat women leans over to retrieve her book from the floor. The man finally pushes himself upright again. Lea turns her face to the window, one hand holding the whistle that's clamped between her teeth. Then her hand falls, the whistle drops and she groans, "Oh, Laddy... what'll I tell them tomorrow?"

THE FAMILY BED

Afterwards, he left the house and walked down the street. He'd tried explaining to the kid: why continue playing the game when it's a lost cause for your own opponent — that's like torture. Finally, he'd had to slap the kid and send him to bed.

They hadn't lived here long and so far he'd only walked around the block. This time he turned left then right then left again. The road lost its sidewalk and he was walking through tumbleweeds. It was summer and his legs were bare, so he stepped into the street and walked in the gutter. The road was on the rim of a canyon, which was why the only houses were on the other side of the street. The houses were small and the yards weedy. Not that his house was spacious and grand. He'd lost another job and this was all he could do until he could find something better than delivery-boy for a print shop. "Don't worry, Dale," Muriel had said, "Barney's so smart — when he grows up he'll finish high school and go to college and have a lot of money!" Dale scooped up a handful of pebbles and started throwing them one by one into the canyon. "Look at him," Muriel kept saying. "Look at him count the money and make change, he does all the figuring in his head. If he doesn't become a movie star, he'll be a big businessman." Dale had to put his hands over his ears or go deaf. Muriel had found the faded, tattered Monopoly game on a shelf in one of the closets of their rental house. "Throw it out," Dale had said, hardly glancing at it. He was busy putting the bed frame together. "Barney loves it," she said, "look, he already has all the squares memorized, he knows how much rent you owe without having to look on the card!"

"Okay, okay, Jesus Christ!" Dale shouted.

They'd sold everything before moving here, but Muriel wouldn't part with her bed — a queen-size with a sagging mattress and a walnut headboard that needed refinishing. They'd bought the bed in the first place at the Salvation Army. He woke up stiff every morning. The kid slept in the living room on a loveseat they'd found in the back yard. He kept the Monopoly game beside him on the floor at night, or sometimes he pushed the box under the couch if it was one of the days Dale threatened to get rid of it. Like tonight.

Muriel had sobbed, "You're teaching him to be a quitter."

"Hey — everyone needs to know when to duck out." He might've hit her, too, if she hadn't flung herself onto the bed, or if he'd ever hit her even once before.

Dale scooped up another bunch of pebbles and threw the whole handful. The rocks spattered into the leaves of a pepper tree growing down the side of the canyon.

"Hey you!" someone called from one of the houses across the street.

Dale turned. "Can't a man take a walk without being yelled at?" he shouted back.

"Come over here — we're having a party!"

She wasn't exactly pretty. Red hair like her head was on fire. That's all he could see from across the street. She was standing on the porch barefooted. When he started crossing the lawn he saw her huge nose and mouth. She laughed. "Come on, come on, the more the merrier!"

"Who is it," said someone inside the house.

"Someone else to help us celebrate."

"What could you possibly have to celebrate," Dale said. He looked past them into the dim living room.

The redheaded woman danced in a circle around him on the porch, then took his arm and led him inside. At first the room appeared to be furnished, but as his eyes adjusted he saw there were only old wooden crates used for tables and shelves, posters taped to the walls, flowers that grew as weeds in the canyon arranged in jars. For a sofa there were two or three large, faded, lumpy pillows propped against a wall, and two or three more pillows on the floor in front.

"I don't have furniture, but at least I don't have junk," Dale said.

"Huh?" said the redhead. "Come on . . . come on and meet everyone."

The other two women in the room weren't any better. One had sooty black hair about a half inch long except on her brow where it was slightly longer, greasy, and combed into a point between her eyes. She also had a million freckles which didn't seem to match the color of her hair. The other was very short and very fat, wearing white shorts that cut into her pink thighs, making a bulging "V" between her legs. She had a husky low voice.

"I'm the talented one in the act," the fatty said. She handed him a drink which tasted like tap water.

"That's what we let her believe," said the redhead, still holding Dale's arm.

"Don't tell me you're actors," Dale said.

"Comics," said the freckly one. "We work little nightclubs and vegetarian restaurants."

"Haven't you ever heard of us?" the fatty said. "The Hot Flashes. Gosh, we plaster our posters all over town."

"Thank God I haven't lived here long."

"Huh? Well, come on girls — let's give him a free introductory show!" They lined up, the fat one in the middle, arms across each other's shoulders and began doing a can-can dance while the fat one sang a wild melody and the other two provided percussion sound effects.

"Hi, what's going on out here?" A tall, sweaty young man was coming out of a dark hall. He was gaunt and looked like he hadn't shaved in three or four days, and there were purplish lines beneath his eyes. The sweat circles under his arms extended all the way down both sides, and he had a red rag tied around his head which was also soaked.

"Don't tell me you raise pigs back there in your bedroom," Dale said.

The sweaty man stared. The three girls broke up their act. "He's joining the party," the redhead said, "helping us celebrate — but we haven't told him yet!"

"Oh!" The sweaty man smiled. "Glad to meecha. My name's Danson. Come on back and meet Rhonda."

Dale followed the sweaty man down the dark hall. The three comics fell in behind, single file. "Who's goosin' me," the freckly one said.

"Pass it on."

Someone pinched Dale's behind. "Knock it off!" Dale turned and the fatty smiled at him.

Then they were at the doorway of the bedroom. All the windows were open, but it was much hotter than the rest of the house. It smelled of heavy sweat and dirty clothes, and a hugely pregnant girl was on the bed, naked from the waist down, her legs spread. Her pubic hair was soaked, as was the dingy towel she was lying on. There was a plastic bowl with some cloudy water steaming near her feet. "Hi," she gasped, then smiled. She leaned to her side so she could raise one arm and wave. Before anyone could say anything else, the girl's smile rippled and her eyes almost disappeared as she squeezed them shut. Her whole face strained. When her eyes appeared again, she began panting, and she repeated the smile. "Thanks for coming, all of you."

Dale held his nose. "Wouldn't you rather be in a clean hospital?"

"Nope." She continued smiling, then grimaced and shut her eyes. Dale shrugged.

"We've performed at grand openings before," the redhead said, "but this is the best."

"Can you see his head yet," the girl gasped.

"Not quite." The sweaty man poked between her legs with his finger while he bent down and squinted.

"Get your glasses, Danny," the girl said. She groaned and smiled.

"You have any air freshener around here?" Dale asked. No one seemed to hear him. "Hey, if this is a party, how about something to eat?"

"Do we have any peanut butter left?" the girl asked, laughing.

"I don't think so." Everyone laughed, except Dale. He turned to go back down the hall and the three comics also trouped back into the living room, singing a Scotch army song through their noses. Muriel said the kid had a singing voice and wanted to buy him lessons — she said she'd get a job to pay for them. "I'm already going deaf as it is," Dale had to tell her again. He picked up his drink from one of the tables made of wooden crates. "Do you have something I could add to this?" he asked. "It tastes like water."

"It *is* water," the freckly one said, "anything wrong with *that*?" She was glaring at him, so he glared back.

"Yes — it tastes like shit, just like all the water in this lousy city."

"You think booze is going to be any gentler on your guts?"

"Yeah, that's right, immediately assume I'm a boozer just because I got laid off and — Maybe I wanted milk, didja ever consider that?"

"Milk is for cows. Maybe I *should've* considered that!" From the bedroom came a shriek, then laughter.

"Look, weirdo, I didn't invite myself here. I thought if we were going to be neighbors — but I can see you don't have a hospitable bone in your body . . . or should I say freckle on your face — "

"Who invited this racist, sexist bastard in here — "

"Hey," the sweaty man ran halfway down the hall. "Knock off the shouting, Rhonda can't concentrate." He didn't wait for an answer. The freckly comic turned her back and began staring at a wall.

"Jeez." Dale shook his head.

"I've just got to go out," the redhead said. "I've got to keep telling people. If I can't find any people, I'll tell the canyon, the rocks and trees. Everything has to know and share what's happening here."

"Why don't you go tell those two what's happening here," Dale said. "*They're* responsible."

The redhead stopped humming and said, "What's that supposed to mean?"

"Look," Dale said, approaching her, "you invited me here — how about taking care of me before you go out looking for someone else already."

"Huh?" She scratched her leg. Her skin was chalky and flaked off. "You're here to share with Rhonda."

"Rhonda has nothing I want."

The redhead slapped his face, then went out, slamming the

door. Dale jerked the door open and shouted, "Can't have a guy come to a party and at least expect a handful of peanuts for his trouble?" She was singing, and her voice grew louder as she crossed the street and stood on the edge of the canyon. She was singing "Waltzing Matilda."

Dale came back into the room and flopped onto the big pillows. Just once, he and Muriel and the kid had started a pillow fight, and he'd knocked the kid clear off his feet, but then Muriel and the kid had ganged up on him from two sides, so he went out and watched TV. That was when they had a TV. The fatty sat beside Dale and touched his arm. "You know, this is the best thing that ever happened to Rhonda. She couldn't get a job, so she slept around. If she didn't get picked up, she had no where to go; then, when she was sixteen, she met Danson."

"You mean *he* has a job?"

The freckly girl turned and sat abruptly on the floor in a lotus position with her eyes shut, and she began to hum. The fatty picked up Dale's glass. "I'll go look for a slice of orange for you."

Dale glanced about. There wasn't much light in the room. In fact, the only light came from an aquarium which was bubbling on a rickety table in the corner. The whole table vibrated because of the noisy motor which ran the air pump. Next to the pillows was a bookcase made of bricks and boards. Most of the books were paperbacks which had been opened so many times the titles could no longer be read on the spines. Muriel kept getting books at yard sales for the kid. "He reads like he's in high school and he's only ten! He reads better'n us!" How many times had he told her to stop squealing in his ear before he went deaf. He pulled the books out one by one to see the titles. *Health for the Millions, Diet for a Small Planet, The Making of King Kong, The Family Bed, Fasting Can Save Your*

Life. There was one hardback, a coffeetable book with a padded cover, *The History of Southern California*. Someone had penciled fifty cents on the inside cover. Dale leaned back and opened that book on his knees. The fatty came back into the room. "Oh, let me show you something in that book." She handed him the water which now had a slice of lemon attached to the rim. "Look," she started fluttering pages with her thumb. "Here it is, look at this, isn't this incredible ... 'for entertainment the early settlers used to capture a bear and chain it to a post then make it defend itself against a long-horned bull.'"

Dale looked into the fatty's eyes for a moment.

"Isn't that terrible?" she said.

"Come on, let's dance."

"What do you think of this idea," the fatty said. "We're going to ask Rhonda to join The Hot Flashes for our next gig."

"You think you can get people to *pay* to see her do this?"

The fatty was sitting crosslegged on the floor near Dale's feet. "I'm going to ignore that," she said. She turned a few more pages of the book. "There used to be herds of deer around here," she said softly. When she closed the book it sounded as though the covers creaked, but it was only another moan from the bedroom.

"Come on," Dale said.

"I heard that sparring deer can get their antlers caught together and then starve," the freckly one said, opening her eyes.

"Ugh." The fatty shivered. "But when you think about it, that's okay because it's natural. The other is ... well, naturally, horrifying."

"It's also natural for a guy to want to have a little fun at a party," Dale said.

"Aren't you having fun?"

The girl in the bedroom screamed, a scream that seemed to go on for hours. Then Dale could hear her panting and she said, "That was a *good* one, Danny."

"Come on, come on!" Dale said. He stood and pulled the fatty to her feet. Her head only came to his chest. Her stomach was touching his groin. "How about putting on some music we can dance to, Janey," Dale said to the freckly one. She shut her eyes again. Dale shrugged. He put both his hands between the fatty's shoulder blades and pulled her as close as possible. The fatty began to hum "The Tennessee Waltz" and Dale swayed with the music, rocking from one foot to the other. "Can't you follow me?" he said.

"You're not with the rhythm."

"Hell with the rhythm." He let his hands move down her back and slip under her T-shirt. He kneaded the rolls of flesh just above her buttock. She didn't yelp, even when he pinched her a few times. But the girl in the bedroom began screaming again, and this time didn't stop. Her voice rose and fell like a siren, grunting like a hungry sow when it dipped too low to actually be a scream, then rising again, shriller and higher.

"Goddamn that hurts my ears," Dale muttered. He pushed his hands down under the waistband of the fatty's shorts and grabbed two handfuls of her butt, squeezing and releasing like bread dough. The fatty continued to hum "The Tennessee Waltz." The freckly one kept her eyes shut. If the redhead was still singing outside, she was being drowned out by the screams in the bedroom. The sweaty man was shouting too. Sometimes the kid knocked on their door at night and Muriel always wanted to let him in. "Everyone's trying to make me deaf!" He pushed the fatty's shorts and underwear down to her knees. She seemed to lose her balance and sat down on her butt, knees apart, looking up at him.

But because of the size of her thighs, he could barely see her crack. "Get ready!" he said, shouting above the screams.

"What?"

"Lose the shirt." Dale dropped to his knees between her legs. He started pulling her shirt over her head and at the same time tried to get her legs farther apart by spreading his own knees. It wasn't easy. Her arms were tangled in her sleeves, so Dale left the shirt over the fatty's head and grabbed her giant breasts with both hands. The fatty had to struggle the rest of the way out of her shirt by herself.

"Hey, listen!" she said. The screams went on and on. Then grunting, moaning, and a sound like gargling, and more screams. "Hey — we're missing it!"

"Wait a sec — you've started something here, you can't just leave." Dale unzipped his pants and pulled himself out. "Come on, come on, we'll hurry." He pushed her to her back.

"Let me help you," the fatty whined.

"I know where it goes." He mounted her and began pumping. She stared up at him, then reached up and cupped his face with both hands and began singing the words to "The Tennessee Waltz." Suddenly the sweaty man started shouting "Here it is, here it is," and the screaming subsided before Dale had come. The fatty kept singing and looking at him, but he went soft, so he abruptly lay down on top of her and made guttural sounds, straining and twitching. Then he sighed, got up, turned around, and quickly put himself away. The fatty also jumped to her feet, pulled her pants up, grabbed her shirt, and ran down the hall. Dale looked at the freckly one, but she closed her eyes again as soon as he turned toward her. She was swaying slightly from side to side.

"Some party," Dale said.

The sweaty man came out of the hall, drying his face on a towel. "It's all over!"

"You can say that again." Dale checked to make sure his fly was zipped.

I'm going to ask you nicely to leave," the sweaty man said. He put the towel across the back of his neck and walked once around the room, kicking the pillows back into place, picking up the coffeetable book. He fed the goldfish, glanced once more at Dale, then went back down the hall toward the bedroom. The freckly girl leaped up and ran after him. A baby was crying. Someone was laughing weakly. Dale started following them down the hall but stopped for a second outside the bathroom. He saw the bucket of slimy blood steaming in the sink.

There was no light in the bedroom. The freckly one and the fatty were kneeling on the bed on either side of the girl, hovering over the plastic bowl and helping to tip it gently, sloshing the water around a baby which was in the bowl.

"What the hell are you doing?" Dale asked.

"I don't want birth to be too traumatic for her," the girl said, "so we're simulating the womb environment and will take her out of it gradually." Her lips looked dark and puffy as though someone had slugged her. But she was smiling. "That's why she's always going to sleep in our bed too," the girl added. The fatty looked up at Dale, wet-eyed and tear-streaked.

"Oh brother," Dale groaned, "don't give me that bullshit." He said it to the fatty, but everyone stared.

"Get the fuck out of here," the young man shouted.

"Danny, the baby — we're supposed to keep our voices smooth and soft for the first several hours."

"Get out, get out!" the young man continued yelling.

"Danny, stop it, please."

"Get out!"

"Danny!" the girl shouted. She picked up her pillow, damp with her sweat, and threw it at Dale. "Get out of here!" Dale swatted the pillow away, then turned and went back into the hall. "Some party," he shouted, but he kept going, out the front door and back down the street toward his own house. By the time he got back to where the sidewalk started, he realized he was humming "The Tennessee Waltz." A coolness had come into the air and splashed over his sweaty face. He entered his front door softly and went over to the couch where the kid slept. The Monopoly game was halfway under the couch and the kid was on his stomach drooling all over his pillow. Dale picked up the game and went back outside. He tried to remember the words to "The Tennessee Waltz" as he walked back to the party. Their door wasn't locked so he went straight in and straight to the bedroom. The baby was nursing on one of the girl's small, pointed breasts. They were all on the bed. The redhead had returned and she was on the bed too. Even the man was on the bed, but he jumped off when he saw Dale, and he came toward the door with his fists clenched. When the young man got near enough, Dale thrust the game into his hands.

The young man stared at it.

"What fun!" the girl cried.

Dale watched them make room on the bed and spread the board out, deal the money around, sort through the properties. They covered up a blood spot on the sheet with a dingy white towel. The fatty came around the bed and kneeled with her back to Dale, her heels pushing into her big ass. They were choosing tokens. "I'll take the cannon," the fatty said, then she turned and pointed it at Dale. "Pow pow."

Dale went into the hall and straight to the bathroom. He took the bucket of afterbirth into the backyard and buried it. He didn't want to go home.

FORMER VIRGIN

When I heard this story a few weeks ago, I wished I could tell you about it. I don't know why. A guy named Roger told me the story about himself and someone named Wanda, but I didn't tell him about you. He might've asked why I don't see you anymore, and what could I have said, that I cried too much? I don't really know why. Do I?

If I *had* mentioned you to Roger, I would've had to tell him that you and I weren't the same as him and me. You knew me a different way. Didn't you? There's a way I could've explained it: Remember the time your wife gave me some of her old clothes? At first I was afraid to wear them, but when I finally came to work in one of the dresses, you said, "I recognize that dress," because no one else would know what you were talking about, so it was okay to say it. You smiled a funny way every time I wore one of them. I still have those dresses, and I still wear them, but no one recognizes them anymore.

Roger wouldn't've understood, but it doesn't matter because I only saw him that one time. How would you look, I wonder, if I told you he and I were having this conversation in bed. But I won't try to imagine it. I wouldn't want you to know.

Maybe the only true similarity is that Roger was Wanda's teacher, just like you were my boss. He was her graduate advisor. I don't know what he advised her in. He read her poems, analyzed her paintings, critiqued her plays, studied her clothing designs, discussed her photography technique, suggested good books and movies, played her songs on his piano? And he started calling her and visiting her in her windy one-room apartment where she served herb tea that tasted like dirt or perfume, and dried figs and humus and pita bread. (Her bed was behind a curtain in the corner.) She had shaved her head a few months before and her hair was a soft one-inch long, making her tiny ears stick out a little. One of her dresses was a black parachute flak jacket. She also had a pair of tight black peg-leg jeans which she usually wore with a size-large V-neck man's undershirt. She put the V around in back. She wore her sweaters that way too. Once she showed Roger a pretty gray pull-over she said she'd bought when she was accepted into graduate school and knew she had to be more dressed up. Then she always wore it inside-out with the V neck in back and the label in front, under her chin.

"Too bad the label didn't say 100% virgin wool," I said to Roger, but I wouldn't want you to hear me say something like that, lying there naked in bed. You'll never know this about me.

But she was no virgin — it was too late for that. Not that it matters. Not that anyone is anymore.

Several times in the few weeks since I saw Roger, I've imagined telling you his story about Wanda, but I can't picture where we'd be. I couldn't have told you at work. You'd know why: In your office I told you things like my credit application was rejected and my car was dented while sitting innocently alone in a parking lot. I like to remember how you smiled and said, "Credit is easy, Cleo," and helped me make a new application. "Once you're credible, you'll wish you weren't." And you said the dent in my car would be a good reminder for me — that's what I deserve for allowing my car to remain innocent so long. But to tell you Roger's story, I would've had to shut the door, and it was a good policy, you said, that we never do that. Lunch was also not a good time for us to talk. Remember, I never said much at lunch? We used to go out with several other people and all sit together at a long booth where you would look at me from the corner of your eye, or across the table, and smile once or twice, or say something about someone else that only I would understand.

Of course there was that time I was at your house, but we had something else to talk about that day.

Most of Roger's story starts when Wanda came to his office after a seminar. She had left class early and he thought she'd come back to ask what had happened during the second hour and to find out when they were going to see the new Italian movie at the Guild. It was spring and had rained that day, so she had her black rubber boots and oiled parasol, and a black leather jacket over her white undershirt. He said her hair looked soft, like the fur on a little, brown laboratory mouse. But her eyes, he said — he could never remember how her eyes looked, even a minute after she walked out of a room.

She sat as usual in the chair beside his desk and pulled her notebook out of her leather book bag. There was nothing held in the rings of the notebook, but between the covers she kept a yellow legal pad. She folded the pages over when they were full of writing, until the first ones got weak and came loose, so she had to fold them in half and put them between pages of her books. She also dug around in her bag for a pen, then tested it on the yellow paper. Tested it over and over, making curly-cue lines down both sides and across the top and bottom. She began coloring in the loops and said, "That woman who sits at the end of the table is really hostile, don't you think so, Roger? I'm sure she thinks I'm a spoiled little rich girl."

"What makes you think so?" Roger said.

"She's always late to class and never says anything. Or she sighs or says *hmmmm* or *Oh!*"

"That's a revealing perception." At this point, Roger smiled while telling the story, and he brushed some hair out of my eyes, which made my stomach kink up and burn like hunger.

"Yes," Wanda said. "Do you think everyone has the wrong idea about us? The man across from me doesn't think I have anything important to say. He thinks I'm just trying to discredit him to make myself look better."

"Oh really?"

"Don't you see the way he looks at me over the top of his glasses — without raising his head — and he stirs his coffee while I'm talking, or spills it. When I tried to clean it up for him once, he said, *forget it — go on with what you were trying to say.* Do you remember that?"

Roger asked, "Is there some problem, Wanda?"

She seemed a little surprised and sat back in her chair, looking at him. He didn't even remember if she wore glasses or not. He said she had a very dainty chin and wide cheekbones. Her eyes may've been brown or green, he said. He'd been trying to remember. But *I* don't have any problem remembering: on your balcony, it was dusk, and as the sun set, your eyes changed from blue to violet.

"Well," Wanda said in her same unsurprised soft voice, "I've been feeling uncomfortably anxious in class to the point where I don't feel I can sit there any more. I'm a distraction and it makes me nervous."

"This is absolutely ludicrous, Wanda," he said.

"What do you mean?" She cocked her head, only slightly.

"Well, you can't stand the thought that everyone might be paying undue attention to you, so you stand and leave the room, which causes everyone to stare after you."

"I didn't mean to disrupt the class."

"But isn't that why you left?"

"Certainly not!" She stopped doodling on her paper.

"I'm not chastising you, Wanda," Roger said. "I'm trying to help."

"I don't want our relationship to be based on you helping me." She still held her pen with both hands in her lap, twisting and turning it between her fingers, unscrewing it, fiddling with the insides, then screwing it back together.

"Do I make you nervous in class, Wanda?"

Again she was speechless for a second, but her hands didn't stop. She looked down at what she was doing to her pen. "I think," she said, her voice even higher and softer, "I shouldn't have chosen to sit so close to you."

Then, after a moment, Roger got up and shut the door of his office. When he turned around again, Wanda was standing behind him, and they embraced.

He said he heard the rain outside. Otherwise the room was silent. He seemed to have a difficult time telling me this part. He thought for a long moment, and I heard my clock humming, and right then, as we lay in bed, I almost told him what I was thinking about: That evening, when you stood and went to the balcony rail, I rubbed my eyes and wiped my nose on my sleeve. The heavy air was salty. I heard you say "Maybe there won't be a fog tonight," and when I could see again, I stared at your glass of red wine balancing on the rail.

They went to her place. Did I forget to mention that Roger was married? It doesn't make any difference; he and his wife had separate bedrooms. He found out that under Wanda's black jeans she wore black silk underwear, but under her white T-shirt she wore a simple, white cotton bra. Then I think he felt a little embarrassed, talking about their sex while lying in bed with me. He stroked my back and down over my rump. I told him it was okay. It makes me glad I'll never see you again.

When they were finished, Roger wanted to talk and Wanda wanted to go out. "Let's do both," she said. She got out clean black underwear and a clean white bra, but put on the same black jeans and white undershirt, then the black jacket and black boots. She stood at the door with her green parasol, jingling her keys in one hand.

She picked the restaurant. He said it was called Earth's Own Garden, and a whole side of the menu was dedicated to herb healing. "Nothing real happens in a vegetarian restaurant," he said to her, and she laughed. Her laugh, he said, was like a music box.

After they ordered he told her about his only other experience with a vegetarian restaurant. Someone was leaving the faculty and they were having a farewell dinner for him. Since he was a vegetarian, they chose a vegetarian restaurant. They were all supposed to meet there, but Roger had an afternoon class which ran later than usual that day, so he decided it wouldn't be worth it to go to the dinner at all. He called the place and asked them to page the party from the university. "I'm sorry," the hostess answered, "this is a vegetarian restaurant — we don't page our customers."

Wanda ordered the smallest salad and sat eating the alfalfa sprouts with her fingers, one at a time. He smiled and said, "What color are your eyes?" She stared at him and he still didn't know.

"You don't seem changed by this," he said.

"Were you hoping I would be?"

"I know *I* am."

"No you're not." She stirred her salad, looking for more sprouts.

He tried smiling again. "Well, it was a first for me — first time on a couch."

She found a sprout and ate it in three bites.

"Next time let's use the bed, okay?" he said.

"I don't like people to see my bedroom."

Roger ordered coffee. "We have grain beverages and herb tea," the waitress said.

"Don't you have anything dangerously flavorful?" Roger joked with her. She had thin brown lips. Wanda wore red lipstick when she went out, but her lips were pretty and pale when, before this had happened to them, he used to drop in to see her, unexpected, on Saturdays.

"I know what," Wanda said brightly. "Let's go to the theater on B Street. They have a French movie — we can talk without disturbing anyone because they'll be reading the subtitles."

"We could go back to your place."

She was already standing, putting on her leather jacket. She turned, her hands in her jacket pockets. He said she looked like a young, lovely punk.

"The heat's not working in my building," she said. "Didn't you notice?"

I wasn't chilly on your balcony until the sun was gone and a wind jumped out of the ocean. I rubbed the bumps on my arms. You never shivered. Your hands were steady as you looked through the telescope mounted on the balcony rail.

The movie had already started. Wanda leaned toward Roger to see the screen between the two heads in front of her. "Wanda, we do have to talk," Roger said. She was holding her wallet in both hands in her lap as she always did in the movies. "I don't want you to misunderstand," he said.

"You mean about our affair?" she said.

"I don't like that word. It doesn't have to be like that — cheap, secret."

Then Roger looked a little embarrassed again and stopped talking, even bent over to give my shoulder a sad kiss.

"It's okay," I told him. "I know there's a difference between her and me."

"Thank you," he said, touching my face again.

Wanda sighed and said, "Wonderful." She was looking at the screen, a wet, black-and-white view of Paris.

"Wanda." He put his hand on her arm and saw that her fingers tightened on her wallet. But she did turn to face him. "Something important is happening to us," he said.

"Do you really think so?" she said.

"I want to know what *you* think."

"I'm flattered . . . aren't you?"

"I just told you it's more than that."

Then Wanda said, "Oh!" and turned to read some dialogue on the screen.

Why wouldn't you stop looking through that telescope? There were no stars. The sky a rose-colored gray. I still remember everything. You knew I would.

"What's happening?" Roger whispered.

"Nothing yet."

"I mean to us."

She didn't answer. Her red lips parted. Her eyes moved across the lines of dialogue.

"I'm going," Roger said out loud. "I hope that you'll meet me outside."

She did come out, and she was smiling at him. She put her wallet in the pocket of her leather jacket and took his arm. But he didn't start walking with her. "Look," he said, "we have to make some things clear."

You never said anything like that. Maybe there was some fog after all, moving inland. "Pull yourself together, Cleo." You finally turned around, but stayed at the rail. "I think you want to look at the world through a Vaseline-covered lens." No lights on the balcony, but I could see your mouth moving.

"It's already clear to me," Wanda said, and she pulled so hard on his arm that Roger had to start walking with her.

"Then tell me how you see us." He said it was the same way they discussed her stories and plays: he told her nothing was happening and she said it was. But this was backwards.

Then she stopped outside a newsstand. "I catch my bus on the next corner, Roger," she said. She gave him a swift kiss on the cheek. "I'll be all right. I have to pick up something here. Drive carefully, it may rain again."

"Wait a minute!" She had already started to go into the newsstand, but he pulled her back. "I know you, Wanda — you starved yourself on grass for supper and now you don't want me to know that you're going to go get yourself some candy bars to eat on the bus!"

"Roger !" she gasped.

After a moment of staring at each other, he said, "It's okay, Wanda," and he touched her face. I shivered. He wasn't touching me then. He was lying on his back talking to the ceiling. He said he didn't remember what she looked like as she listened. His words came out slowly, his voice low, hard to understand. "Wanda, dear," he said to her, "maybe you can't face the world without your alfalfa sprouts . . . it's okay. I'd just like to be closer to you than anyone else has been — to be allowed to see you eat, sleep, maybe even cry once in a while." He *wanted* to see her cry. What does it mean?

Did he stop mumbling or did I stop listening? We lay there a while, then he said, "And you can guess what happened next, otherwise I wouldn't be here with you — Oh, I'm sorry."

"It's okay."

After a while I said to Roger, "How about if, after nailing you, someone told you you're not the center of the universe to anyone but yourself," even though you looked at me and smiled, your words spoken so softly, and the background was a dying day. You may remember what I looked like, but it's not how I look anymore.

Roger didn't say anything else. I think he left soon after that. I stayed there in bed for a long time. But only virgins cry.

LET'S PLAY DOCTOR

The nurse shaves away her pubic hair.

"I wonder if Joey will like this." Dee props herself up on her elbows and watches. The nurse doesn't use shaving cream or water, and yet it doesn't hurt. "Looks like a baby," Dee says, and laughs.

Then she has to stand on the floor and bend over across the examination table while the nurse shaves between her buttocks, holding the sides apart with two fingers. She must be a good nurse — not a single nick, scratch, or drop of blood.

"I guess you'll be lying on your side for a while," the nurse says.

"Yes, a double-whammy!" Dee is seemingly unable to avoid saying anything without the breathless half-laugh. She's just repeating what Dr. Shea said last week when he decided to remove the cyst near her tailbone after he repairs her hernia.

"You know, neither the hernia nor the cyst has ever bothered me, never any pain or anything. They seemed to bother Joey more than me. He was afraid he was going to hurt me or something."

"You don't look old enough to be married." The razor makes a scratchy sound.

"Looks can be deceiving, you know," Dee says. "We've been married three years."

"Just about time for another honeymoon."

The nurse stops shaving for a second as Dee giggles. "We never had a real honeymoon."

"Never too late to start."

"I'll tell him," Dee laughs again.

"Hold still, okay?" The nurse holds her buttocks farther apart, the razor moving intricately around Dee's anus. "You realize you won't be able to, or shouldn't try to have intercourse for at least three weeks."

"Oh, I know that. Joey knows too."

She'd asked Dr. Shea last week in the final pre-surgery exam. He'd probed the hernia gently, then she rolled over and he touched the cyst, lying just under the surface, and he'd explained the procedure, then tapped her bottom and told her to get dressed.

"What about sex?" she'd said. Joey never told her to ask.

"I'm afraid you'll have to wait a few weeks, after the surgery. Tell Joey I'm sorry." Dr. Shea is as thin as a young tree, and when he smiles he's *all* smile.

"That's okay," Dee said. "He doesn't care. I mean, it's no big deal. He's not worried about it. I mean, it's not as though it's going to change anything. Is it?"

"Won't make a bit of difference." Dr. Shea began lowering the examination table, with Dee still on it, lying on her side, wearing light blue underwear and a paper examination gown. She'd shaved her legs that morning, taken a shower, and sprayed a little deodorant in her crotch. He kept his hand on her hip while he lowered the table. A nurse was in the room, holding Dee's chart.

"It's no big deal," Dee repeated.

Another nurse comes in to put silly paper slippers on Dee's feet and a blue paper poncho over her head. "We're ready for you." The three of them walk to the operating room and Dee climbs on the table.

"Dr. Shea's still at the hospital, but the anesthesiologist is here," says a third nurse, already masked. The three nurses turn their backs and begin to scrub. Dee can hear their voices under the running water. Whoever they're talking about had to be reminded about something over and over and everyone's beginning to wonder if she'll ever get it right and how many chances is Dr. Shea going to give her before he — But maybe she's providing him with other services. *Him?* Well, why'd he hire her then? *Him?* The three nurses laugh. Dee turns her head and smiles at the big man who comes in and introduces himself, but she can't understand his name through his mask. He attaches some round things to her chest so everyone in the room can hear her heart beat. She keeps one eye on the door, but Dr. Shea doesn't arrive before the other doctor has already attached an IV and shoots something into the tube so the drowsiness begins like an eclipse.

Then she can hear Dr. Shea's high-pitched voice and the nurses mumbling. One of the nurses says, "What's ten inches long and white? Have you heard this one already?"

"Nothing," Dee says. She can't see anything because the paper poncho is pulled up over her head.

"Is she awake?"

"Hi, Dee!" Dr. Shea says.

"So what's the punch line?" a nurse asks.

"That's it. What she said."

"You knew that joke, Dee?" Dr. Shea says. "Okay release it," he says, in a different voice.

"I remember another joke," Dee says with a chuckle. "But it's too nasty. You know what? I can't feel you doing anything."

"I'm almost done. Go ahead, tell your joke."

"You sure? Okay. How do you make a hillbilly girl pregnant?"

"I don't know. How?"

"Come on her shoes and let the flies do the rest."

One nurse groans. Dr. Shea says, "What? I didn't catch it."

"Don't make me repeat it, it's awful, isn't it? Come on her shoes and let the flies do the rest. You can change the hillbilly to anything — Italian, Mexican, whatever — but I use hillbilly cause I'm from Kentucky, so no one can say I'm making fun of anyone else . . . " She closes her eyes. She can't feel him touching her. Not like last week. He has very soft hands and long fingers, well-manicured and without heavy calluses. Of course he does, he's a surgeon.

"Did Joey tell you those jokes?" Dr. Shea asks.

"Joey? No, I never tell him nasty jokes. I get 'em from a book . . . in the library, that is, I go to the library every night while Joey's at work."

"I gotta get me that book," a nurse says.

"Very hard to find. Not all libraries . . . "

The bookstore is a block *past* the library, in between a cult movie theater and a health food store. A bakery and coffee shop inside the bookstore — where apparently people are allowed to sit at tables and read new magazines — seem to make the store warmer than most. It's a fairly small bookstore, but has a whole wall of magazines, organized by sexual preference. Dee always walks past them, slowly, back and forth, but hasn't yet ever taken one and sat at a table with a tempting croissant. Of course the joke book is on the humor shelf and she reads a few jokes every time — but not at one of the tables — and when the smell of the baked goods gets too overpowering, she leaves. The air outside seems to be shockingly cool — sometimes she gasps.

She wakes puking as they wheel her back to an empty examination room. A nurse walks beside her holding a little dish to catch the vomit. She can't hear Dr. Shea and can't move to look for him. The gurney is narrow and she's on her side. They tell her not to roll one way or the other. She continues puking. Joey arrives to take her home, but she's still puking and can't leave, so he sits beside her all afternoon, holding her hand and reading *Sports Illustrated* while she pukes. There's probably poetry in that somewhere.

Eventually, she's home. She heard Dr. Shea giving Joey some instructions. He said she could have a bath on Saturday. Joey drove carefully, but she puked once on the way home anyway. She sat on the edge of the bed, doubled over, then fell sideways, curled in a ball on her side, noticed the bouquet of carnations Joey had put on the night stand, then closed her eyes and the nausea began to fade. Dr. Shea had told Joey that if she didn't calm down tonight, call his service and they would get in touch with him. She reaches blindly to the night stand to make sure the plastic vomit bowl is close at hand. Joey comes in to say he has to go to work. He sits on the side of the bed and strokes her head.

"Touch my places," she says, "The scars."

"I don't think that would be a good idea."

"Okay, it doesn't matter." She moves one hand, slowly, from where it was tucked between her thighs and pushes it under her pillow, beneath her head. "You won't have to call the doctor tonight."

He pulls the sheet over her shoulders. It's an early summer evening. When he's gone, she opens her eyes once more. The carnations are white and pink, but look gray in the twilight. She was a virgin when she met him.

It might be later, but not too much later. She seems to be watching herself as she gets out of bed, not appearing to need any help, apparently not weak or sore. She brushes her long hair, seeing herself — she might be in the bathroom looking in the mirror, but she can see the *back* of her head, the brush swishing through her hair, which hangs to her butt. Her hair was blond when she was younger, even when she got her driver's license. It's been light brown for several years, but looks blond again now. She breaks off one of the carnations and puts it behind her ear. The flower is some bright, exotic color, but she can't really tell what color it is. Her reflection seems to be coming from a wall of glass, like a picture window. She leans close, shading her eyes to help herself see through. Apparently she already left the house, locked up, walked briskly down the sidewalk, as she does every evening after Joey goes to work. If she passed the library, she didn't recognize it, and the bookstore has changed too — she can't see any books through the window. In fact, she can't see through the window. It's black, huge, and opaque, and all she can see is herself trying to look through.

"Aren't we going to go inside?"

The voice doesn't startle her. It's Dr. Shea. He's with her. Either they came together or he met her here. He looks too young to be a doctor, especially in his green scrub suit, which makes his neck look longer and his smile even more toothy. "Show me where you learned your jokes."

Suddenly she's hot, burning up, and presses both hands to her face. "It's okay," he says, "From now on *I'll* teach you all your jokes." He takes her hand.

The bookstore is extremely hot and humid. It's like a heavy coat hanging on her shoulders. The heat seems thick around her and she paddles with her free hand, passing thousands of racks of books, looking for the wall where the magazines are. "I know they're here somewhere," she says. Even though it's so oppressively hot, she's not sweating. But when they find the magazines, they walk back and forth because she doesn't recognize any of them. "This isn't right, where are they?" It doesn't even seem like she's searching for the magazines. She's looking at his hand holding hers as though she's still standing behind herself. He strokes her knuckles with his thumb.

"Don't you want to look at one of them?" he asks.

"Yes, of course."

"You don't need to be afraid. We'll say it's doctor's orders."

She has a magazine in her hands and Dr. Shea moves behind her, very close, his cheek against hers. The smells from the bakery at the back of the bookstore become potent. She sees a whole pan of buttery cinnamon rolls coming out of the oven. She doesn't let go of the magazine; she can feel the slick, heavy pages in her hands. Dr. Shea kisses her neck. "Let's check your wounds," he murmurs. She's looking at the magazine but doesn't see anything. Dr. Shea lifts her shirt and runs his finger along the line where he had cut her open. She had bandages on when she got home from the hospital, but they're gone now. She can see the place, a red line where the two flaps of her skin are sewn together with invisible thread, his finger moving back and forth across it. She shudders. "Did I make you do that?" he says. She must be mute. Or there's nothing more to say. She can see him smiling, like maybe she's watching from a different angle now, but she's still holding the magazine and he's digging his finger between the stitches then pushing it inside. She doubles over, pressing her butt into him, and he seems to bend over around her. The magazine could be a mirror or maybe she's looking out of the pages, watching herself and Dr. Shea, but sometimes she can't tell which one is her. She's never moved her hips like that. His hand moves into her gently, cupping each organ in his fingertips. He's a surgeon, so he'd know if something was wrong with her.

"Now the other place," he says, turning her around. He holds her buttocks and rubs the wound on her tailbone with his thumb. There's blood on the front of his scrub suit. Bread is baking. The hot odor of it makes her dizzy for a minute. Then he turns her sideways and maybe holds her with his knees, his chin over her head, but his legs and arms and neck are just warm places pressing against her, and the room is so hot anyway it seems hard to tell if it's really him — except for his hands. Each of his hands is on one of her wounds, reaching inside, feeling the slippery pieces of her. She's wiggling and arching her back, but he doesn't tell her to be still. Every once in a while she can feel the magazine in her hand. She smells the bread baking and looks at the blood on his shirt. She asks if it's hers without having to say anything. "You started your period during the surgery," he says. His hands are pushing harder, farther, his fingers spread, softly touching everything they find, although her heart is too far away, and his hands aren't reaching that direction. She must have her eyes closed because she can't see anything anymore, not until his hands meet each other in the middle. He must be clasping his hands together, making a gentle fist that seems to throb, matching the sound of an uncontrolled heartbeat coming from somewhere else, which everyone in the bookstore must be able to hear. She can see her own mouth open and her entire body arch, her head thrown back and she is alone, writhing and moving freely through the pea-soup heat, holding a heavy magazine. Her arm is tired. It's dark and somehow she got back to her bed before Joey came home. She can hear his key in the front door and she can see her hand lying on the mattress beside her, the weight of the magazine tingling in her palm, a pounding soreness in her guts, underneath the bandages. He comes in to ask if there's anything she needs. The room is freezing and she begins to sob but doesn't answer him.

HIS CRAZY FORMER ASSISTANT
AND HIS SWEET OLD MOTHER

Until today, the person I've replaced here was a mystery. Obviously he didn't want to talk about her. Once he said, "She went bats, skiing down the wrong side of the hill, you know?" Another time he wasn't smiling and said, "She must've had a lot of problems, a very disturbed girl." He did call her a girl that one time. She was probably twenty-four or twenty-five, same as I am now, but I think I really *am* a girl. But other than that, the only times he referred to her was like, "The woman who was here before did this or that . . . ," which he doesn't say often because I have my own ways of doing things, and he's about as flexible as they come, or so I hear. His listeners never even noticed when he switched researchers. A good, serious title — researcher — for someone who reads newspapers and tabloids and check-out counter magazines for shtick for his talk show. He doesn't have a *writer*, so *researcher* has to be the title for what I do.

I also do know that this previous *woman* stopped coming up with any good material. And it's so *easy* to find material — we can fill a week of shows in one morning. That gives us all the time we need to schedule and plan his talks for college clubs or afternoon ladies' societies. For some reason, he wants me to go with him tomorrow, fifty miles out in the desert to a country club that booked him six months ago. I can't figure out why the hell he wants me out there. I've gone with him before, so it's not unusual, but all of a sudden now I'm wondering. What a cruddy attitude.

She *was* fired legitimately. Nothing strange about that. He said she wasn't coming up with *anything*, but I found what she was working on when she left: jokes about some rapes at the local college. Fraternity gang rapes — they get the girl drunk or doped and ask if she wants to rest a while before going home, or they offer her a ride, but end up getting a quickie in the parking garage before their car will start — and the defense attorney decided not to prosecute *any* of them. The same term, the school gets put on *Playboy*'s List of Party Schools, the fraternity's national head-quarters refuses to impose any disciplinary action, all of a sudden there're three or four sexual harassment charges brought against some faculty members. And this *woman* wants him to do a rape bit. Like a phone answering-machine joke: "Sigma Q rape service, you ask for it, you'll get it!"

I showed him her material today during donut-and-coffee hour in the lounge. He took the notebook and said, "I've seen this," but sat there reading it all, very slowly, much slower than he reads my material, and he didn't laugh. Well, of course, it wasn't funny, not the material, but amusing at least to imag-ine this crazy *woman* coming up with the idea and *thinking* it was funny. Then, without looking up, he said, "It's kind of a long story."

"Something I shouldn't ask about?" I said.

"You can ask." He looked up and finally smiled. "And you'll even get an answer, if you want."

"If I asked, I would want an answer."

"So, *are* you asking?" His eyebrows don't go *up* when he's teasing, they go *down*. It's incredible. And one of the reasons why I'm never there when he actually does the show — I can't stand the way it's his same comfortable voice (except a little more animated, for live radio) but his face is somewhere else, without expression or with the *wrong* expression.

"Tell me," I said. *Some*one has to end the playing around, usually me. All of a sudden that sounds bad.

"It was just one of those screwed-up things," he said. "I don't know what I did — if anything — to get her started. But this's the crap she came up with." He was still staring at the notebook. The edges were curled-up and brown. The concrete evidence of one of those times when one person's runaway imagination can pile a lot of shit onto someone else. "I tried saying stuff like: 'Get your mind out of the gutter,' and, 'Do you ever think of *any*thing else?' or, 'A one-track mind is great for your social life, but doesn't work on the radio.' That's all I said — " It still seemed like he was reading the material. He wasn't looking at me. I know why I was a little on edge — because it wasn't like us, it was like watching him do the show. His voice was talking to me like I was the audience he never has to face. I could've explained that to him, but by the time he started bugging me about being uncomfortable, he wasn't doing it anymore.

"Then I got fed up," he went on. "I wasn't serious, though, just a little tired of it, sort of wanted to jolt her to her senses, you know? So I said, 'Look, if you want to fuck, come out and say it, don't use this garbage.'"

Then he looked at me, and finally his face and eyes were part of the conversation again. "There," he said. "That's exactly why I didn't tell you. You'll look at me different."

"No I won't."

"Tell that to your eyes."

"Next time I see them, I will. Anyway, what happened?"

"Guess," he said, grinning.

I shivered, then told myself, This's the way we *always* talk. "She tattled."

"Yup. To the station manager. He paid her off so she wouldn't file formal charges, then had a 'private talk' with me."

"Meaning no written record."

"Meaning nobody knows nuttin'."

"Except me."

"You don't know anything either, right?" He said.

"It'll be all over the tabloids tomorrow," I answered.

He started ripping the pages out of the notebook and shredding them. "This isn't going to change anything, is it?" he said.

"Why would it?"

"I mean, you'll just forget it and all?"

"Sure," I said.

"So you're still coming with me tomorrow?"

"Sure, but — "

"Ah ha!" He tossed the shredded rape material into the air like confetti and leapt to his feet. "A hesitation, teetering on the brink! Why just yesterday I was slapping you around in here and you were loving it."

What he meant was our brainstorming session. We always have a good time. I mean, laughing at stupid ideas — that's how the good ones shine through. He'll pretend to twist my arm or choke me around the neck for a dumb idea. Or we'll have a fake argument on some shtick and we'll arm-wrestle over it. It's his show, so it's up to him who'll win. But that's all he meant.

"I *knew* it!" He was saying. "Open my big mouth and you're like a naked hermit crab looking for a new shell to back into." My arm was lying on the table. Suddenly he slammed his hand down on it, clamping my wrist down so I couldn't pull away. I hadn't been *planning* to pull away, but I jumped and *did* pull when he grabbed me. But he was stronger. "But *what*?" he said.

"I was just wondering why you wanted me to go."

"Oh." He let my arm loose. "I just can't face it alone."

I guess he meant the retirement village country club.

———

Naturally, I was a zombie afterwards and remember nothing about his act at the country club. I probably sat backstage, spine erect, knees and ankles trembling, pressed together, even though I was wearing slacks. These horrible chocolate brown pants I always saved for a special occasion. They're so tight, size three. I wear a five but they were the only brown ones on the rack, so chocolate they almost smelled sweet — God, that's sick — size three, but they *fit*. A miracle. A mistake. If the sleek brown pants fit, wear them — but only on special occasions. To dinner, to a party ... to his sweet old mother's mobile home, surrounded by zinnias and petunias and white rocks, second row from the end in the Deer Meadow Rancho Estates in the middle of the California desert. Not the same place as the talk he gave. Twenty miles east of that. An unannounced detour. But she was expecting us. At least she was expecting *him*.

I kept thinking I wanted to go back and study her first expression when she saw me (in these pants), to freeze time right before the split-second it must've taken her to pretend to recover. But I didn't actually see her face, I was behind him. Was it horror (What's he done *now*?") or disgust ("*this* again?") or lost innocence ("oh my *God* ... !"). She never asked where his wife was. At one point, she showed me his baby pictures while he smiled benignly behind her, over her head. She said, "I didn't know you were bringing anyone, but I'm glad I made enough." She'd prepared strawberry shortcake. For his birthday.

"Did you know it was my birthday?" he said.

How much else do I not know?

I said, "How old?"

"A milestone. Thirty-five." His mother was rattling something in the tiny kitchen, maybe she was trembling, how thin were the walls between us. He said, "From the look of your expression you'd think I just said *sixty*-five."

"But I'm not surprised that you're thirty-five."

"My mother's not going to bite you."

You haven't even told her who I really am! She was coming back with a tray. I should've stood to help her, teacups teetering in a stack, steaming teapot, three plates of dessert with the top part of the shortcake sliding off the mounds of strawberries and whipped cream. She only came up to his chest, his heart, had the whitest white hair I've ever seen, and her skin didn't seem old — more like a wrinkled baby just out of a long bath, cleaner than it'll ever be again. Her eyes, behind glasses, watched the desserts tipping, sliding, falling over as she lowered the tray.

"Drat, they didn't stay put."

"But taste just as good," he said, taking one, motioning me to do likewise. I didn't. I waited to be served, waited to be *introduced*. Didn't he see what he was *doing* to her? "Here you are, Jodi," she said, handing me a shortcake that she'd quickly put back together. She knew my name because he'd told her, as we came in the door — I'd offered to wait in the car — "This's Jodi," that's all, no explanation, no job description, not even a last name, just some twenty-four-year-old *girl* (in tight pants) he brings home instead of his wife on his thirty-fifth birthday. I think I was all ready for her to grab his arm and pull him inside then slam the door in my face, but through the prefab walls I'd be able to hear her scream at him, or maybe cry, until he came out, red-faced and eyes averted, to take me home (or to the nearest bus station) before he could come back and have his birthday shortcake. When I did see her, he'd already gone inside and she was smiling, holding the door, so I went inside too, into a small room that looked even smaller because of the fake wood paneling on the walls, and she'd hung dozens of pictures and diplomas. That's what I did, I studied the walls while they exchanged greetings, but she never asked about his wife nor who the hell I was, and he never volunteered any information. He's supposed to be *good* at ad-libbing, he never needs a script, we never write his material down word-for-word. I stared at the glare on the glass in the picture frames. She said, "I have lots more too," and opened a drawer where she kept the baby pictures.

There were only two pieces of furniture for sitting — a soft chair and a small sofa. We ended up with me smack in the middle of the sofa, him in the chair, so she brought a straight-backed chair from the kitchen and sat down opposite him, the three of us clustered around the coffeetable where she'd put the dessert tray. I imagined trying to take a careful bite of shortcake, tipping it over, flipping the cake cream-side-down onto the floor, and she jumps up screaming, "Whore, whore!"

He crammed another forkful flawlessly into his mouth. "Good thing you bought into this resort, Mom, we needed a vacation, didn't we, Jodi?"

"What!" I guess I practically shouted. He looked at me, then smiled, kept smiling at me. I hadn't even taken a bite yet. Why was he treating me that way? His mother said, "I'm so glad you could arrange it. Are the strawberries sweet enough?"

"They're fine."

"I've made strawberry shortcake for his birthday for thirty years now," she said. She was looking at my whole shortcake, my clean spoon, my cooling tea. A new crease on her forehead? "We used to just go out the back door and pick the berries, but now I have to buy them."

"You had a farm?" The first whole sentence I'd said, I think.

"No, no, just a small garden, and a berry patch."

He started humming, like background music while she explained how they used to live in Riverside before it was a city. I faced her and nodded occasionally, but I was listening to him — I recognized the tune, "A Lonely Little Petunia in an Onion Patch." We'd done a bit once on the show using that as background. Something about supposing flowers had wars, would the young radical liberals (the buds, I guess) be called "people-children"? It was dumb, so *dumb*. Rose-hippies. During our '60s nostalgia week. Planning it, I laughed so hard I had to lie on the floor. I almost wet my pants (not *these* pants). Afterwards he helped me get up. The ideas were like popcorn that day. Why was he humming it? Looking at me again, his mother telling a story about how he tried to get out of weeding the garden, then he interrupted her, right in the middle, busted right into a sentence. "That was a good show, wasn't it? Mom can't get my show way out here."

"That's too bad," I said.

"I'd tell you about it, Mom, but poor old Jodi might not survive it again. She might just lie down laughing till she died."

My breath was stuck, I couldn't breathe *out*. Hadn't she gasped? She was chewing a mouthful, touching her lips with a napkin.

"I'm his assistant," I said softly. Someone has to say it.

"No, she's my taster," he said. My mouth dropped open, but I shut it again quickly (jarring my whole head when my teeth snapped together), as he was saying, "You know, like old kings had, to prevent anyone from poisoning them." Didn't *every*one look at my untouched dessert then? "But in our case," he said, "if she doesn't die laughing, I know I'm not good enough."

Wasn't she believing the worst *yet*? Obviously if she hadn't so far, she wasn't going to burn holes through me with her eyes and ask if I'd taken a bath in brown paint (or melted chocolate). But, nearing seventy, was she old enough to still believe in the purity of her baby boy?

She said, "Good enough at what?"

A simple answer could've cleared everything up — put her at ease, let her mind rest — but he said, "Oh, anything and everything, right Jodi?"

My head dropped, I almost cried on that beautiful shortcake she'd probably spent all morning making.

"Wouldn't that be a good bit, Jodi? Why couldn't you stick around someday and do the show with me . . . yeah — we wouldn't even give you a name, just call you The Taster." He put his plate on the coffee table and stood up, hands in his pockets, sounded like he was rattling quarters and dimes (she might've thought so), but it was the charm bracelet he carries there. Once he used it like handcuffs to lock my hands to the back of a chair. We were proba-bly working on our gay policeman bit, after I'd read about a town in Tennessee whose crime rate doubled when some gossip leaked that one of the cops was homosexual. They didn't know which cop it was. Then the cops were all afraid to go out and arrest people.

"Another piece?" she asked him.

She went to the kitchen with his plate. When I looked at him, he was standing there grinning, pouring the charm bracelet from hand to hand. Has she seen it? Didn't she have a million ques-tions? Where did he get it? I'd asked him twice. Once (while I was tied up with it), he said, "It's *mine*. Shouldn't a charming guy go on collecting charms?" Another time when we were sliding it back and forth at each other from either end of the long table, he said his wife gave it to him after he gave her combat boots for Christmas.

"What about it, Jodi," he said, "The Taster? We'll have you give the okay before I can listen to any caller's comments?" His mother was already coming back. I heard her close the refrigerator and turn the kitchen light out. Was he going to get rid of the bracelet?

"C'mon," he said, "you've never been too shy to shoot me down. Go ahead, what's that question all over your face?"

"Kinda dumb, isn't it?" I said softly, the only question I could think of, knowing she was back, putting his plate on the coffee table in front of his knees, so it was too late to ask if she was going to want to know why I don't wear any underwear with these pants. I can't! The lines show. But I always wear pantyhose!

"*Dumb*?" He sat down. "C'mon, Jodi, if you really thought it was dumb you'd put a headlock on me till I gave it up."

I expected it, I was ready for it: *he* would put the headlock on *me*, pressing my ear to his belt buckle until I bled all over the front of his pants, until I gave in and said, "okay okay, we'll do it," while her mother tried to cut her wrists with her teaspoon.

"Change places with me, dear," she said. "I can't see you well with that bright window behind you." I heard her move around the coffee table to the chair he'd been in, then the sofa rocked and I almost fell sideways *onto* him when he sat beside me instead of going over to her chair.

"New sofa?" he asked. He stretched his arm across the back.

"The old one wouldn't fit in here," she said.

"How about if we get them to put one of these in the lounge,

Jodi, instead of those awful vinyl chairs — you always say your skin sticks to them. A love seat like this, wouldn't that be neat?"

"No." I said it looking at her. "The chairs are fine."

"That's why you spend half the time on the floor, on the table, on the windowsill — " He laughed and she smiled. She probably wanted to cry. After refilling his teacup, she added to mine, making the tea rise to the brim, one more drop would've spilled it. "Oops." She continued smiling and emptied the teapot into her own cup. Then the silence. I felt the sofa shift but I kept my balance, eyes shut, just waiting for him to end the slow torture by casually remarking, through a mouthful of strawberries, "Yes, Mom, Jodi and I have to sleep together, in case one of us has an idea in the middle of the night," while I jump up shouting, "Pervert, sleazeball!" And his little old mother falls over in a dead faint across the coffeetable, on top of my untouched strawberry shortcake. We bend over her, look up simultaneously to say in unison, "You killed her," our faces close enough for a quick kiss.

She was telling him something about his sister who lived in Oregon, he was leaning back, behind me, I couldn't see him, but I waited for him to interrupt again, to start humming "Love in the Afternoon," or "Mothers Don't Let Your Babies Grow Up to be Cowboys," maybe even put a hand on my back — she wouldn't be able to see it from where she was. He might slowly and gently massage each vertebra until I felt loose and relaxed as a ragdoll, his mother talking about his nieces and nephews and their school activities (already dating, is that a school activity, doesn't she wonder where it might lead?). Maybe I'd be ready to fall asleep, smell the whipped cream and strawberries as my body bent farther forward, my head sinking to my knees, then he would push his fingers into my armpits, laughing "Gotcha!" His mother, stone frozen, her last strawberry and picture-perfect dollop of whipped cream poised on her spoon halfway to her mouth. The sofa shifted, he said, "Showtime, Jodie." I screamed, "Don't touch me again!" But he and his mother sat there eating strawberry shortcake as though no one had screamed anything.

HER FIRST BRA

1981

There was one more card from Millard in August, some sort of mushy sunsets-at-the-beach or dew-on-flowers missing-you crap, and he wrote, *hope to see you again someday*. Three weeks later, Dale picked it up from the floor under the kitchen card table and said, "Who's this from, your mother?"

"Yuckity yuk." Loralee was slicing hotdogs to go into canned beans. Dale ate lunch at about ten a.m. when he got home from his new job delivering fresh tortillas to restaurants.

"Well, who is it?"

"It's a photographer I did a session for. I guess he liked me."

"A *session*? What's that mean? You're working as a model? Since when?"

"About six months."

"Why didn't you tell me?"

"I thought I did." She put a plate of tepid franks-n-beans in front of him, then started sorting through the mail, putting the utility and credit card bills in one pile for Dale to pay from his checking account, the rent and food came from hers. She had a session that afternoon. The guy on the phone yesterday had asked how old she was and she'd answered *I'm VERY bold, why'd'you ask?* then the guy digressed to something else, the color of her hair and eyes, how tall she was, her measurements. She'd changed her ad again. It said, *young, versatile female model for private photo sessions with imaginative photographers, amateur or professional.*

"How much have you made?" Dale asked.

"Not much. The rent went up, remember?"

"Well let's make out a *budget* or something, maybe we don't have to sell anything to buy grass."

"Sessions aren't predictable, Dale. We can't budget for them. I thought you were *off* grass, anyway."

"Well they use it for cancer patients, don't they? Maybe it'll help."

"Help *what*? God, what a hypochondriac, it really gets old."

"I'm getting this shortness of breath all the fucking time, dammit, I'm hot then cold, then I start sweating my fucking ass off. What would you call it?"

"Maybe it's menopause."

"Har-de-fucking-har." He put three huge spoonfuls into his mouth in rapid succession before chewing and swallowing.

She picked up his empty plate and put it with the dirty pan beside the sink. "Dale, I tried to tell you what'll probably happen, but you wouldn't believe me." She boosted herself to the counter and swung her feet into the sink to shave her legs. "Luckily I don't think you'll even miss me."

"What're you yammering about?"

Sometime during that summer, Dale had sat in front of the TV while some station showed the whole Royal Wedding. As she passed through the living room, Loralee heard play-by-play announcers murmuring over trumpety fanfare music, saw flashes of white horses, an ornate, made-from-a-pumpkin carriage, an endless velvet runway, and gargantuan white dress.

She'd actually only had three jobs all summer, and none of them had really cashed out. The first just wanted her feet — feet walking, feet splashing puddles, feet showing over the side of a pick-up truck, feet on gas pedals, feet kicking a ball, feet in high heels. He said he'd done sessions with guys and older people and little kids, and some animals. When he took her out for lunch after the session, she touched his leg with her bare toes under the table, but nothing happened, so the *Feet!* exhibit he said he was working on must've been real. The second wanted her to look through the crotch and branches of an old burned tree, wearing a light cotton dress smudged with soot, but the photographer was a woman and women were never the sickos, at least not so Loralee could tell or figure an angle on. The third worked out a little better because he said from the start he wanted a nude, but he also made her sign a form promising she was over 18. Still, he liked her shaved twat and fucked her afterwards, but only gave her $20 for cab fare when she asked, although she was parked around the corner from his house.

This latest one handed her two fifties before she came through the door. The session was at his house — he had his living room furniture pushed to one side and a corner converted into a set resembling a dressing room in a fancy department store. A three-sided mirror and stool, clothes with tags draped over accordion partitions, with big umbrella photography lamps preventing anything from throwing or showing a shadow.

"Okay, listen to this," the guy said. He had long hair parted in the middle, the kind that either looks dirty or, if it's clean, is so fine it's like baby hair that was never cut. He also had one of those halfway mustaches that usually only sixteen-year-old boys can grow. All he needed was a fringed vest and some granola. "Okay, listen," he repeated, "it's like, you're shopping, it's a big day because . . . see, you've come to the store without your mother — "

"My *mother*?"

"Yeah, listen, you've come shopping, you took a bus or rode your bike, but you came to this upscale store where you get one of those personal shoppers. You see, you're here to get your first . . . training bra." Suddenly he ducked his head and looked through a camera on a tripod. She wasn't even on the set yet.

"Does anyone even use training bras anymore?"

"Sure they do, and listen, you're all excited, this is a big day for you, a milestone, know what I mean? Today you become a woman . . . and all that." He stood up but continued to look at the set, not a Loralee.

"And I suppose my dressing room has a hidden camera or two-way mirror. And then what, la-de-da, my personal shopper is a man?"

"Maybe," he said slowly. "We'll see. The importance of this is — this is such a big day for a girl. It makes her feel like . . . anything can happen. Um, hang your old clothes on the hook there, like you would in a dressing room. And here you go, try these on." He pulled a plastic Sears shopping bag from behind one of the partitions.

"I doubt Sears has personal shoppers," she said, looking inside. There were three or four cupless bras and matching underwear, one set white with purple flowers, one baby blue, one with pink polka dots, and one set basic white with lace. The bras were just stretchy material with elastic straps and a hook in back.

"You can have them when we're finished," he said. "Do you have any that nice?"

"No I can't say that I own anything like these. In fact, I don't have a bra."

"You don't?" His face and sad brown eyes and repulsive mustache seemed to leap at her, but he hadn't moved closer, just was looking at her. "Oh God, that's great. Perfect. Like . . . this's real, isn't it? Your first bra."

"Yeah, whatever. Where should I change?"

"Well . . . the dressing room, of course."

She looked back at him for a moment while he touched his limp hair then touched his mustache then put three fingers over his lips and dropped his eyes.

"Of course, I'm such an airhead."

He dragged another stool over so he was sitting behind the camera. After her jeans and t-shirt were hung on the hook and her socks stuffed into her shoes (he said leave them under the stool, and let one sock come trailing out of the shoe a little), she glanced at the camera while putting on the flowered bra and underwear with her back to him, but of course everything showed in the mirror, tits and mound with just a little new growth.

"Your first bra," he murmured, the camera clicking, zipping to the next frame and clicking again. "How does it feel?"

She turned to hide a laugh as a small burp. The bra actually fit her but the underwear was not bikini style. The high waisted panties made her tits look even smaller, the bra like an elastic headband put around her chest.

"Oh God," he moaned, "God-in-heaven." The camera clicking and clicking. Something in her gut popped, drilled through, leaving behind a vibrating hot Jello-y place in her middle. She turned slowly back and forth in front of the mirror, stretching to check her ass over each shoulder which also stretched the bra.

"*Oops!*" One tit popped out when the bra rode up. "Where's my personal shopper, I need to know if this one fits."

The guy was huddled on his stool, his face almost to his lap, no longer clicking, sort of whimpering.

"Come on, please, mister? It's my big day, help me pick one that fits."

He slid off the stool onto his knees and shuffled toward her. His head came up to her stomach. His eyes were murky and glistening, sweat on his upper lip had dampened the disgusting little mustache. He held her around the waist with one hand, pulling the flowered underwear tight against his chest, bending her knees slightly and throwing her off balance so she had to hold onto his shoulders and lean backwards slightly. With two fingers he eased the bra back over her exposed tit.

"There, it fits like that," he breathed.

"Are you sure?"

He moved his hands slowly up her body until he was holding her around the ribcage, a thumb on each nipple. He moved the thumbs back and forth, hardening the nipples under the stretchy purple-flowered material. His face tilted up. His two watery eyes right behind each thumb. "Yes, this is how it goes. Like this. Like this."

"I know, um, fifteen is sort of late for my first bra, but my mother still thinks I'm not old enough, isn't that *lame*?" she said, making her voice airy and higher. The flowered underwear were wet between her legs. She tried to grind her twat against his chest but zingers of adrenalin were zapping her almost continuously and she was in danger of falling over backwards.

"It's OK," he whispered, "maybe you were fourteen just yesterday. But you had to be ready. You knew when you were ready."

"I'm ready."

"Today you were ready. Today was the day. Oh, but if only your little titties wouldn't grow any more," he sobbed, "so impatient for this day, but now they'll be ruined." He slid his hands to her back and pulled her stomach against his face, blubbering against her skin below the bra.

"Hey, mister," she breathed softly. "Today's not over yet." She touched a bald spot on his crown with a single finger. "Remember, today's my big day. And there's still a half hour of it left."

He lurched to his feet with her in his arms and smiled through his tears down into her face. He bent and kissed her gently, touching her lips with the awful mustache, while carrying her out of the set and down a hall. The room they went into was dim, but after placing her on the bed, he turned on the night stand lamp and she could see the white lace canopy, the matching white lace lampshade and bedspread and curtains, antique-looking dolls in white or peach or baby-blue satin dresses lined up on a shelf, plus little Troll dolls and glass princesses, horses and china puppies, a brush and comb set on the dresser, a life-sized white teddy bear sitting in a corner.

"This isn't *your* room is it?" Loralee asked, propping herself up on her elbows. He was kneeling again, beside the bed.

"No . . . it's yours."

"Huh? *Oh* . . . ," she lay back slowly. "I know — it's the room my mother doesn't know I left to go buy my first bra, right?"

"That's right." He took off his shirt. He was as skinny as Dale but not a single hair on him, except his armpits. "Just touch them against mine while they're still little, while it's still the big day." He got on top of her. She couldn't see or feel any hard-on inside his baggy green army-surplus pants, but his hips were below hers, on the mattress between her knees, so she wouldn't've felt it anyway. He pressed his gaunt chest against hers, his head down against her neck, then without raising his body eased the bra up so her bare breasts were against his chest. He rocked slightly so their nipples brushed back and forth. And he started to tremble. She could feel his heart like a fist on a windowpane, banging to get out. His swaying continued for five or ten minutes.

Loralee's buzz was long gone. She checked her watch by raising one arm in the air behind his shoulders.

Then he was easing the bra back over her, with his chest still pressed to hers. "Okay," he whispered in her ear. "I didn't hurt you." He backed up off of her and stood beside the bed. "I'll leave you in your pretty room, with your bears and dolls." He clicked off the light and retreated toward the door.

"Hey!" A crude voice blasting through the room. Loralee sat up. "I *would* like a doll like one of them. Where could I get one?"

"A doll shop." He was a shadowy form by the door, putting his shirt on.

"How much would it cost?"

"Some of them are as much as $200."

"I could just get a *fifty* dollar one, though ... couldn't I? or a hundred?"

He didn't answer, buttoning his shirt, then he looked up, but she couldn't see his eyes. It was too dark.

"A girl should have a doll like that before she gets too old ... don't you think?"

He slowly reached for the door knob. "Too old?"

"Yeah, like ... I should have one *now*, several years before I'm ... say, *eighteen* ... don't you think?"

He sniffed. He cleared his throat. "How did you drive over here if you're fifteen?"

"Well...this *is* a big day for me, isn't it. Um...learner's permit?"

He opened the door and a crack of light lay on the floor between him and the bed. "I...okay. Okay, just a sec." Then he went out and closed the door.

She lay back on the bed with a suddenly thudding pulse, but not the same thing as the earlier neon lightning bolt of adrenalin. The wave of nauseous weakness passed, a feeling that almost stunk, and she thought about the symptoms Dale described, then she got off the bed. Her clothes were folded on the sofa in the living room with exactly one hundred dollars in cash placed on top, a fifty, two twenties, a five and five ones. Of course the first two fifties were still stashed in her jeans.

Outside his front door she wrote his address on one of the bills, but it turned out to be one of the ones and she spent it by accident, stopping at the corner store for a can of tuna and loaf of bread for dinner. She didn't realize the bill with the address was gone until she was putting the three fifties away in her underwear drawer, in an envelope she would take to the bank the next day. But what did she think she was she going to do with the address — write and say if he didn't pay more she'd tell someone he'd boinked jailbait? He hadn't actually done the deed.

In November Loralee got her hair cut into a pixie style and used some of her savings for white jeans, a white jean jacket, and several new tank tops. She had her ears pierced and wore just the two pearl studs which came with the piercing. She let Dale pay for the piercing and call it her Christmas present, but in December he also bought her a corduroy skirt and jacket set that was one size too big, so she exchanged it for a denim mini and peasant-style top, both with designs made of sequins and glitter, both from the junior department. Dale said she looked like a baby pop star in *Teen Beat* magazine.

"That'll work," she answered.

"Whadda you talking about?"

"Oh, just thinking. If I want to start a real modeling career, I hafta have an angle, you know? My own shtick. Like, do junior high fashions."

"You can't start a real modeling career just because you get a few new clothes and say you want to be a model."

"You don't know jack about it. I've had some gigs. How many gigs have you had lately?"

Dale stared at the TV screen. It wasn't even on. He still had hair down to his collar, except where he didn't have hair at all, and it looked wet even when it wasn't. The flattened cushions in the chair that had come with the furnished apartment had stains now where his head rested. Sometimes he still tapped a drumstick on the coffee table while he sat there. It seemed the drumstick appeared and disappeared by magic, but she'd found it once, by accident, stashed under the seat cushion.

Loralee loaded some celery sticks with peanut butter, wrapped them in a paper towel and placed them on Dale's lap on her way to the sofa. "Dale, we have to talk."

"About me going down in flames?"

"No, but maybe *we* are. You know? It's only been, what, three and a half years. We could just call it one of those things. We're both young, we could, you know, still be like our ages."

"Instead of old married farts?"

"Speak for yourself, but I guess that's the general idea."

The drumstick appeared, but he didn't start tapping. He

held it up and placed the tip against his lips like a long finger saying *Shhhhh*. "No."

"No? That's it, just *no?*"

He took a bite of celery then replaced the tip of the drumstick against his mouth while he chewed. It sounded like a horse chewing corn. It sounded kind of nice.

"It wouldn't be like we hate each other's guts and go to court to fight over the car and stereo," Loralee said. "And it doesn't have to be *now*, we could do it when we're both ready, when we can both afford it, you know?"

"We can barely afford this shit *together*."

"I know, but I've been working on this plan."

"You mean becoming a famous cover girl by next week?"

"There's lots of types of modeling, Dale, and I think I've found my niche, something I can even capitalize on, expand the potential for real profit."

"Now you sound like some fatcat." He swallowed what looked like a hard lump.

"I'm just saying I've discovered a way to make what I'm good at more lucrative — does that word pass the lowlife test? And when I make enough of a stash, how about I share it with you then we, you know, go our separate ways?"

"What if I want to stay with you?" He was just sitting there looking down into his lap like an imbecile who watches himself pee, holding a celery stick with globs of peanut butter in one hand and the drumstick in the other.

"Please, don't go Karen Carpenter on me." Loralee stayed on the sofa for only a few seconds longer, then went into the bathroom, shook her short hair and watched it all fall back into place. For the first time in her life she was glad for the strip of freckles across her nose. She'd get some of those rubbery bracelets the girls on her bus wore to school — they looked like they were made of Jujubes and were cheap, sold in packages on the rack by the cash register at the grocery store. These investments could be doubled, maybe tripled quickly. It was going to cost the next sick bozo more than a hundred to do more than look.

IS IT SEXUAL HARASSMENT YET?

Even before the Imperial Penthouse switched from a staff of exclusively male waiters and food handlers to a crew of fifteen waitresses, Terence Lovell was the floor captain. Wearing a starched, ruffled shirt and black tails, he embodied continental grace and elegance as he seated guests and, with a toreador's flourish, produced menus out of thin air. He took all orders but did not serve — except in the case of flaming meals or dessert, and this duty, for over ten years, was his alone. One of his trademarks was to never be seen striking the match — either the flaming platter was swiftly paraded from the kitchen or the dish would seemingly spontaneously ignite on its cart beside the table, a quiet explosion, then a four-foot column of flame, like a fountain with flood-lights of changing colors.

There'd been many reasons for small celebrations at the Lovell home during the past several years: Terence's wife, Maggie, was able to quit her job as a keypunch operator when she finished courses and was hired as a part-time legal secretary. His son was tested into the gifted program at school. His daughter learned to swim before she could walk. The newspaper did a feature on the Imperial Penthouse with a half-page photo of Terence holding a flaming shish-kebab.

Then one day on his way to work, dressed as usual in white tie and tails, Terence Lovell found himself stopping off at a gun store. For that moment, as he approached the glass-topped counter, Terence said his biggest fear was that he might somehow, despite his professional elegant manners, appear to the rest of the world like a cowboy swaggering his way up to the bar to order a double. Terence purchased a small hand gun — the style that many cigarette lighters resemble — and tucked it into his red cummerbund.

It was six to eight months prior to Terence's purchase of the gun that the restaurant began to integrate waitresses into the personnel. Over the next year or so, the floor staff was supposed to eventually evolve into one made up of all women, with the exception of the floor captain. It was still during the early weeks of the new staff, however, when Terence began finding gifts in his locker. First there was a black lace and red satin garter. Terence pinned it to the bulletin board in case it had been put into the wrong locker, so the owner could claim it. But the flowers he found in his locker were more of a problem — they were taken from

I know they're going to ask about my previous sexual experiences. What counts as sexual? Holding hands? Wet kisses? A finger up my ass? Staring at a man's bulge? He wore incredibly tight pants. But before all this happened, I wasn't a virgin, and I wasn't a virgin in so many ways. I never had an abortion, I never had VD, never went into a toilet stall with a woman, never castrated a guy at the moment of climax. But I know enough to know. As soon as you feel like *some*one, you're no one. Why am I doing this? *Why?*

So, you'll ask about my sexual history but won't think to inquire about the previous encounters I *almost* had, or *never* had: it wasn't the old the vases on the tables. Each time that he found a single red rosebud threaded through the vents in his locker door, he found a table on the floor with an empty vase, so he always put the flower back where it belonged. Terence spread the word through the busboys that the waitresses could take the roses off the tables each night *after* the restaurant closed, but not before. But on the whole, he thought — admittedly in retrospect — the atmosphere with the new waitresses seemed, for the first several weeks, amiable and unstressed.

Then one of the waitresses, Michelle Rae, reported to management that Terence had made inappropriate comments to her during her shift at work. Terence said he didn't know which of the waitresses had made the complaint, but also couldn't remember if management had withheld the name of the accuser, or if, when told the same at this point, he just didn't know which waitress she

ships-in-the-night tragedy, but let's say I had a ship, three or four years ago, the ship of love, okay? So once when I had a lot of wind in my sails (is this a previous sexual experience yet?), the captain sank the vessel when he started saying stuff like, "You're not ever going to be the most important thing in someone else's life unless it's something like he kills you — and then only if he hasn't killed anyone else yet nor knocked people off for a living — otherwise no one's the biggest deal in anyone's life but their own." Think about that. He may've been running my ship, but it turns out he was navigating by remote control. When the whole thing blew up, *he* was unscathed. Well, now I try to live as though I wrote that rule, as though it's *mine*. But that hasn't made me like it any better.

There are so many ways to humiliate someone. Make someone so low they leave a snail trail. Someone makes a was. He said naturally there was a shift in decorum behind the door to the kitchen, but he wasn't aware that anything he said or did could have possibly been so misunderstood. He explained that his admonishments were never more than half-serious, to the waitresses as well as the waiters or busboys: "Move your butt," or "One more mix-up and you'll be looking at the happy end of a skewer." While he felt a food server should appear unruffled, even languid, on the floor, he pointed out that movement was brisk in the kitchen area, communication had to get the point across quickly, leaving no room for confusion or discussion. And while talking and joking on a personal level was not uncommon, Terence believed the waitresses had not been working there long enough for any conversations other than work-related, but these included light-hearted observations: a customer's disgusting eating habits, vacated tables

joke, you don't laugh. Someone tells a story — a personal story, something that mattered — you don't listen, you aren't moved. Someone wears a dance leotard to work, you don't notice. But underneath it all, you're planning the real humiliation. The symbolic humiliation. The humiliation of humiliations. Like I told you, I learned this before, I already know the *type*: he'll be remote, cool, distant — *seeming* to be gentle and tolerant but actually cruelly indifferent. It'll be great fun for him to be aloof or preoccupied when someone is in love with him, genuflecting, practically prostrating herself. If he doesn't respond, she can't say he hurt her, she never got close enough. He'll go on a weekend ski trip with his friends. She'll do calisthenics, wash her hair, shave her legs, and wait for Monday. Well, not *this* time, no sir. Terence Lovell is messing with a sadder-but-wiser-chick.

that appeared more like bat-tle-grounds than the remains of a fine dinner, untouched expen-sive meals, guessing games as to which couples were first dates and which were growing tired of each other, whose business was legitimate and whose prob-ably dirty, who were wives and which were the mistresses, and, of course, the rude customers. Everyone always had rude-cus-tomer stories to trade. Terence had devised a weekly contest where each food server pro-duced their best rude-customer story on a three-by-five card and submitted it each Friday. Terence then judged them and awarded the winner a specially made shish-kebab prepared after the restaurant had closed, with all of the other waiters and waitresses providing parodied royal table service, even to the point of spreading the napkin across the winner's lap and dab-bing the corners of his or her mouth after each bite.

The rude-customer con-test was suspended after the

complaint to management. However, the gifts in his locker multiplied during this time. He continued to tack the gifts to the bulletin board whenever possible: the key chain with a tiny woman's high-heeled shoe, the four-by-six plaque with a poem printed over a misty photograph of a dense green, moss-covered forest, the single black fishnet stocking. When he found a pair of women's underwear in his locker, instead of tacking them to the bulletin board, he hung them on the inside doorknob of the women's restroom. That was the last gift he found in his locker for a while. Within a week he received in the mail the same pair of women's underwear.

Since the beginning of the new staff, the restaurant manager had been talking about having a staff party to help the new employees feel welcome and at ease with the previous staff. But in the confusion of

Yes, I was one of the first five women to come in as food servers, and I expected the usual resistance — the dirty glasses and ash-strewn linen on our tables (before the customer was seated), planting long hairs in settling in, a date had never been set. Four or five months after the waitresses began work, the party had a new purpose: to ease the tension caused by the complaint against Terence. So far, nothing official had been done or said about Ms. Rae's allegations.

During the week before the party, which was to be held in an uptown nightclub with live music on a night the Imperial Penthouse was closed, Terence asked around to find out if Michelle Rae would be attending. All he discovered about her, however, was that she didn't seem to have any close friends on the floor staff. Michelle did come to the party. She wore a green strapless dress which, Terence remembered, was unbecomingly tight and, as he put it, made her rump appear too ample. Her hair was in a style Terence described as finger-in-a-light-socket. Terence believed he probably would not have noticed Michelle at all that

the salads, cold soup, busboys delivering tips that appeared to have been left on greasy plates or in puddles of gravy on the tablecloth. I could stand these things. It was like them saying, "We know you're here!" But no, not *him*. *He* didn't want to return to the days of his all-male staff. Why would he want that? Eventually he was going to be in charge of an all-woman floor. Sound familiar? A harem? A pimp's stable? He thought it was so hilarious, he started saying it every night: "Line up, girls, and pay the pimp." Time to split tips. See what I mean? But he only flirted a little with them to cover up the obviousness of what he was doing to me. Just a few weeks after I started, I put a card on the bulletin board announcing that I'm a qualified aerobic dance instructor and if anyone was interested, I would lead an exercise group before work. My card wasn't there three hours before someone (and I don't need a detective) night if he were not aware of the complaint she had made. He recalled that her lipstick was the same shade of red as her hair and there were red tints in her eye shadow.

Terence planned to make it an early evening. He'd brought his wife, and, since this was the first formal staff party held by the Imperial Penthouse, had to spend most of the evening's conversation in introducing Maggie to his fellow employees. Like any ordinary party, however, he was unable to remember afterwards exactly what he did, who he talked to, or what they spoke about, but he knew that he did not introduce his wife to Michelle Rae.

Terence didn't see Maggie go into the restroom. It was down the hall, toward the kitchen. And he didn't see Michelle Rae follow her. In fact, no one did. Maggie returned to the dance area with her face flushed, breathing heavily, her eyes filled with tears, tugged at his arm, and with her voice

had crossed out "aerobic" and wrote "erotic," and he added a price per session! I had no intention of charging anything for it since I go through my routine everyday anyway, and the more the merrier is an aerobic dance motto — we like to share the pain. My phone number was clear as day on that card — if he was at all intrigued, he could've called and found out what I was offering. I've spent ten years exercising my brains out. Gyms, spas, classes, health clubs . . . no bars. He could've just once picked up the phone, I was always available, willing to talk this out, come to a settlement. He never even tried. Why should he? He was already king of Nob Hill. You know that lowlife bar he goes to? If anyone says how he was such an amiable and genial supervisor . . . you bet he was genial, he was halfway drunk. It's crap about him being a big family man. Unless his living room had a pool table, those beer mirrors on the shaking, begged Terence to take her home. It wasn't until they arrived home that Maggie told Terence how Michelle Rae had come into the restroom and threatened her. Michelle had warned Mrs. Lovell to stay away from Terence and informed her that she had a gun in her purse to help *keep* her away from Terence.

Terence repeated his wife's story to the restaurant manager. The manager thanked him. But, a week later, after Terence had heard of no further developments, he asked the manager what was going to be done about it. The manager said he'd spoken with both Ms. Rae and Mrs. Lovell, separately, but Ms. Rae denied the incident, and, as Mrs. Lovell did not actually see any gun, he couldn't fire an employee simply on the basis of what another employee's wife said about her, especially with the complaint already on file, how would that look? Terence asked, "But isn't there some

wall, and the sticky brown bar itself—the wood doesn't even show through anymore, it's grime from people's hands, the kind of people who go there, the same way a car's steering wheel builds up that thick hard black layer which gets sticky when it rains and you can cut it with a knife. No, his house may not be like that, but he never spent a lot of time at his house. I know what I'm talking about. He'll say he doesn't remember, but I wasn't ten feet away while he was flashing his healthy salary (imported beer), and he looked right through me—no, *not* like I wasn't there. When a man looks at you the way he did at me, he's either ignoring you or undressing you with his eyes, but probably *both*. And that's just what he did, and didn't stop there. He's not going to get away with it.

law against this?" The manager gave Terence a few days off to cool down.

The Imperial Penthouse was closed on Mondays, and most Monday evenings Terence went out with a group of friends to a local sports bar. Maggie Lovell taught piano lessons at home in the evenings, so it was their mutual agreement that Terence go out to a movie or, more often, to see a football game on television. On one such evening, Maggie received a phone call from a woman who said she was calling from the restaurant — there'd been a small fire in one of the storage rooms and the manager was requesting Terence come to the restaurant and help survey the damage. Mrs. Lovell told the caller where Terence was.

The Imperial Penthouse never experienced any sort of fire, and Terence could only guess afterwards whether or not that was the same evening

Wasn't it his idea to hire us in the first place? No, he wasn't there at the interview, but looked right at me my first day, just at me while he said, "You girls probably all want to be models or actresses. You don't give *this* profession enough respect. Well," he said, "you will." Didn't look at anyone else. He meant me. I didn't fail to notice, either, I was the only one with red hair. Not dull auburn — flaming red. They always assume, don't they? You know, the employee restrooms were one toilet each for men and women, all the customary holes drilled in the walls, stuffed with paper, but if one restroom was occupied, we could use the other, so the graffiti was heterosexual, a dialogue. It could've been healthy, but he never missed an opportunity. I'd just added my thoughts to an on-going that Michelle Rae came to the sports bar. At first he had considered speaking to her, to try to straighten out what was becoming an out-of-proportion misunderstanding. But he'd already been there for several hours — the game was almost over — and he'd had three or four beers. Because he was, therefore, not absolutely certain what the outcome would be if he talked to her, he checked his impulse to confront Ms. Rae, and, in fact, did not acknowledge her presence.

When a second complaint was made, again charging Terence with inappropriate behavior and, this time, humiliation, Terence offered to produce character witnesses, but before anything came of it, a rape charge was filed with the district attorney and Terence was brought in for questioning. The restaurant suspended Terence without pay for two weeks. All the waitresses, except Ms. Rae, were interviewed, as well as several ex-waitresses — by

discussion of the growing trend toward androgyny in male rock singers — they haven't yet added breasts and aren't quite at the point of cutting off their dicks — and an hour later, there it was, the thick, black ink pen, the block letters: "Let's get one thing clear — do you women want it or *not*?" Just what is the *thrust* of this conversation?" What do you *call* an attitude like that? And he gets *paid* for it! You know, after you split a tip with a busboy, bartender, and floor captain, there's not much left. *He* had an easy answer: earn bigger tips. *Earn* it, work your *ass* off for it, you know. But who's going to tip more than 15 percent unless…well, unless the waitress wears no underwear. He even said that the best thing about taking part of our tip money was it made us move our asses that much prettier. There was another thing he liked about how I had to earn bigger tips — reaching or bending. And then my skirt was "mysteriously," "accidentally" lifted from this time the restaurant was already experiencing some turnover of the new staff. Many of those interviewed reported that Michelle Rae had been asking them if they'd slept with Terence. In one case, Ms. Rae was said to have told one of her colleagues that she, Michelle, knew all about her co-worker's affair with the floor captain. Some of the waitresses said that they'd received phone calls on Monday; an unidentified female demanded to know if Terence Lovell was, at that moment, visiting them. A few of those waitresses assumed it was Michelle Rae while others said they'd thought the caller had been Mrs. Lovell.

behind, baring my butt in front of the whole kitchen staff. He pretended he hadn't noticed. Then winked and smiled at me later when I gave him his share of my tips. Told me to keep up the good work. Used the word *ass* every chance he got in my presence for weeks afterwards. Isn't this sexual harassment yet?

When the district attorney dropped the rape charge for lack of evidence, Michelle Rae filed a suit claiming harassment, naming the restaurant owner, manager, and floor captain. Meanwhile, Terence began getting a series of phone calls

Of course I was scared. He knew my work schedule, and don't think he didn't know where I live. Knew my days off, when I'd be asleep, when I do my aerobic dance routine every day. I don't mind *whoev*er wants to do aerobic dance where the caller immediately hung up. Some days the phone seemed to ring incessantly. So once, in a rage of frustration, Terence grabbed the receiver and made a list of threats — the worst being, as he remembered it, "kicking her lying ass clear out of the state" — before realizing the caller hadn't hung up that time. Believing the caller might be legitimate — a friend or business call — Terence quickly apologized and began to explain, but the caller, who never gave her name, said, "Then I guess you're not ready." When Terence asked her to clarify — ready for what? — she said, "To meet somewhere and work this out. To make my lawsuit obsolete garbage. To do what you really want to do to me. To finish all this."

Terence began refusing to answer the phone himself, relying on Maggie to screen calls, then purchasing an answering machine. As the caller left a message, Terence could hear who it was over a speaker, then

with me — but it has to be at my place where I've got the proper flooring and music. It was just an idle, general invitation — an announcement — I wasn't *begging...any*one, him included, could come once or keep coming, that's all I meant, just harmless, healthy exercise. Does it mean I was looking to start my dancing career in that palace of high-class entertainment *he* frequents? Two pool tables, a juke box, and big-screen TV. What a lousy front — looks exactly like what it really *is*, his lair, puts on his favorite funky music, his undulating blue and green lights, snorts his coke, dazzles his partner — his doped-up victim — with his moves and gyrations, dances her into a corner and rapes her before the song's over, up against the wall — *that* song's in the juke box too. You think I don't *know*? I was having a hassle with a customer who ordered rare, complained it was overdone, he could decide whether or not to pick up the phone and speak to the party directly. He couldn't disconnect the phone completely because he had to stay in touch with his lawyer. The Imperial Penthouse was claiming Terence was not covered on their lawsuit insurance because he was on suspension at the time the suit was filed.

When he returned to work there was one more gift in Terence's locker: what looked like a small stiletto switchblade, but, when clicked open, turned out to be a comb. A note was attached, unsigned, which said, "I'd advise you to get a gun."

Terence purchased the miniature single-cartridge hand gun the following day. After keeping it at work in his locker for a week, he kept it, unloaded, in a dresser drawer at home, unable to carry it to work every day, he said, because the outline of a gun was clearly recognizable in the pocket of his tux pants.

wanted it *rare*, the cook was busy, so Terrence grabs another steak and throws it on the grill — tsss on one side, flips it, tsss on the other — slams it on a plate. "Here, young lady, you just dance this raw meat right out to that john." I said I don't know how to dance. "My dear," he said, "*every*one knows how to dance, it's all a matter of moving your ass." Of course the gun was necessary! I tried to be reasonable. I tried everything!

One Monday evening as Terence was leaving the sports bar — not drunk, but admittedly not with his sharpest wits either — three men stopped him. Terence was in a group with another man and three women, but, according to the others, the culprits ignored them, singling out Terence immediately. It was difficult for Terence to recall what happened that night. He believed the men might've asked him for his wallet, but two of the others with him say the men didn't ask for anything but were just belligerent drunks looking for a fight. Only one member of Terence's party remembered anything specific that was said, addressed to Terence: "Think you're special?" If the men had been attempting a robbery, Terence decided to refuse, he said, partly because he wasn't fully sober, and partly because it appeared the attackers had no weapons. In the ensuing fight — which, Terence said, happened as he was running

Most people — you just don't know what goes on back there. You see this stylish, practically regal man in white tie and tails, like an old fashioned prince ... or Vegas magician ... but back there in the hot, steamy kitchen, what's *wrong* with him? Drunk? Drugs? He played sword fights with one of the undercooks, using the longest skewers, kept trying to jab each other in the crotch. The chef yelled at the undercook, but Terence didn't say a word, went to the freezer, got the meatballs out, thawed them halfway in the microwave, then started threading them onto the skewer. Said it was an ancient custom, like the Indians did with scalps, to keep trophies from your victims on your weapon. He added vegetables in between the meatballs — whole bell peppers, whole onions, even whole eggplant, started dousing the whole thing with his brandy. His private bottle? Maybe. He said we should put it on the down the street, but was unsure whether he was chasing or being chased — Terence was kicked several times in the groin area and sustained several broken ribs. He was hospitalized for two days.

Maggie Lovell visited Terence in the hospital once, informing him that she was asking her parents to stay with the kids until he was discharged because she was moving into a motel. She wouldn't tell Terence the name of the motel, insisting she didn't want anyone to know where she was, not even her parents, and besides, she informed him, there probably wouldn't even be a phone in her room. Terence, drowsy from pain killers, couldn't remember much about his wife's visit. He had vague recollections of her leaving through the window, or leaning out of the window to pick flowers, or slamming the window shut, but when he woke the next day and checked, he saw that the window could

menu, he wanted someone to order it, his delux kebab. He would turn off all the chandeliers and light the dining room with the burning food. Then he stopped. He and I were alone! He said, "The only thing my delux kebab needs is a fresh, ripe tomato." Isn't this incredible! He wanted to know how I would like to be the next juicy morsel to be poked onto the end of that thing. He was still pouring brandy all over it. Must've been a gallon bottle, still half full when he put it on the counter, twirled the huge shish-kebab again, struck his sword fighting pose and cut the bottle right in half. I can hardly believe it either. When the bottle cracked open, the force of the blow made the brandy shoot out, like the bottle had opened up and spit — it splattered the front of my skirt. In the next second, his kebab was in flames — maybe he'd passed it over a burner, I don't know, he was probably *breathing* flames by then — so not be opened. Terence never saw his wife again. Later he discovered that on the night of his accident there had been an incident at home. Although Terence had instructed his eight-year-old son not to answer the phone, the boy had forgotten, and, while his mother was giving a piano lesson, he picked up the receiver just after the machine had clicked on. The entire conversation was therefore recorded. The caller, a female, asked the boy who he was, so he replied that he was Andy Lovell. "The heir apparent," the voice said softly, to which Andy responded, "What? I mean, pardon?" There was a brief pause, then the caller said, "I'd really like to get rid of your mom so your dad could fuck me. If you're halfway like him, maybe I'll let you fuck me too." There is another pause on the tape. Investigators disagree as to whether it is the caller's breathing or the boy's that can be heard. The boy's voice,

naturally as soon as he pointed the thing at me again, my skirt ignited, scorched the hair off my legs before I managed to drop it around my feet and kick it away. What *wouldn't* he do? Looks like he'd finally gotten me undressed. It's ironic, isn't it, when you see that news article about him — I taped it to my mirror — and how about that headline, "Pomp and Circumstance Part of the Meal." There sure were some circumstances to consider, all right. Like he could rape me at gunpoint any time he wanted, using that cigarette lighter which looks like a fancy pistol. I wanted something to always remind me what to watch out for, but I didn't take the lighter. Why not? I'll kick myself forever for that. There was so much to choose from. Now one of his red satin cummerbunds hangs over my bed while he still has the lighter and can still use it!

obviously trembling, then said, "What?" The female caller snapped, "Tell your dad someone's going to be killed."

During Terence's convalescence, the Imperial Penthouse changed its format and operated without a floor captain, using the standard practice of a hostess who seated the guests and waitresses assigned to tables to take orders and serve meals. The restaurant's menu was changed and now no longer offered flaming meals. When Terence returned to work he was given a position as a regular waiter, even though by this time most of the male food servers had left the restaurant and were replaced with women. Michelle Rae was given a lunch schedule, ten to three, Wednesday through Sunday. Terence would call the restaurant to make sure she'd clocked out before he arrived for the dinner shift.

When he said "staff meeting," he didn't mean what he was supposed to mean by it. You know, there was a cartoon on the bulletin board, *staff meeting*, two sticks shaking hands, very funny, right? But long ago someone had changed the drawing, made the two sticks flaming shish-kebabs on skewers. So the announcement of the big meeting was a xerox of that cartoon, but enlarged, tacked to the women's restroom door. *Be There or Be Square! Yes, You'll Be Paid For Attending!* You bet! It was held at that tavern. Everyone may've been invited, but I'm the one he wanted there. There's no doubt in my mind. What good was I to him merely as an employee? I had to see the real Terence Lovell, had to join the innermost core of his life. Know

During the first week he was back at work, Terence came home and found that his wife had returned to get the children. In a few days she sent a truck for the furniture, and the next communication he had with her was the divorce suit — on grounds of cruel and unusual adultery.

what? It was a biker hangout, that bar, a biker gang's headquarters. One or two of them were always there with their leather jackets, chains, black grease under their fingernails (or dried blood), knives eight inches long. They took so many drugs you could get high just lying on the reeking, urine-soaked mattress in the back. That's where the initiations were. No one just *lets* you in. Know what he said the first day we started working, the first day of the women food servers? He said, "You don't just work here to earn a salary, you have to *earn* the right to work here!" So maybe I was naïve to trust him. To ever set one foot in that bar without a suspicion of what could happen to me. That same ordinary old beer party going on in the front — same music, same dancing, same clack of pool balls and whooping laughter — you'd never believe the scene in the back room. It may have looked like a typical orgy at first — sweating bodies moving in rhythm, groaning, changing to new contorted positions, shouts of encouragement, music blaring in the background. But wait, nothing ordinary or healthy like that for the girl who was chosen to be the center of his dark side — she'll have to be both the cause and cure for his violent ache, that's why he's been so relentless, so obsessed, so insane . . . he was driven to it, to the point where he had to paint the tip of his hard-on with 150 proof whiskey, then use the fancy revolver to ignite it, screaming — not like any sound he ever made before — until he extinguished it in the girl of his unrequited dreams. *Tssss.*

The only thing left in Terence's living room was the telephone and answering machine. When the phone rang one Monday afternoon, Terence answered and, as instructed by his attorney, turned on the tape recorder:

caller: It's me, baby.

Lovell: Okay...

caller: You've been ignoring me lately.

Lovell: What do you want now?

caller: Come on, now, Terry!

Lovell: Look, let's level with each other. How can we end this? What do I have to do?

caller: If it's going to end, the ending has to be *better* than if it continued.

Lovell: Pardon?

caller: A bigger deal. A big bang. You ever heard of the Big Bang theory?

Lovell: The beginning of the universe?

caller: Yeah, but the Big Bang, if it started the whole universe, it also *ended* something. It may've started the universe, but what did it end? What did it *obliterate*?

Lovell: I still don't know what you want.

caller: What do *you* want, Terry?

Lovell: I just want my life to get back to normal.

caller: Too late, I've changed your life, haven't I? Good.

Lovell: Let's get to the point.

caller: You sound anxious. I love it. You ready?

Lovell: Ready for what?

caller: To see me. To end it. That's what you wanted, wasn't it? Let's create the rest of your life out of our final meeting.

Lovell: If I agree to meet, it's to talk, not get married.

caller: Once is all it takes, baby. *Bang.* The rest of your life will start. But guess who'll still be there at the center of everything you do. Weren't you going to hang out at the bar tonight?

Lovell: Is that where you want to meet?

caller: Yeah, your turf.

Terence estimated he sat in his empty living room another hour or so, as twilight darkened the windows, holding the elegant cigarette-lighter look-alike gun; and when he tested the trigger once, he half expected to see a little flame pop from the end.

REVELATION COUNTDOWN

The photographer, without any pants, takes a pre-dawn picture of his motel room. But then he winds the film back and re-exposes the frame to destroy the image of the rumbled, soiled sheets. There's no evidence to suggest that someone's breath and heartbeat fluttered against his body all night, like holding a sleeping bird in two cupped hands.

He has a large-format Pentax, two lenses (wide and wider), twenty rolls of film, two gasoline credit cards, seven pair of underwear, nine pairs of socks (two extra if his feet get wet), fourteen pears in a cooler, a two-pound package of carrots, twenty-four serving-size cans of V8 and grapefruit juice, and an AT&T book of immaculate, comfortable landscape photographs he's been allotted on free week. Then he'll have to lose the flab (and other foul bad habits) he's been reminded these kinds of trips tend to cause.

1

A cloudbank postpones daybreak. The sun sends a five-pointed star of light through a pinprick hole in the slate-iron sky, spotlighting a lone, white mountain between the equally dark desert and foothills. When he's able to turn off the headlights — as the world fades into view, and after he's traveled past the fleecy of the overcast — a cloud like a long, curved finger zaps down to touch a point on the earth, somewhere beyond the toothy ridge of hills on the horizon. His hand leaves the steering wheel as though to find the camera, but pauses, scratches his head, rests in his lap a moment, then goes back to the wheel.

Just down the block from the gas station phone booth, a portable sign has been wheeled to the sidewalk, an arrow of blinking lights points off the road to a small, white church with a tall, needle-thin steeple. The sign's body is opaque, fluorescent white, so the plastic letters are sharply conspicuous. The black letters say *Revelation Countdown*, and below that, in red, *world chaos by 7, angels 7:30, Wed. 19th, The road leads to heaven or hell, renounce sins now!* A man is on other side of the sign, his legs all that are visible, just his feet and ankles. He's changing the message.

Celebrating softly in his chest, only a faint smile on his lips, the photographer frees the camera from its protective padding, the shot is made, the film wound forward. Back to the van, back on the freeway. He eats a box of donuts he picked up at the gas station mini-market, drinks a coke, stuffs the evidence into the brown sack with a damp receipt.

Since the snub-nosed van has no hood poking into his view in front, the big sloping windshield is like living inside his wide-angle lenses — his peripheral vision sharper. If he passed anyone on either shoulder of the freeway, he'd clearly be able to see that expression of disapproval or disappointment.

2

A herd of six deer cross the road in front of him, then stop on the side, turn to stare back at the photographer. His engine idling, his window up, his breath fogs the glass a little, but he wipes it away, takes out the camera, watches the deer through the view finder until they wheel, bolt away, their tails up. Later a coyote runs along the shoulder before veering off into the chaparral. An owl sits on a fence post. At the end of that fence, a long drive-way stretches toward a distant house. A sign over the driveway announces live Hereford embryo transfer. A hushed chortle in his throat, the photographer sets up his tripod for the shot. His eye steams up the view-finder. Something like hunger is a tickle in his stomach, and he can smell the sweet cream from his break-fast éclair still on his fingers.

The last few steps back to the van, his loafers are like fif-ty-pound army boots. His clothes feel dank and clammy. Sitting on the rear bumper, he hangs his head but is unable to vomit. He takes a bite of pear. Chews slowly, many times, so he never has to swallow it. Leaves it on the bumper while he walks three and a half times around the van. Washes the windshield and drives on.

3

The salt flats stretch horizon to horizon, punctuated by spots of pale sage, animal holes, rigid quills of grass, four or five shadows of small clouds passing through like migrating animals.

The photographer sits in his van eating a candy bar. Gingerly feels his feet to see if his socks are damp, then slips his loafers back on, carries his camera along, across the freeway to an abandoned motel, licks chocolate from his fingers before taking three or four shots of the empty swimming pool and deck, filmed with a thin layer of snow, marked only by his own footprints walking an undi-rected, looping, criss-crossed pattern around it. Underneath he's smiling at himself for having to step back and use a cable-release so his trembling won't shake the camera. His heart jumps around like something alive in there.

The abandoned motel has a pay phone which still works. Coming back to the van, he sees two or three candy wrappers on the front seat, puts the camera in the van, does ten jumping jacks, watching his face in the window, then opens the door and flops across the seat on his back, his pulse a dull thud, his feet still outside on the freeway shoulder. Watches the air-freshener dangling from the rear-view mirror. Tries to clean his teeth with his tongue. His toes feel slimy. The extra socks were packed for him in a small vinyl suitcase with toothpaste, mouthwash, deodorant, aftershave, and shampoo.

4

In the middle of a dry basin, a bare tree stands alone, its many thick branches forking off into many more thinner branches splitting off into thousands of distinctly separate twigs. On the hard ground, the tree's roots look like snakes slithering all over the surface, branching out into a swarm of thinner roots, dividing into a gnarled roadmap of winding trails, crossing each other, winding together, but all heading for the open prairie beyond the shade of the furthest branches.

The photographer leaves his van and walks past the tree before he uncaps the camera, kneels, and takes several shots of a family tree etched onto a grave headstone. Lying on the ground, he's under the chilly wind. The hard, bumpy soil is even a little warm, hollows and swells fitting with his body, seems to move with his breath.

The sun on the van's windshield glares in his eyes as he approaches. He digs into the first aid kit for aspirin. Takes a few of the vitamins provided for him as well. Can't seem to get the Band-Aids, gauze, iodine, and cotton swabs packed as neatly as they were in order to close the lid of the box. He shoves it under the seat.

5

The moon is full. It's rising over a little pueblo village, illuminating the walls and roofs as though they're lit from within. But while looking for a public phone, the photographer lets out a mellow chuckle when he finds a bulbous silver water tank rising on stilts in an empty lot beside a fireworks stand. A cartoon tiger swells his chest and flexes his bicep on one side of the silver ball, on the other: *Golden Hill Fighting Tigers*. With his camera on a tripod, the photographer is on his side, looking up at the resplendent fireworks stand, the glowing water tank hovering above it, a scattering of stars bold enough to stay visible in the velvet sky. He holds his breath, holds his body as taut as the shutter opens, then the click is a huge release of air, a flood pouring out of him. He rolls to his back, smiling, sighs, and shuts his eyes.

Standing by his van, he takes off one shoe and scratches the bottom of his foot. The restaurant across the street offers a fattening array of chicken-fried steak, homestyle fries, sausage biscuits, peach pie. Maybe he can get a salad. His stomach growls and turns. The sudden chill of night seems to tighten his whole body. He stretches over his head, reaches to touch his toes, stretches again, then takes a deep breath with his hands pressing on his ribs as though they're sore.

He hangs up the phone and curls on his side with a stabbing knot in his stomach. The room smells like perspiration, dirty clothes, stale breath. His snoring sounds like a large insect and wakes him several times as he begins to doze. Later, when the window is gray and the TV in the next room is silent, the photographer wakes. Slowly he stretches his legs out, kicking the scratchy sheets and blanket down, his stomach gently softened, refreshed, as though soothed by someone's generous hand. Or her mouth. Open slightly. Her tongue barely touching, licking his sweat like a kitten lapping whipped cream. He touches himself the same time she does, but neither pulls their hand away in shame. Her whole hand. Her fingertips. A single, ardent finger. Then just her breath. He can't tell when she's no longer there. She returns again and again. Like dawn . . . never shocking, always astonishing . . . not ever methodical, always natural . . . never fragile, always delicate . . . and yet somehow extraordinarily untamed . . . When it's still before sunrise, she'll be waiting for him on the bed with the wet slicked-down hair, jeans, and torn sneakers, smiling as he puts on yesterday's socks, yesterday's pants; then they'll go exploring at a time when the air is still as much water as it is light, like the touch of her mouth still damp on his skin.

6

So at midmorning he relishes a hotdog in the parking lot of the DipDog drive-thru. Wipes his fingers on the leg of his pants. The DipDog sign is a fat arrow, high on a post, drooping to point down at the tiny food stand, which is steaming from its windows and several spots in its roof. A juicy scent of the hotdogs being grilled, a tint of mustard and onions in the crisp air. He takes his shot of the DipDog sign, then returns to the van to touch himself, wetting his fingertips on his tongue, touching again, his chest and nipples and soft stomach, and his penis. Then takes another shot of the DipDog arrow.

7

In the restroom at the Kuntry Kitchen, the condom machine is illustrated with a drawing of a woman in high-cut lace underwear and push-up bra, her back arched, knees half bent, a hand on her hip, head turned and leering over one shoulder. The machine offers "The Screamer." The words under the illustration say, "If she's a moaner, it'll make her a screamer. If she's a screamer, it'll get you arrested."

Beside the condom machine is a cologne dispenser. Drop in a quarter, press a button, and position yourself to be squirted by your favorite scent: DRAKKAR, POLO or STAG MUSK.

The photographer leans against a wall bracing himself to steady the camera, and gets a shot of the two machines. If someone came light-footed through the door to join him . . . her reckless laugh, her bold hands touching the machine as though reading it by braille . . .

He buys a condom, puts it in his pocket. Stands aside and lets each of the three colognes shoot into the room. Mixes the air with one hand, then walks through the cool mist.

8

The morning newspaper from someplace in Idaho carries a story about a man arrested for masturbating in a rest stop restroom. A state trooper had followed him into the restroom, observed him through a crack in the door. The man refused the trooper's offer to go to a motel room and was then arrested for infamous crimes against nature. The photographer rips the article out of the paper. At the first rest stop he comes to, the photographer pulls off. He pauses on his way to the men's room at a row of eight or ten pay phones. Every phone except one is occupied by a truck driver, the smallest around 200 pounds. All in cowboy or baseball hats, jeans, plaid shirts, boots, sweaty hair. Broken pieces of technical truck language can be heard under the freeway roar. The empty phone is in the middle. Someone else *could* dash up to use that middle phone, half the size of any of the truckers surrounding her, leaning luxuriantly against the box, listening only to the dial tone as she touches her stomach below her short T-shirt with two unrestrained fingers which then dig below the waistband of her jeans and reappear to slip between her lips. He takes a picture, laughing. Then moves on. Takes a roll of tape from his camera bag and goes into a toilet stall with his camera. He tapes the article to the door, sits on the toilet, uncaps his camera, unzips his pants. She waits outside, squatting in the shade beside the building, drawing in the dirt with a stick or sitting on top of the posted state roadmap, tapping her heels against Boise or Twin Falls. When he comes out, she'll take his hands and touch between his fingers with her tongue, close her eyes, hold his sticky palms to her cheeks.

9

The last five frames in his camera hold another church sign: *Our Preacher Speaks: a.m. An Empty Field, p.m. Under the Pulpit.* In a Wyoming 8-room motel, the photographer looks at the phone beside the bible on the nightstand. Goes to the jukebox joint next door. Dark with blinking lights and tinkling conversation. The photographer sits watching the television behind the bar. The two cowboys on his right have selected a car race. The photographer's eyes go round and round with the speeding cars. The beer is fresh in his mouth. The salty peanuts alive on his tongue.

The bar atmosphere is quickened as a huge Indian with long black hair, turquoise kerchief, and leather chaps comes in, pelted by shouts of welcome and invitations to share a pitcher of beer. But the Indian gets his own pitcher, sits on the photographer's left, watches the television for a moment, then asks the bartender if he could change the channel. The bartender looks at the two cowboys. They shrug, put their mugs to their mouths. The Indian stands, leans across the bar. His arms are enormously long. He reaches over the bar, past the bartender, above the bottles lining the counter, and spins the dial. The Indian settles back as an old Bogart movie flickers on the screen. Someone heading toward the restrooms pauses behind the Indian, says something, calls him Snake, her hand unabashed on the back of his neck, under his hair. The Indian shows small, white teeth when he smiles. During the ad, he says, "On vacation?" He's looking at the photographer.

"Not exactly. In a way, I guess."

"Take vacation any way it comes," the Indian says. "That's how to do it. Five minutes. Ten. Anything you can get."

"Well, I'm just sort of coasting toward home."

The Indian smiles. "I saw you today, taking a picture of the Wilson Brothers Ranch sign."

"Don't worry. I'm not a developer or insurance adjuster."

"Anyone can take a picture of a cow," the Indian says. "But that sign ... the longer it stands out there, the rust running down is giving that metal bull a pretty fine set of testicles."

The photographer smiles, pushing a palmful of peanuts into his mouth.

"You otta try the taxidermy shop across the street," the Indian says. "There's some wildlife photos for you."

As the photographer is saying, "Thanks, I will," the atmosphere peaks again as three or four uniformed men come in, move deliberately to the bar, standing behind the Indian and on both sides of him, squeezing the photographer away. With his arms pinned behind his back, they lift the Indian from his stool and take him outside. The photographer pays for his beer and follows, but when he gets to the door, one of the uniformed men is there, shakes his head. "I can't go?" the photographer says.

"Not yet."

"I have to make a call."

"Phone's there." The man nods toward the restrooms. The sounds coming from outside are muffled thuds, low grunts, grinding and shuffling of feet on the gravel parking lot. Then a low whistle. The uniformed man says, "Okay, it's all over," and leaves in front of the photographer. The Indian is spread-eagle over the trunk of a car, then is put into the back seat and pushed over so he's no longer visible. The car leaves. Broken glass gleams in the parking lot under the yellow lights.

He wakes far past dawn, sheets soaked, but doesn't take time to shower or use the phone before taking his camera across the street to the taxidermy shop.

10

The taxidermist, with skin like tanned leather, doesn't speak. Stands behind the counter with level eyes locked on the photographer. The glass eyes of every stuffed creature in the shop focus to a point in the middle of the counter, where a customer would stand at the cash register paying for a stuffed memory.

The photographer says, with a brittle laugh, "Hey, is this where people come to become stuffed-shirts?"

"Job's been done." Any one of the glassy-eyed heads could've said it. The taxidermist's mouth hadn't moved.

"What season is it?" the photographer asks. "What are they hunting right now?"

The taxidermist doesn't answer, but the voice, now obviously coming from a dark back room, says, "Stray tourists."

The taxidermist stays parallel with the photographer as he moves to look more closely at a stuffed trout mounted on a board, its body arched, head and tail pointing down, mouth open in a silent moment of unvanquished excitement — except for the hook to the left in its jaw. As the photographer reaches to touch the fish, the taxidermist pulls it a little further back on the counter. Not entirely out of reach, but the photographer's hand stops.

"You know what they say," the photographer says, "nothing's certain but death and taxidermy."

The taxidermist's thin lips don't move, but again the disembodied voice from behind: "In some cases, you can't tell which happened first."

The photographer tries to look behind the taxidermist through a partially opened door in the back of the shop. A man's shoulder, part of the back of his head, his arms moving, doing something with what could be the wing of a large, stiff bird.

The taxidermist blocks the photographer's view. The photographer's eyes roam to all the stuffed heads along the walls behind the counter, on the beam above the counter, eight-pointed stags, heavy-horned rams, birds in flight. When he's finished looking, another man is standing behind the taxidermist behind the counter, wearing an identical leather apron, also staring at the photographer. The second man's head is huge, without hair. He says, "Too much fat, not enough meat."

The photographer edges away to the side wall where a bulletin board is filled with a patchwork of greenish Polaroid photos of hunters and their trophies. Eyes closed, the big-horned sheep could be sleeping with its chin resting on a hunter's knee. The photographer stares at each Polaroid for a few moments, lingering longest over one of what appears to be a swan, the hunter holding the wings spread out in front of himself, a six-foot span, the elegant neck flapping limp against its breast. His eyes return to it again and again, two of his fingers pinching and tugging on his lower lip. The first taxidermist comes out from behind the counter. Wipes the dust from the nostril of a stag elk. The second taxidermist says, "Those loafers'll be needing to be polished again real soon."

The photographer jumps when the first taxidermist pinches the flesh above his belt.

A truck pulls into the gravel lot outside. Then another. Several others. Doors slam. Loud laughter. The first one, coming through the door backwards, pushes the photographer out of the way with the butt of the deer slung across his shoulders. An elbow in his stomach. Someone steps on his feet. Another and another come in with animals across their backs. Blood-soaked white bellies or shot through the eye. Antlers clacking, boots shuffling, the smell of fur and musk as still more hunters push through the door wearing their kill on their backs. The photographer backs up against a wall, the taxidermist still beside him, still holding onto his love-handle, still silent. The other taxidermist is circulating among the hunters, measuring antler racks, examining entry wounds, tagging ears. The tip of an antler scratches the photographer's cheek. He can't move.

They start stacking the carcasses against the walls, three high, knee deep, legs tangled on the floor, boots shuffling in mud and dried blood. A big guy in a red plaid shirt hoists his pants higher and belches, then asks if anyone's seen Straight Snake, that boozing bastard, fucking wives while the men are on a weekend hunt and all they've had is deer cunt. As the mob swirls among the dead deer, the big guy stops in front of the photographer, "Don't worry, sweetheart, I'll give her a big kiss for you." The guy's cracked, cold lips are on the photographer's, his beef-jerky breath inside the photographer's mouth, his hand grabbing the front of the photographer's pants. The animal smell is thick and feral, there's blood on the photographer's shirt, but the men are leaving, stopping traffic to cross the road to the jukebox joint where the parking-lot gravel contains human teeth. When the taxidermist lets go of his flap of flab, the photographer edges sideways out the door.

He gets up before dawn to unplug the phone and open the window. Cold clean air rushing in to meet festering air in the room could cause a storm. His rank breath. Rancid sweat. He returns to the bed and lays facing away from the window, feeling a breath come like a feathery touch over his shoulder and back. As though she came through the window in the wind. Fits herself behind him. Half his size, but holding him, breathing his air deeply into her body, her hands tender on his soft waist. Her heartbeat resuscitates his.

But he's within one day's drive of home and it'll be his move, after all, which sends her back out the window.

———

In all, it only took him five days to get home. On the outskirts of town, he stops. One at a time pulls all nine remaining pair of socks onto his feet, peels them off, stuffs them into the folded laundry bag. Throws away all hotdog, hamburger, and candy wrappers, all coke cans, all donut boxes, all gum papers. Finishes his last film toward a distant dusty mountain range, a hundred miles on each frame, from north to south.

He sits at the Formica kitchen table eating meatloaf and peas. His shirt smells cottony. From the utility room, the slosh of water, hum of the drier. He looks out the kitchen window, but it's dark and he only sees the reflection of a kitchen with a photographer looking out. But it's not nighttime — it's because the hedge, which needs monthly clipping, has grown above the window. He stands to see over the leaves, chewing his last bite of meatloaf, looking into the back yard where an old bicycle has been taken out of the attic and turned into an exercycle for him, its rear wheel propped up, unable to get anywhere, no matter how hard or fast the pedals are pumped.

NOT HERE

The girl told him about a river in Wisconsin . . . clear and guileless, cold and honest, and some asshole like you or me standing on the bank somewhere, slitting open a fish, dumping the guts. But that's where he went, three weeks every year, for ten years. Ever since she had said, "Pretty nifty sneakers, Mister Fisherman . . . they'll look great with a grey suit." And then a few hours later, "Say what you mean, you coward, you bastard."

His very first time out, he'd almost landed a twenty-pound brown trout in a pool at the foot of a short falls. What an incredible pumping sensation, the five or ten seconds he'd had that thing on the line. But that fish was long gone, dead, caught by someone else, fried, or turned to mulch on the muddy bank of the river. And the girl never even heard about it. He didn't really continue to believe he'd be able to go back and hook into the same one in the same pool — some years shallower, some years overflowing and creating a marsh so he couldn't get near enough to get his bait into the deepest holes.

Does anyone ever call you Ronnie?

Sometimes my mother does.

I wouldn't ever call you Ronnie, but in these movies that's

what you are — Ronnie. Lookit that face, Jeez-Louise, you poor kid, going on vacation with a bunch of adults. Didja ever get to hold the fishing pole yourself?

I think so.

Don't you remember?

Not really. I remember we went to Florida. And Galveston. And Las Vegas. Mostly we went to Las Vegas. But this was before it was such a big deal. There was a little amusement park across the street from our hotel. I went there every day.

By yourself?

Yeah.

Poor little Ronnie, always on vacation with the adults, no kids to play with.

I've got you to play with now.

But you're still going on those adult vacations, aren't you? Some bus tour through New England sitting beside Mr. and Mrs. Booth from Duluth.

You take me on a non-adult vacation. Where would we go?

It's not where that's important — but how. Walk around Greenwich Village at three a.m. The coast of Maine at dawn. Or ... you think you've been fishing? Forget three days of drinking beer and trolling for one stuffed trophy. Stand in a glacier river up to your thighs.

Brrr.

No, you'd be addicted. Didja know when you cook a fresh-caught trout, it curls up and tries to swim outta the pan?

How do you know?

I've done it! You held your mother's hand and walked on the beach in pants and shoes; I was two eyes looking outta a layer of woodsmoke and mud, wet to my knees all day, blood all over my hands — either mine or a fish's — fingernails caked with salmon eggs. That's why I don't like caviar. I always want to take it off the silver platter and bait-up my hook.

Yeah, I can't take you anywhere, can I?

You think that's funny?

———

From Indianapolis, he could get almost anywhere in the same amount of time, give or take a day or two. Maybe it was time to try somewhere else. Besides, he wanted to avoid the stock truck. Ten years ago, it had all been just like she'd described it . . . the fishy smell of stagnant mud, slosh of icy water in his sneakers, flash of silver scales under the bright, shallow rapids, sharp gills cutting his fingers, the roar of the falls and his heartbeat in his ears. But the fish farms and stock trucks made the sensation more and more difficult to find: dumping hundreds of stunned, grain-fed monsters into the river from a bridge, screaming children running down the road with too-expensive rods and reels, mothers with nets letting their toddlers scoop the dazed fish from the shallow inlets where they'd been carried by the current.

Last year he saw two women on the opposite side of the river, both in dresses and heels. They'd pulled their car off the road and were standing there fishing from the unlikely position of a bluff which was six or eight feet above the bank of the river. He'd heard their shrieks every five or ten minutes, looking up to see them flip another huge, shining rainbow trout out of the water, sling it over their heads so it flopped in the dust near the front tires of their car. Then they threw a gunny sack over it, somehow released the hook, added the fish to the bleeding load in their ice chest, and put the can't-miss treble hook loaded with salmon eggs back into the water.

He lay awake that night listening to the river, hearing as well the car radios and laughter around campfires. He couldn't close his eyes without seeing his bait disappear under a riffle, then feeling the strike and the struggle, his heart racing, his legs going weak like softened wax, even his fingertips buzzing. Maybe what those screaming women had felt was the same as the tug in his heart, the gush of adrenaline in his guts at the moment of the bang-bang-bang of the strike.

Sometimes, even now after catching thousands of fish, it seemed like he hadn't had that feeling in years.

———

D'you remember anything about fishing on that boat with your father and uncles?

No. Not really.

Okay, we'll have to start at the beginning. This is a hook.

Well, I know that much.

D'you know how to tie it off?

I guess not.

I'll show you. See how small this hook is? You don't need it any bigger. See this one? That's a treble hook. That's only for kids under five and real dweebs.

Why?

Can't miss with a treble hook. Fish can't steal the bait. Any way he hits it, he's caught. You can pay me back for this, you know.

What do you mean?

You can teach me things. Like which fork to use in a restaurant.

It doesn't matter a lot.

I watched you last night, I did what you did.

How do you know I used the right fork?

I trust you.

Ellen used to scold me for using the same fork for the whole meal. But I wasn't trying to be a snob by taking you to a place with fifteen forks. The food's good there.

Yeah, well that spinach thing had too much butter.

Florentine.

Yeah, that. It had too much butter.

I'm sorry, I sounded like a snob again.

No, how the hell am I gonna learn what these fancy dishes are if you don't tell me. I can't be a chef and go on making something called spinach-thing or crab-thing or veal-named-after-a-king-thing.

You're going to be a chef?

I decided last night.

He wasn't even to Champaign yet. Why not, instead of spending three weeks fishing in Wisconsin, go ahead and take three or four extra days and drive to Southern Louisiana. Stop in Tennessee or Arkansas on the way, catch a few, take snapshots, no one would be the wiser where he'd caught his fish. He always had to have snapshots of the day's catch or the largest . . . and took pictures of the signs to show where he'd been. Gail, his second wife, flipped through the pictures and always said the same thing, "Well, I'm glad the trip was relaxing and good for your nerves. Maybe you won't be so edgy for a while now." She liked to stay home by the pool. They'd been next door neighbors in the apartment complex. Living together and then getting married had just seemed to happen.

Darcy. She liked her own name. She didn't color her hair. She wore no make-up. There was a raccoon mask around her eyes from wearing sunglasses. A scar on her chin from a dogbite. She didn't wear nail polish. Clipped her nails short. Weighed one hundred pounds but could lift a forty-pound sack of dog food and carry it from her truck to the storeroom of the kennel. And could do more things with an egg than he'd ever had the imagination to hunger for. She wore no perfume but smelled of spices when she'd been cooking. He used Darcy's father's kennel to board his first wife's dog when they went on trips.

Gail spent a month every year at a country-club health resort. He'd gone with her a few times, at first. It was never the same month as his fishing trip. She asked why he didn't go fishing while she was at the club, if he hated going there so much. He said he didn't hate it. He always said things like that instead of answering.

He pulled into a two-pump gas station in Cooks Mills. A woman was getting off a Greyhound bus. A man got out of a sedan, took two suitcases from the bus driver, put them into the trunk of the sedan, then got back into the car behind the wheel. The woman turned and looked at the bus. The bus driver didn't wave. The bus pulled between Ron and the woman. After the bus went past and pulled out onto the road, the woman was already inside the car with the man. She had her head tipped back over the seat.

Darcy was a chef now in a restaurant in New Orleans. He'd almost left his first wife for her, a long time ago, ten years ago. He'd left his anyway, but it was too late. Three or four years too late. The girl was gone. To New Orleans. She'd written him sad letters once a month for a year and a half. He always intended to answer, but there never seemed to be the right thing to say. By the time he finally did leave his marriage, the last correspondence — a postcard of geese flying in formation between two blank billboards on a two-lane highway, with her printed message saying simply, *more later* — was at least two years old.

———

DiCarlo's? Is this a boarding facility?

Yeah, about once a week some ding-dong calls here for a pizza. Whadda *you* want? I mean, can I help you?

I'm going to England. My wife's dog has to be boarded.

Wife's dog? So *you're* not gonna claim it?

It's a Pomeranian.

I don't blame you. You look like you should own ... a spaniel.

Why?

That suit — I'll bet you didn't pick it out. Someone who owns a Pomeranian chose that suit. You'd probably like to put on a red flannel shirt and jeans and go wet your line in a creek somewhere.

Do you speak to all your customers this way?

Just certain ones — when I think it's worth my while. Besides, you got lucky, my father's not here today.

Hey ... put your foot up here.

Why?

Your shoe's untied.

So it is. I'd make a great impression stepping on it and falling on my face.

Put your foot up here.

Careful you don't get your finger caught in the knot.

———

He stayed on back roads, so he could stop and take pictures of places he might've fished. Bucksnort Trout Pond in Tennessee.

Catch-a-Rainbow Bait-n-Tackle in Arkansas. Pioneer River Fishing Resort in Texas. He was zig-zagging, but heading south. He drove down Louisiana between eleven p.m. and six a.m. The yellow, diamond-shaped highway signs illuminated by his headlights all said "Church" instead of things like "Icy" or "Slow Trucks." Maybe there aren't any slow trucks where there are a lot of churches. Everything was totally dark except those signs and the on-coming truck headlights in the distance. When they passed, they almost blew him off the road. The gear in his tackle box rattled.

———

Hey, Ron, I got a great idea.

Tell me.

Let me cater your family Thanksgiving.

You've got to be kidding. My in-laws will be there, my wife's sister and her family. Theres no way —

Hey, I can cook, can't I? I could put it on my resumé, that I catered a big Thanksgiving bash for a prominent lawyer.

I'm not prominent, I'm pretty average.

Just think on it, Ron, you could come into the kitchen and catch the cook bending over, basting the turkey, with nothing on but the apron — and get basted yourself at the same time. Start a new holiday tradition.

I'll never feel the same about gravy.

———

At the intersection where an uphill off-ramp became a downhill on-ramp — after crossing the service road which went over the interstate — a man was standing on a rock in the rain watching

cars on the freeway through a massive pair of binoculars. The
street was slick and shiny. The tires hissed. The man's wet clothes
whipped in the wind like flags on a pole.

Fishing can be good in the rain because the fish can't look
up through the disturbed surface of the water and see the murky
movement of the fisherman. Most years he got at least one rain-
fall during his trip, but not last year. The trip had been put off a
month because his mother visited, so it was too late into the summer. A thunderstorm always made the river seem quieter, softer.
Wet clothes were never uncomfortable. Of course, daytime noise of
campers also made the river seem smaller and the splashing rum-
ble less loud. But before dawn, there was usually just the crunch
of his footsteps and roar of the swift water. That was the time of
day, just last year when he came into the clearing beside the small
waterfall that tumbled into a deeper pool. A girl was sitting on
the ground, untying her shoe, taking out the shoelace and using
it to string together her morning's catch of three trout. As the
white lace passed through the gills, it came out bloody red. Blood
trickled down the side of the fish, dripping from its twitching tail.
Darcy would be over thirty by now.

So, does just one guy cook all these things?

There's usually a head chef. I'm not sure. Maybe a lot of
apprentices. I've never been in the kitchen before.

Let's ask if we can go see!

It's kind of busy right now.

I wanna know who puts the parsley on . . . *just* right. And who
decided to put mustard in this sauce.

How could you tell?

Taste it!

I did. I wouldn't've been able to name the ingredients.

I'd cut back on the dill weed too.

Not here, Darcy.

Huh? Your hand, not here.

Oh. Sorry. Hey, can you leave work early tomorrow? We can go to the fly casting practice pond in the park.

I thought you preferred live bait.

I do. It seems more fair, cause if you're not good enough, at least the fish gets some food as his reward for winning and getting away.

Do you feel bad when that happens?

Bad? Not bad. Excited, trembling, pumped, high . . . then suddenly the line goes slack and you don't know what to do with all that energy except go for it again. Hey, how do you think people who get to be apprentices to a chef or something?

I don't know. Ask. Apply. Send out resumés. Bring in a baked Alaska.

Yeah, like: here's my portfolio! Pull a dish of shrimp scampi out of a briefcase.

Darcy — not here.

Oh, Jesus. I can't keep my hands off you, can I. I'm just so excited thinking about being a chef. D'you think I should go to chef school or try to get hired as an assistant and work my way up? I tend to prefer just doing it. Hey, whadda you think those people over there are eating? Am I talking too loud?

———

A man in a sleek red car pulled into the rest stop but didn't park nor turn the engine off. He was speaking into a walkie talkie. A streamlined black car pulled alongside. The man in the red car spoke to the people in the black car, laughing, his face open with joy. The woman beside him in the red car stared straight ahead, unsmiling, her profile a sharp cut-out against the tinted window on her other side. The man's excited words and laughter sounded like someone across the river, shouting to a buddy and holding up a silver trout, its body twisting back and forth, throwing arcs of water from its flashing tail. The woman put two fingers on each of her temples. Her hair was an elaborate, frosted shape.

———

When you feel the strike, set the hook. Don't let it swallow the bait. If you set the hook right, the fish won't be hurt much — you can let it go and catch it again tomorrow.

How will I know — What does a strike feel like?

God, that's like asking what chocolate tastes like, what pine trees smell like . . . what a kiss feels like . . . it only feels like what it feels like, there's no other way to describe it.

Try. I'd like to hear you try.

Okay . . . Bang. It feels like *bang*.

Like a gunshot?

No. Silent. No pain. Like your heart breaking open.

That's not pain?

Like the happiest time in your life all squished down into two seconds. *Bang.*

I've never had a conversation like this before.

Why? Am I drunk? D'you get me to talk about stupid stuff when I'm drinking just so it'll be funny and different and a few yuks to pass along to your lawyer buddies?

C'mon, Darcy. It's just a fun conversation. Hey, I don't get to talk to anyone like this.

But do you tell your friends about me?

No. I don't talk about you. I don't tell anyone about you.

Why? Ashamed?

No ... well, maybe, in a way. I wouldn't be able to describe you. They'd get the wrong idea and I'd be ashamed of *that*.

You can't describe me? C'mon, try.

I don't know. I couldn't describe you to anyone and make you seem real. It wouldn't be the whole you. They'd wonder what the hell I was doing with you.

Well, hey, should I be insulted? No, I guess it's *their* problem. But could you describe how I make you feel?

Bang.

I like that! Let them misunderstand that one!

Anything I said would be misinterpreted unless someone knew you.

Try. C'mon, try. Let's hear it. I'll be some fat, bald lawyer you've taken out for a ... what's that word ... *upscale* ... some upscale lunch ... steak for lunch. Steak and french fries and two pieces of lettuce they call a salad. Is that pretty typical?

I guess.

So, okay, impress me with your extra-curricular exploits. Who's this girl you're seeing? What's she like?

She ... uh ... okay, she told me how to scrape the blood out of a fish's spine with the back of a thumbnail ... and ... she taught me how to tie flies ... and she ... she'll have to learn not to lick her fingers while she cooks if she ever wants to become a gourmet chef ... and she always wants to mess up my hair at the wrong time ... and ... dogs listen to her and love her and respond to every inflection in her voice, every tiny signal of her body language . . . and . . . and she comes and comes and comes when I fuck her. God, I've never talked like this to a woman before.

Something wrong with it?

No, I like it.

———

A girl wearing a black leotard and overalls hopped out of a small truck. The overall straps were unhooked, trailing behind her. The bib was a loincloth flapping in front. She had a camera, squatted and took a picture of a single stock of red-gold wheat grass, standing in front of and framed by the hollow burned-out trunk of a still-living tree. The grass had its fleecy head bowed, lacy arms outstretched. The girl went back to her truck, returned without the camera, carrying a tennis racket. After a forehand smash, backhand, and answer with the forehand, the wheat grass was no longer there. She picked shards of fiber from the face of the tennis racket. Then she climbed back into the cab, one of the overall straps dangling out, but she slammed the door on it and drove off, the buckle trolling the pavement beneath the truck.

———

Darcy, I have to remind you . . . we won't be the only two people in the place.

And?

Just remember that. It's different than when alone.

Oh yeah, no public displays of affection. Got it.

I've always been this way, Darcy, it's not just you. I don't think it's right for people to hang all over each other in public places.

Do I hang on you?

Well . . . yes, sometimes you're a cuddly little thing.

In public, Ron, in public, do I hang on you? Have I ever *hung* on you?

No, I guess not.

You see, I know how to behave. You may think I don't know what's proper, but I do. I was raised *proper* . . . in Texas. That's why I can cook a meal with whatever ingredients I'm given . . . that's why I can take stains out of underwear . . . You think I don't know how to behave?

No, I think you probably do.

I'll tell you how proper my behavior is. Two years after I graduated from high school, before we moved up here, I sent a sympathy card to my old high school principal when his wife died. He wouldn't've even known me, but I knew what was proper. Don't you think that was proper, Ron?

Yes, it was proper.

Yeah, then my principal was arrested and convicted of killing her.

Really? Did you know that he'd killed her?

Of course not. If I'd known, I would've sent one of my all-occasion cards.

———

At the counter, a woman was buying *People* magazine, Lifesavers, chocolate cupcakes, prunes, mixed nuts, beef jerky, and toilet paper. While the clerk waited for the money, she turned and called out the door, "Want anything, Chuck?" The clerk waited. The woman left the counter, stood in the doorway. A huge Winnebago was parked in the closest slot. She shouted, "Hey, Chuck, Whadda you want?" The driver of the Winnebago had his head down on his arms on the steering wheel, his face tucked in. The woman was wearing baggy red shorts. The fronts of her thighs were burned pink and clashed with the shorts.

Wow — good thing you wanted me to wear a dress.

Well, I read this place is supposed to have one of the top ten chefs in the world. I thought you'd like to taste the best — know what you're shooting for.

Haven't you ever been here before?

No.

Why not?

No occasion, I guess.

What's the occasion now?

I don't know. That I got you to wear a dress?

Ho ho. You'll pay for that later.

How?

Maybe . . . by coming up from behind me, lifting the back of this damn skirt and making me bend over.

D'you think anyone's had a conversation like this in here before?

Has anyone ever done anything like *this* in here before?

Ooh — Maybe that's why they put the napkins over our laps.

Hey Ron . . . I notice you didn't tell me not to do stuff like that in public.

And you forgot about proper behavior.

When you've got a hard-on, it's only proper for me to touch it, isn't it?

Jeez I can't believe we're talking like this in here.

Well, we could leave and go to this place I know of — it has plastic placemats with fall-colored leaves on one side and green Christmas trees on the other.

If you're rich enough — and in a place like this, it's taken for granted — there are two things you're considered incapable of doing: pulling out and pushing in your own chair and unfurling a napkin and putting it on your own lap. I had mine done before they got to me.

———

Sometimes a particular current, swirling around a rock, felt like a bite. Or the bait hitting a submerged log — that felt like a bite. But nothing on earth could really be similar to the real thing, the strike. It couldn't be shared, it couldn't be felt watching someone else get it. Once another guy with a canvas fishing vest was working the other side of the river and stopped just opposite him. The other guy caught two fish while Ron felt nothing on his line. His bait insisted on drifting back into a stagnant place. He kept lifting it out, tossing it toward the spot where he saw the other guy hook his two fish. But he never saw or heard nor felt the other guy's strike. There was just suddenly the whir of the other's reel, the gentle swishing splash of the fish being drawn toward the shore, and a rustle in the grass as the guy held the fish down on the ground to remove the hook.

His worst year fishing was last year when he'd had to move his trip from early June to mid-July because his mother was visiting from Seattle. The stock truck came and dumped fish twice a week. Up and down the river, children could be found at almost every decent hole pulling the whale-sized trout out of the river with treble hooks or nets or even by hand. He'd been under the bridge once, standing in waders three feet from the shore. The road above him rumbled, a truck door slammed. He looked up and saw the bulging net of wet silver fins and sleek, twisting bodies. "Hold your hat out," the stock truck man yelled. "Here's what you're waiting for!" The fish splashed into the water all around him. A few hit his body first then bounced off into the river. Just after that he'd thought he was getting a bite, tried to set the hook, but the bait came flying out of the water, hit his face, and the hook nicked the corner of his eye.

The night before his mother had gone home, he'd needed to go to the store and get hooks, line, and salmon eggs. Gail had grabbed her purse and said, "I'm coming with you. I need a few things."

"At a sporting goods store?"

"I've got to get out of here," she whispered. "She's driving me crazy. Thank God she doesn't try to visit during the holidays."

On the way home, Gail wanted to stop and get hamburgers at a fast food restaurant, eat them there, then go home and tell his mother they didn't feel like having dinner that night.

"I think she wants me to bring back a pizza," he said.

"Are you going to do whatever she asks?"

"I don't mind. Pizza, what's wrong with pizza?"

"Well, I don't want any pizza," Gail said. "Let's just tell her we already ate."

"I'm hungry."

"Then stop here for hamburgers. Or how about fish and chips. She doesn't have to know. Then we can say we're not hungry and we're not going to eat."

Gail had stayed in the bedroom while Ron and his mother shared the pizza and watched TV. The next day his mother's plane went back to Seattle and Ron packed his car for his fishing trip. Gail watched and said, "If it's warmer there this time of year, I wouldn't mind going with you." He said, "I don't know if it's warmer, I've never been this time of year."

"It's got to be warmer," she said.

"You can never tell," he said.

Gail walked away but came back with a paper towel and began washing the car's mirrors. The heels on her sandals clicked in the driveway. She said, "Wouldn't it be fun to teach me to fish?"

Ron slammed the trunk. The paper towel in Gail's hand wasn't wadded in a ball. She had folded it into a square. "I'm leaving right now," he'd said.

He parked in an empty parking lot in front of a big, dark Big Deal store in Alexandria, Louisiana. There were only two lights on poles in the parking lot. The street was unlit and none of the houses or buildings had lights in the window or over the porches. Perhaps people moved into town in the morning and left it at night. He was still sitting up, his head back against the seat. It was around three a.m. His sleeping bag was unrolled and unzipped, spread around him and tucked under his chin. The car thermometer said it was thirty degrees outside. He reclined the seat a little but could still see out the windshield. A man and a woman with quiet footsteps were walking through the parking lot. They were not touching each other. They passed right in front of the car. The woman's hair was long, down her back, blowing slightly in the breeze. She watched the ground as she walked. When she stopped to pick something up, the man kept walking. She put whatever it was into her pocket then hurried a little to catch up. The man said, "I saw that. Whaddaya want that for?" The woman took whatever it was out of her pocket again, then it fluttered down from her hand an they kept walking.

Wait a minute, Darcy.

No I've heard enough.

C'mon, you're over-reacting, I didn't say —

You don't have to say anything else, Ron. Waiting for the dog to die is perfectly understandable.

It's just a saying. It didn't mean anything.

Then say what you mean.

I don't know what I mean.

Where're my shoes? These're yours.

Darcy . . . What'd you do to your hand?

Nothing.

There's blood on it.

Oh. I didn't notice. The dogs were barking. I put my fist through the window.

Why?

The dogs were barking.

That's not the reason.

Maybe not.

He walked around downtown New Orleans in his khaki fishing vest and plaid shirt, high top sneakers, and jeans. He paused to read the posted menu of each big restaurant. Most required coat and tie. Two girls came out of the Bon Ton Café in shorts and cotton blouses, sunglasses on their heads, toenails painted pink. They smiled at him. A poodle on a leash was sniffing his shoes, then lifted his leg and peed while its blue-haired owner read the Bon Ton menu. The girls laughed and crossed the street. The old lady apologized. "I think my shoes smell like fish," Ron said. Gail usually washed everything, including the shoes, when he got home. But last year, he'd tied the shoes together by the laces and hung them with his reel. They were the same shoes he'd worn on his first fishing trip. He only wore them fishing. He'd worn them once to Di Carlo's boarding kennel. Darcy had left blood fingerprints on them, but after his first fishing trip he hadn't been able to tell if the blood was still there. She'd been holding a shoe in each hand, her pants pulled up but unzipped and gaping open, her underwear was white, her belt unthreaded and hanging down to her ankles, blood smeared across one of her hands, holding his shoes. She let the shoes drop, but not all the way. The laces slipped through her fingers. The shoes dangled in front of her, she held each by the tip of a lace, between thumb and forefinger. Then the shoes thumped on the floor, Darcy turned, he lunged and caught her hanging belt, she grabbed it in both fists and whipped it out of his hands, dragging him halfway off the bed before he finally let go.

BETWEEN SIGNS

LIVING LEGENDS OF THE ENCHANTED SOUTHWEST
WATCH AUTHENTIC INDIANS,
HANDMADE CRAFTS, LEATHER,
PAN FOR GOLD WITH REAL PROSPECTORS

He'll drive with one hand. With the other, unbuttons her shirt. Then when trucks pass, close, going the opposite direction, he'll drive with no hands for a moment, waving to the truckers with his left hand, his right hand never leaving her breasts. She'll arch her back, smile, eyes closed. The wind of the passing trucks will explode against the car like split-second thunderstorms.

Swim
Ski
Relax
Play
In Lostlake City

DO NOT PARK
IN DESIGNATED
PARKING AREAS

Someday she'll return, using this same road, and it will be late spring, and the migrating desert showers will wash the windshield of collected bugs and dust over and over, and the smell of wet pavement will lift her drooping eyelids, and she'll not stop until she's knocking on his door and it's opening and he's standing there. She'll feel the explosion of his body or the explosion of the door slamming.

15 Restaurants
11 Motels
Next 2 exits

RATTLESNAKE-SKIN BOOTS
TURQUOISE BELT BUCKLES
BEADED MOCCASINS, SNO CONES

They took nothing. Credit cards bought gas and food, plastic combs, miniature toothbrushes, motel rooms, tourist T-shirts, foaming shaving cream, and disposable razors. She watched him shaving as she lay in the bathtub. Then he shaved her. Rinsing her with the showerhead, soaping her over and over again. Shoved a blob of jelly, from a plastic single-serving container taken from the diner, far inside her, went to retrieve it with his tongue, drop by drop, taste by taste, but there was always more where that came from.

See Mystic Magic Of The Southwest...THE THING?

While she takes a turn driving, he'll lay his head in her lap and watch her play with herself. The sound is sticky and sweet like a child sucking candy. The sun will appear and disappear. A band of light across her bare knees. She'll hold his hand and his fingers will join hers moving in and out. The seat wet between her thighs. A cattle crossing will bounce his head in her lap and her legs will tighten around their joined hands. Air coming in the vents is humid, thick with the warm smell of manure, straw, the heat of bodies on the endless flat pasture under the sun. He'll roll to his back to let her wet fingers embrace his erection.

VISIT RUBY FALLS

MAKE A BEE-LINE TO ROCK CITY

Don't Miss CATFISH WILLIE'S RIVERBOAT
Restaurant, Lounge, Casino
Fresh Catfish & Hushpuppies
Beulah, Tennessee

Rip Van Winkle Motel just 35 miles

He has no sunglasses. His eyes are slits. Bright white sky and blinking lines on the road. Touches blistered, chapped lips with his tongue. Digs into his pocket, sitting on one hip and easing up on the gas. Crackle of paper among the loose change. He unwraps the butterscotch and slips it into his mouth, rolls it with his tongue, coats his mouth with the syrup. When he passes a mailbox on the side of the road, he looks far up the dirt driveway beside it, but can't see where it leads. At the next mailbox, five miles later. He stops for a second. The name on the box says Granger, but, again, the driveway is too long to see what it leads to.

Triple-Dip ice cream cones
Camping, ice, propane
Truckers Welcome

SLIPPERY WHEN WET   **FALLING ROCK**

They weren't allowed to rent a shower together, so they paid for two but when no one was looking, she slipped into his. Someone far away was singing. They stood for a while, back to back, turned and simultaneously leaned against the opposite walls of the shower stall, then slid down and sat facing each other, legs crossing. She told him he looked like he was crying, the water running down his face, but his tears would probably taste soapy. She said once she'd put dish detergent into a doll that was supposed to wet and cry. From then on it had peed foam and bawled suds. He reached out and put a hand on each of her breasts, holding her nipples between two fingers. A door slammed in the stall beside theirs. Water started and a man grunted. He rose to his knees, pulled on her arms so she slid the rest of the way to the floor of the shower, the drain under her back. He eased over her, his mouth moving from breast to breast. Then he lathered her all over, slowly, using almost the whole bar of soap, her ears and neck, toes, ankles, knees, lingering between her legs where the hair was growing back and sometimes it itched so badly while they drove that she had to put her hand in her pants and scratch. She was slick to hold. He didn't rinse her before pushing his cock in. The sting of the soap made them open their eyes wide and dig their fingernails into each other's skin. Staring at each other but not smiling.

Taste Cactus Jack's Homestyle Cookin

Relax in Nature's Spa
CHICKEN HOLLER HOT SPRINGS
Sandwiches, Live Bait

ROAD CLOSED IN FLOOD SEASON

Finally she stops and buys half a cantaloupe at a roadside fruit stand. After eating as much as she can with a plastic spoon, she presses her face down into the rind and scrapes the remaining flesh with her teeth. The juice is cool on her cheek and chin. Part of a tattered map, blown by the wind, is propped against the base of a telephone pole. He had laughed at her for getting cantaloupe margaritas, but then he'd sipped some of hers, ordered one for himself, said it tasted like her. She breaks the rind in half and slips one piece into her pants, between her legs. The crescent shape fits her perfectly.

MARVEL AT MYTHICAL RELICS
INDIAN JEWELRY
VELVET PAINTINGS

TEXMEX CHICKEN-FRIED STEAK
TACOS, BURRITOS
FREE 72 OZ STEAK IF YOU CAN EAT IT ALL!

When the dirt road gets so bumpy he has to keep both hands on the wheel, she'll take over using the vibrator on herself. He'll watch her, and watch the road. The road always disappears around a bend or beyond a small rise. The car bounces over ruts and rocks. She won't even have to move the vibrator, just hold it inside. She'll say he chose a good road, and her laugh will turn into a long moan, her head thrown over the back of the seat. One of her feet pressed against his leg. Her toes will clutch his pants.

VIEW OF SEVEN STATES FROM ROCK CITY

Poison Spring Battleground
next exit, south 12 miles

PIKE COUNTRY DIAMOND FIELD
All The Diamonds You Find Are Yours!

For three days he's had a postcard to send home, but can't find the words to explain. It's a picture of the four corners, where Colorado, New Mexico, Arizona, and Utah meet. He hadn't gotten down on hands and knees to be in all four states simultaneously. But he had walked around them, one step in each state, making a circle, three times. When he arrives at Chief Yellowhorse's Trading Post and Rock Museum, he buys another postcard, a roadrunner following the dotted line on Highway 160. This one's for *her*, wherever she is, if she even left a forwarding address. The rock museum costs a dollar. A square room, glass cases around the edges, dusty brown pebbles with handwritten nametags. Some of the rocks are sawed in half to show blue rings inside. A bin of rose quartz pieces for a nickel each. Black onyx for a dime. Shark's teeth are a quarter.

HOGEYE, POP. 2011
HOGEYE DEVILDOGS FOOTBALL
CLASS D STATE CHAMPS 1971

**BEHOLD! PREHISTORIC MIRACLES!
INDIAN POTTERY, SAND PAINTINGS
COCHINA DOLLS, POTTED CACTUS**

Found Alive!
THE THING?

They'll toss their clothes into the back seat. Their skin slippery with sweat. She'll dribble diluted soda over and between his legs. Tint of warm root beer smell lingering in the car. She'll hold an ice cube in her lips and touch his shoulder with it. Runs it down his arm. It'll melt in his elbow. She'll fish another ice out of her drink, move it slowly down his chest. When she gets to his stomach, the ice will be gone, her tongue on his skin. She'll keep his hard-on cool by pausing occasionally to slip her last piece of ice into her mouth, then sucking him while he slides his finger in and out of her. The last time she puts the ice into her mouth, his hand will be there to take it from her lips. He'll push the ice into her, roll it around inside with a finger until it's gone. The road lies on the rippling desert like a ribbon. Leaving the peak of each of the road's humps, the car will be airborne for a second.

Cowboy Steaks, Mesquite Broiled

**Black Hills Gold, Arrowheads,
Petrified Wood, Chicken Nuggets,
Soda, Thick Milkshakes, Museum
WAGON MOUND TRAVELERS REST**

He had to slow down, find a turnout, pull her from the car, and half carry her to the shade of a locked utility shack. She dropped to her knees, then stretched out full length on her stomach. He sat beside her, stroking her back. Her body shuddered several more times, then calmed. When she rolled over, the hair on her temples was wet and matted with tears, her eyes thick, murky, glistening, open, looking at him. She smiled.

INDIAN BURIAL MOUNDS NEXT EXIT
GAS, FOOD, LODGING

Rattlesnake Roundup
Payne County Fairgrounds
2nd Weekend in July

DUST STORMS NEXT 18 MILES

The waterpark is forty-eight miles off the main interstate. He's the only car going in this direction and passes no others coming the opposite way. The park was described in a tourbook but wasn't marked on the map. Bumper boats, Olympic pool, three different corkscrew waterslides, high dive. The only other car in the lot has two flat tires. Small boats with cartoon character names painted on the sides are upside down beside an empty concrete pond, a layer of mud and leaves at the bottom. Another layer of dirt at the bottom of the swimming pool is enough to have sprouted grass, which is now dry and brown, gone to seed. The scaffold for the waterslides is still standing, but the slides have been dismantled. the pieces are a big aqua-blue pile of fiberglass.

Ancient Desert Mystery...THE THING? 157 miles

LAND OF ENCHANTMENT
NEW MEXICO T-SHIRTS

BULL HORNS
HANDWOVEN BLANKETS
CACTUS CANDY
NATURAL WONDERS

She'll look out the back windshield. The earth is a faint, rolling line against a blue-black sky. His hair tickling her cheek. She'll be on his lap, straddling him, her chin hooked over his shoulder, his cock has been inside her for miles and miles. Sometimes he'll push up from underneath. Sometimes they'll sit and feel the pulse of the engine, the powerful vibration. The air coming through the vent, splashing against her back before it spreads through the car, is almost slightly damp. Smells of rain on pavement, clean and dusty. Out the front windshield, both sky and land stay so dark, there's no line where they meet. No lights and no stars.

If we go west fast enough, will it stay predawn forever?

We can try.

Did you ever pester your parents, When'll we get there, daddy?

And I'd've thought it was torture if he said never.

GOSPEL HARMONY HOUSE CHRISTIAN DINNER THEATRE

MERGING TRAFFIC   **DEER XING**   **SHARP CURVES**
NEXT 10 MILES

They started walking toward the entrance of the Walmart store, but she turned off abruptly, crossed a road and climbed a small hill where someone had set up three crosses in the grass. They were plant stakes lashed together. Kite string was tangled on a tumbleweed. When she got back to the parking lot, five or six big cockleburs were clinging to each of her socks. She sat on the hood of the car picking them off. When he came from the store with two blankets, toilet paper, aspirin, and glass cleaner, she said, There weren't any graves up there after all. He put the bag in the back seat, turned and smiled. Kiss me, she said.

Meteor Crater and gift shop, 3 miles ⬛➡

WARNING:
THIS ROAD CROSSES A
U.S. AIR FORCE BOMBING RANGE
FOR THE NEXT 12 MILES DANGEROUS
OBJECTS MAY DROP FROM AIRCRAFT

BIMBO'S FIREWORKS
Open all year

He spreads a map over his steering wheel. This road came forty-five miles off the interstate. He pays and follows the roped-off trail, stands looking at the cliff dwellings as the guide explains which was the steam room, which compartment stored food, which housed secret rituals, where the women were allowed to go and where they weren't, why they died off before the white settlers ever arrived, and the impossibly straight narrow paths which connected them directly to other cliff-dwelling cities and even now were still visible from the sky, spokes on a wheel converging on their religious center.

Bucksnort Trout Pond
Catch a Rainbow!

Krosseyed Kricket Kampgrounds

TWO GUNS UNITED METHODIST CHURCH
SUNDAY WORSHIP 10 A.M.
VISITORS WELCOME

She doesn't even know how long she's been sitting by the side of the road. The car shakes when the semis go past. Sometimes she can see a face turned toward her for a split second. The last time she went behind a rock to pee, she found three big black feathers with white tips. Now she's holding one, brushing it lightly over her face. Her eyes are closed. Somehow the scent of the feather is faintly wild. When she returns—in a year, two years, five years—in a heavy sleep long past midnight but long before dawn, he'll never know any time passed at all. Like so many nights before she left, her footsteps will pad down the sidewalk. The nurse who shares his life will have put on her white legs and horned hat and gone to the hospital. Using the key he made for her, which she still carries on her chain, she'll let herself in. Move past the odor of hairspray in the bathroom. Drop her clothes in a heap in the doorway—simple clothes she'll easily be able to pull on in the moments before she leaves him. Then she'll stand there, listen to his body resting. Watch the dim form of him under the sheet become clearer. She'll crawl to the bedside, lean her elbows and chin on the mattress, his hand lying open near her face. She'll touch his palm with the wild feather, watch the fingers contract and relax. Until his hand reaches for her, pulls her into the bed and remembers her. She opens her eyes and squints, although dusk has deadened the glare on the road. Slips the feather behind one ear. She doesn't remember which direction she'd been going before she stopped here to rest.

BRIDGE FREEZES IN COLD WEATHER

The Unknown is Waiting For You!
See The Thing? just 36 more miles

STATE PRISON
Do Not Stop For Hitchhikers

Yield

The music channel hasn't had any music for a while. She sat up, stared at the screen, counted the number of times either the interviewer or the musician said *man*, lost track quickly, changed to the weather station, turned the sound down. She massaged his shoulders and back, each vertebra, his butt, his legs, the soles of his feet, each toe. He said, I'm yours forever. Said it into the pillow. Anything you want, he said. She lay her cheek against his back and watched a monsoon, palm trees bending to touch the tops of cottages, beach furniture thrown through the windows. He had rolled over and was looking at her. His eyes looked almost swollen shut. Anything, he said. She looked back at the screen, yachts tossed like toys, roofs blown off, an entire pier folded sideways along the beach. She said, I've never been in something like that.

He pinned her wrists in just one of his hands, hurled her facedown. She was open and ready as though panting heavy fogged air from her cunt, and he slammed himself in there, withdrew completely and slammed in again and again. With each thrust she said, Oh! And he answered when he came, a long, guttural cry, releasing her wrists to hold onto her hips and pump her body on his cock.

They lay separate for a while. Now, she said, hold me . . . with both hands. Hold me like something you'd never want to break. Tomorrow I'll drop you off at the nearest airport.

SPECIAL PERMIT REQUIRED FOR:
Pedestrians
Bicycles
Motor Scooters
Farm Implements
Animals on Foot

> *Home of Johnny Johnson*
> *Little All-American 1981*

ICE CREAM, DIVINITY, GAS, PICNIC SUPPLIES
REAL INDIANS PERFORMING ANCIENT RITES

He'll set the car on cruise control and they'll climb out a window, pull themselves to the roof of the car, to the luggage rack. Their hair and clothes lash and snap in the rushing wind. Dawn has been coming on for hours. The sun may never appear. The sky behind them pink-gold on the horizon, bleeding to greenish, but like wet blue ink straight above them. She'll unbutton her shirt and hold her arms straight up, lets the wind undress her. They'll take turns loosening their clothes and feeling the thin, cool rushing air whip the material away. Bursting through low pockets of fog, they come out wet and sparkling, tingling, goosebumped. They'll slide their bodies together, without hurry and without holding back, no rush to get anywhere, saving nothing for later, passing the same rocks, bushes, and fence posts over and over. As the car leaves the road, leaping and bounding with naive zest, they'll pull each other closer and hold on, seeing the lovely sky in each other's eyes, tasting the sage and salty sand on each other's skin, hearing the surge of velocity in the other's shouted or breathless laughter, feeling the tug of joy in their guts, in their vigorous appetites. The sky still deep violet-black, the dawn still waiting, the car still soaring from butte to pinnacle to always higher peaks.

HESITATION

It's not that he left after fucking her because he wanted to get away from her. It's not that he wouldn't've enjoyed the heat of her beside him or her hand creeping inside his underwear in the morning when they would both be groggy and he was hard but not urgent. He would've liked her to hold it while he slept. But what if he were with her and the phone rang at one or two in the morning, and what if it were his ex-wife calling? Once he lay spread eagle and said, Tie me up and do whatever you want to me. She actually put her tongue in his armpit, sucked his toes, rubbed his hard-on between her breasts. The jewel in her pierced nose scratched gently on his stomach as she nipped and licked around his navel, growling like a puppy, laughed, and said she was eating away the cord he'd forgotten to cut. So she can't piss her poison into you no more, the girl said, it's not like she's your fuckin' mother. It's not that he still went out with his ex-wife because he liked her company. It's just that he'd destroyed someone's whole world and he owed that much in return, so she wouldn't feel like a worthless person, so she wouldn't feel totally abandoned. More than once he wet the girl's neck with his tears. She touched his cheeks and kissed his face and sometimes he held her hard, but the worst time he just stared at the ceiling through his brimming eyes because the woman had said he was selfish and always got what he wanted but never wanted to take care of her and never wanted to give her what she wanted and he was always constantly shoving that thing at her but why didn't he hold her hand or take her to hear the symphony play outside at the waterfront at night — so why should she want to have sex with him? — and now he's ruined her plan for her life because they were supposed to grow old together in their lovely home and now she'll be alone and even though she was going on a vacation cruise to the Mediterranean next week, think how awful it would be for her knowing he'd be with that weirdo filthy girl, doing whatever he wants, how was that supposed to make her feel? It would ruin her trip, she said. It's not that he thought the woman had actually guessed his reverie that the girl helped bring to life as soon as the Rome-bound jet was off the ground: a hungry, vibrant creature wearing an evening gown slit up the back to her bare ass who wandered around among the crowd at the opera until she chose him out of a whole theater full of people and followed him to the downtown pier, begging him to fuck her on the rail above angry, violent breakers lapping at the pylons one hundred feet from shore as embarrassed tourists hurried past in salty, milk-warm darkness, pretending not to notice. It's not that he felt guilty or wrong for making love to the girl like that, after all those years of his own spit. It's not like he vacillated at all, it's not as though he'd had any qualms, that he wasn't flying on adrenalin as he and the girl made up those fantasies while eating take-out ribs in the living room in their underwear, promising them to each other as gifts. It's not as though he wasn't absolutely exhilarated when she rolled him over and used colored pens to draw a tattoo on his butt. He saw it in the mirror later, a heart all wrung up like a dish cloth, with blood dripping out, a little smeared because she'd pressed her face over it before the ink was dry. She said, You mean none of those friends of yours ever said you've got a sexy ass? I'm gonna ask them why. It's not that he was reluctant to introduce her to his friends because he was ashamed of her. It's not that he thought they wouldn't like her, wouldn't think she's smart enough or sophisticated enough for him. He said after twenty years of knowing him with his wife, they weren't ready for him to appear suddenly with a new girl. They'd be uncomfortable. He wouldn't want to do that to them. He said maybe they always thought if their kids turned out like her, they'd feel like complete failures or kill themselves. Yeah, she said softly. He just meant he had to prepare them first. He couldn't imagine what they would think if he dropped in or showed up at a party unannounced with her. The girl suggested, maybe they'll wonder: wow, what's *he* got that *I* don't got? Maybe she didn't understand when he said don't ever tell anyone that another girl once fell in love with her. And don't ever tell anyone that a former lover took Polaroid snapshots of her during foreplay before he beat her up. Don't talk about the head shop in Ocean Beach where she used to work, her alcoholic mother who held her down and shaved her head long before that style became popular, or why she was kicked out of bartender school. And don't show them her wrists where the scars stand up, cherry red, shiny just-born skin that sometimes she ran her tongue along while watching his collection of Bogart movies. Don't laugh and tell anyone they're called hesitation marks. Don't say it was the first new skin of a whole new girl, that there's a chart in some hospital basement saying twenty-six sutures, lacerations on right and left forearms, suicide gesture suspected. Don't mention at a dinner party that blood tastes like silver, if silver had a taste, that's what it would taste like — like blood. Don't talk about incest or abortions or hitchhiking or sugar-daddies or bull-dykes or body art or dildos. He only warned her because they would've wondered about her, would've thought funny thoughts about her, and he wanted them to know her as he knew her. He says in her case maybe first impressions wouldn't've told the whole story. It's not that he asked her not to wear sleeveless shirts in public because he didn't think her tattoos were cute. And it's not that he was wavering, the night he'd sent her home, as usual, but she crouched in the bushes outside his bedroom until dawn because she'd moved again and couldn't remember where she lived. If he'd known it was her he wouldn't've called the police. It's not that he doesn't care enough to call someone now, but how could he describe her to the police? He doesn't have a photograph of her to put up on telephone poles, and, even though he's not embarrassed of her fantasy, he wouldn't want to show them the videotape of it: the dark room with dozens of candles, the twenty-four-hour road race from Le Mans on the television, him on the floor in jeans and bare feet, eating anchovy pizza and drinking 7-Up from a can, the girl arriving like a thief through the glass slider behind the sofa, wearing a crotch-length mini and spike heels with ankle straps, nothing underneath, and completely shaved, kisses his neck and ears but his eyes never move from the TV screen, he continues sipping the 7-Up as she unbuttons his jeans, but not the top button, takes his cock and balls out of the fly, strokes him and licks the cheese from his fingertips as he finishes the soda and settles back against the sofa, leans sideways to see the TV, doesn't even close his eyes as she sucks his cock, but his toes curl and uncurl, then she straddles him, slides her shaved pussy right down over him, but the end of the fantasy was ruined — the part where the cars go into their final lap and he gets up, bends her onto her knees and fucks her from the rear — because a door opens in the background and someone says *Yoo-hoo*, and the woman he'd been married to comes into the picture, and there's absolutely no pause before the girl falls sideways, almost onto the candles, as he struggles to his feet to hurry after the woman who has run from the room. The video camera kept filming until the tape was finished. He doesn't reappear in the picture, but it does show the girl leaving through the slider, splashing through the glass like water. He used to tell the girl he needed her. He used to talk about how she was the only one he could turn to, the only one on his side. He used to say no one else had ever given him as much as she did. Once he'd told her she was a dream come true. Once he said she'd saved his life.

DOG & GIRLFRIEND

She is trained to stay off the bed. Somehow she understands this rule to mean only her back end. She's perfectly capable of keeping her little feet on the floor and taking a nap with the rest of her body on the bed. She also uses this position, when I'm in bed, to ask for things. So she gets up there, puts her head on the blankets, two silly feet still on the floor, and says she wants to die. She thinks she's pregnant again.

But I'm hardly in a position to respond. She didn't say I'm *ready* to die. She's just mad, so I'm letting her cool off, which proves she didn't mean it. I'm still busy after being tubed.

Familiar position. Isn't it? How much other trouble will it cause? He would only touch me with his cock. He wouldn't mind getting *it* dirty. I never had that talk with my mother about freshness. I scratch down there in my sleep. It takes a long time, but I shave the whole shebang, nose to toes.

What if I'd told my girlfriend it was her father? My girlfriend might've said, What do you think you're doing, trying to take my mother's place so then you can say *come back to the womb*? Clever girlfriend.

I'm treating myself for yeast infection. Staying inert on the bed long after ejaculating the medication.

How'd you get the man, she wanted to know. Dressed like a female impersonator, let him get tanked, then said my sex-change operation was in progress, wasn't complete, getting a hairy chest, but no cock yet.

I finally get out of bed, take the leash off the hook by the back door and my dog says she's ready to chase squirrels. Maybe she forgot what she told me while I was on my back. Dogs don't remember, unless the incident in question is accompanied by a traumatic occurrence or great reward, putting into her memory: *repeat this*, or: *don't*. Which I don't think happened. Sure, the medicine is white like semen, but when I say, *you want puppies?* she looks into the trees shouting, for the squirrels to come down and face off.

She's wrong, I wouldn't say *come back to the womb*, even if fucking someone who could've been her father might make me somehow her mother. If she hadn't left, I'd say, I don't want you in my womb, I don't want anyone in my womb. But you *would* let him go *part* way in, my dog says, that's more than *I* did. She's still proud of that. She refused the stud and had to be artificially inseminated.

So, is the hair on my body repulsive? Thick, stiff and black, armpits, crotch, legs. That's par. Then I hit thirty and it's coming in on my chin and upper lip. On the big knuckles on my big toes. A ring around each nipple. Next it'll be sprouting from my earlobes. But my girlfriend shouldn't've said, yeah, some dykes like hairy women, but not *me*. Maybe it was her first time being a girlfriend as well as being a first girlfriend. My dog wanted to hump the stud. We're a fine pair.

Every time I came out of the bathroom, I shouted, Where are you! I'd been hiding it. I got the depilatory system down pat. Then the top of my head started going thin. So I figure, what's the use, and tell all. I think my clit's getting bigger too. Punishment for renting a stud and getting my dog pregnant. The doctor said your hormone levels are within normal ranges for a woman your age. But a true girlfriend shouldn't have said, If you turn into a man,

I'm history. She also said, You don't want me, you want to *be* me. And she said, Lips that touch wangers will never touch mine. She was a girlfriend not a poet.

My dog squats to pee. She has a pointed little vulva. She lets me watch her poop. When I'm on the toilet, she sometimes comes in for a drink, sniffs delicately, then wanders back out. Just wondering where you were, she always says. She instinctively stays close to me, but I'm not sure it makes her happy like it should.

I always wash before medicating. I undressed and got into the tub. I hate it when I'm trapped in a room with my dirty underwear. She'll sniff it, then drink, either from the bowl or warm water from the bath. Come here, I said, hooking my chin over the edge of the tub.

When she licks my face, I say, Let Mommie be your puppy. Sometimes I imagine her tongue is shaving my upper lip. It's what a girlfriend should've done. I don't know why I wanted her to be my girlfriend. Or any girlfriend. Yes I do. She was going to make me beautiful.

Everything around me is pretty. Especially when I'm on my bed. Gauzy winter light from north-facing curtainless windows, dead tree branches making whispery shadows on white walls, inky blue toner on B&W framed photos of dead trees from another dead year, everything quiet, frozen, and dormant. Stiff, dried stalks of wheat bleached white, kernels hard and fat, standing upright in a white urn. My shelves are beautiful too, pale unvarnished oak, and my soft gray rug the color of a dove's breast. & my dog & my girlfriend. Long hair, tinted with both blond and chestnut highlights; huge dark, sincere eyes. She stares at me so seriously. The applicator already filled. I lifted my leg, exposed it from under the sheet, hadn't shaved for two days, she licked carefully around my ankle. When her tongue hit the stiff, thorny stubble, she moved down to my foot, between each toe. I sat up on the side of the bed, legs spread, and said go ahead. She didn't even sniff. She went into the kitchen for a drink. Then she came back and said you never want to go on walks anymore, always in bed.

She said I kicked her out of bed in my sleep every night. Then said she wouldn't sleep where a man had squirted. Forgetting I washed the sheets daily. Everything has to be white, bleached, and dry. It's an insidious bacteria, craving warmth and moisture. Don't we all. So she caught my infection anyway. Dirty bitch, she said. I looked at my dog, my dog looked at me.

Two feet on the floor, the rest of her body in bed with me, she was watching me inseminate myself for yeast infection. I used to roll my dog over and say, you have hair where I don't, and no hair where I do. Armpits, groin, all nude. Now? We're almost even. If I'm not a man, maybe I'm a dog. I could've been my girlfriend's dog. I'd be a beautiful dog. In that case, my dog wants to know why *I'm* allowed on the bed and *she's* not. Look, bitch, you want to be *me*? I used her old insemination tube and gave her a shot of yeast medication. I heard you can use yogurt too. She ordinarily loves yogurt. She said, You can't be the father of my puppies.

Everyone's afraid I'll do anything to be related to them.

To make it up to her, I'll let her almost nab a squirrel, but she's not allowed to go all the way. I don't want her catching some disease then giving it to me. As punishment, we're both getting spayed next month after we finish our periods.

MY HUSBAND'S BEST FRIEND

She ordered meatball soup. There was one meatball. I said it was a bull testicle. I couldn't ruin her appetite.

We were there to talk about: My search for a career across the continent, her lover 2,000 miles away waiting for a commitment. My husband wondering if being married was what he wanted, our new unintentionally similar haircuts, her budding friendship with my husband. Also: my memories of being fired from a job I loved, her anger at her brother for giving her a nightgown for Christmas, my childhood remedies to prevent my body from maturing, her new stock portfolio that she tried not to audit every day, my husband's recent curiosity about sex with two women at once. And maybe something else.

We shared a chocolate mousse. I carefully shaved the pudding with my spoon in an upward motion. My side looked like Half Dome. On her side she plunged in and ate whole spoonfuls at a time. I gave her the cherry on top. We stopped talking for a while, sat looking around. The waiter kept filling our coffee cups. My fingers were trembling; I switched to decaf. I wished I would stop handling everything so well, just go ahead, fall to the floor, twitching, foaming at the mouth. Things were winding down. Then she took my hand.

WHAT IF

The neighborhood was on fire.

1985

The neighborhood was called Normal Heights. It had once been
the location of the old normal school, and it sat on a plateau above
the county's major river valley, thus normal-plus-heights. No one
thought the neighborhood's name was odd, although few, if anyone, knew that normal schools had been started by the French
in the seventeenth century, and the English adjective "normal"
derived from the Latin word *normal*, which signifies a carpenter's
square, a rule, a pattern or model. Teacher-training schools were
called *normal* because they were to be *model* schools in which pu-
pils apply theory to practice. Puritans starting colleges in America
wanted only *practical* education, nothing too ethereal, abstract,
speculative, and ... useless.

So it was an old neighborhood, as old goes in Southern California. The streets were lined with palm trees and eucalyptus,
jacaranda and Brazilian pepper. The one business district along
Adams Avenue had pizza and Chinese take-out, Mexican hole-
in-the-wall cafes that would've been called *cantinas* if they were
in Mazatlan, a vegetarian restaurant run by a suspect group of
possibly brainwashed young men, and a produce-plus-health-food
corner grocery. There had been a Polish restaurant once, but such

places, offering large sausages, hadn't survived in California in the seventies. Just off Adams Avenue, about three blocks on a residential street, a small walled monastery overlooked the valley.

You could walk to the post office and pass antique shops, used bookstores, and three laundromats where the thick, steamy smell of clean cotton wafted out the doors and young women just like you stood over heaps of miniature sets of pants, overalls, and t-shirts, their bangs plastered to their foreheads. There was a bar called Elbow Inn. And another one called Paddy's Wagon. There was a spiritual healer who read palms and tarot cards and offered midwifery, and a pet store called The Blue Lagoon. There were courtyards where five or six identical, miniature Spanish-style cottages were arranged around a square of grass, one with a fountain that no longer ran now used as a planter for geraniums. There was a closet-sized establishment that sold only juices of any combination: celery and carrot, mango and lettuce, tomato-lime.

If you walked the other way, you'd go by a real estate and law office — small storefronts, with brick planters of marigolds and petunias beside their doors. Then a few thrift stores, a copy shop with only two Xerox machines behind a counter, a model train store, and, across the bridge that spanned the freeway, a library, a community vegetable garden, and a bookstore that had been the first in the country to have a coffee shop inside, featuring a large selection of gay magazines not carried by the library. Beside the bookstore, a one-screen theatre where you had seen *A Hard Day's Night* as a first-run movie when you were eight, and now could probably see it again since the theatre showed classic and cult movies, a different pair every night, and published a calendar that everyone in the neighborhood had stuck to their refrigerator with a magnet.

Where you'd grown up, the place you'd left when you left home, not too many years before this, there were no sidewalks or juice stores or natural groceries or landmark theaters. People had chickens and big, rocky, weedy hillside yards where they could fabricate a shelter and a barbed wire fence and have a horse. For ten or twenty years after leaving home, there's little nostalgia about where you came from; you get caught up with the striking-out-on-your-own, the discovering who you are and what you have to offer and who's going to want it, and you don't do too much longing for what you left behind. So it didn't matter a lot that nobody in Normal Heights had a horse. Instead, there were a lot of cats, sitting in windows of living rooms and storefronts, on stoops, on fences, and sometimes dead. Once someone's cat had gone up a fifty-foot palm tree. Not one of those smooth, slender palm trees that bend over in hurricanes, but the kind with a thick jagged façade caused by cutting off the dead lower fronds as the tree grew higher, so the trunk was like a huge cylindrical cheese grater until the skirt of leaves at the top where the cat's face looked down. It could've been your cat, if you had a cat, and after trying to lure it down with a can of sardines extended on a tree-trimming device a neighbor donated, something else had to be done. Fire trucks no longer came for treed cats. In a neighborhood with nothing taller than two stories, fire trucks didn't have ladders, did they? But somehow someone got the idea to call an antenna repairman, and he went up with boots and leather gloves, ropes and a pulley, climbing the way he would scale a sheer rock face, got the cat into a canvas bag and lowered it to the ground. That cat lived, for a while longer. But while walking to the post office or laundromat or juice store, you would often see one in the gutter, sometimes just skin and hair, other times swollen and staring, a frozen snarl aimed skyward, the buzzing of amassed flies like a wind-up motor still sputtering inside it. But probably most of the time someone found the cat still fresh and carried it home. One time a woman screamed and screamed in the street for several hours after a cat was mauled by a pizza delivery car. No one could even tell if the cat was hers, because someone else wrapped the body in a towel and held it while the screaming woman went on screaming. It was a day that didn't sound like Normal Heights and people came out of houses and apartments to ask her to shut up. Meanwhile the pizza delivery boy sat on the curb beside the woman with the dead cat wrapped in a towel until his pizzas were cold.

A funky Normal Heights version of Monopoly might've seemed fun at first, with the spiritual advisor and massage therapist as the cheap-rent Baltic and Mediterranean Avenues, and the theatre with carved gilded woodwork and velvet-draped balcony seats as the Boardwalk. But it would've been all wrong. First of all, across the bridge, the theater and gay bookstore and library did not like to be called Normal Heights; they said they were in *Kensington*. If you lived in Normal Heights you probably couldn't afford to live in Kensington, although you could use their library, view their classic movies, and sip the coffee in their bookstore. Maybe that part *was* like Monopoly, but it wasn't like Normal Heights. A Normal Heights Monopoly game would have to have a different way to win: no one who lived in Normal Heights was striving to own all of Normal Heights and raise the rents so high that no one else could afford to live there, then squeeze the money out of everyone until they all had to move away. Maybe somebody wanted to live there forever.

You would love living in Normal Heights, even if it could not be forever. Even if nothing happened to change the course of your life, the rhythm of the journey you'd already started probably would've taken you to another neighborhood someday, by the time you turned thirty, a neighborhood that was different but good, or even better, in its own way. A neighborhood that could've saved your marriage.

From the neighborhood down to the valley, the walls of the canyon were native, semi-arid chaparral, home to possums and snakes, birds and coyote, some foxes, feral cats who'd survived the streets of Normal Heights and now would be food for the coyote, and one mythical albino deer, but it hadn't been seen for years until it was spotted once again farther west toward Presidio Park, where it was hit by a car. The floor of the valley used to be dairy farms beside a creek they called a river. Photos from a hundred years ago showed the entire valley filled with water when the sluggish stream proved its ultimate authority. Even Southern California has its hundred-year floods. Now the valley had a freeway and hotels, two shopping malls, a small convention center, a tiny golf course whose days were numbered because the land was too valuable for pitch-n-putt, and a stadium.

In the stadium that day there would be a baseball game, and after the game, a concert performed by the symphony. Naturally you'd be going to both events in the stadium, because your husband played a brass instrument in the symphony. Brass instruments are expensive, but nothing like violins and cellos, which can cost as much as a house, even houses in California, if the instrument is good enough. So the string players, playing an outdoor concert, always used their second rate instruments — called, affectionately, their *axes*. Brass players frequently only had one ax. Of course his ax would be in the car when you headed off to the stadium on the day Normal Heights was on fire.

It was what he did, play a horn in a symphony, and probably would be what he got to do forever. You know he had to be good to play in a symphony, to be allowed to do for a living the thing he felt best doing. With roughly thirty symphonies in the country that paid a living wage — and in this case it meant a salary that allowed him to live in Normal Heights but not La Jolla, La Mesa, La Costa, or even down the street in Kensington — and hundreds if not thousands of musicians vying for each seat in each orchestra, he had to be good. He was lucky, that way. Fortunate, blessed, privileged. Even though you knew he'd worked for it.

Remember: you had made a game, a board game, based on the practical life of a classical musician. Each player tried to get into bigger and bigger orchestras, starting with community orchestras, then regional, on up to small cities, etcetera. For each audition at each level, the player had to have gathered enough poker chips representing lessons (paid for with money earned at freelance gigs) and hours practicing (earned by landing on the proper squares on the board or gaining practice hours via the "phone-call" and "mail" stacks of cards). The auditions were based on roll of the dice, with wider and wider odds as the size of the orchestra increased. It was an elaborate, multi-faceted game that could go all night and on into the next, when you would play it with other friends from the symphony, each time tweaking the rules a little to smooth out the rough spots. No player ever won the game by obtaining a chair in one of the top six orchestras, but still, they had jobs in this city's *real* orchestra, which was more than hundreds of musicians in this city and thousands of others all over the country could say.

But it wouldn't be fair if *he* was the only one accomplishing what he set out to do. That particular summer, that particular day, it could've been a week or even just a day before you would hit that *finally-finally-finally* phase of euphoria, when, in the nick of time, just before you turned thirty, you'd get the call: your first one-woman show or exhibit or book. It might've been sculpted ceramics — mostly abstract figures of wild horses with legs and necks too long, too thin, or too thick, and manes like plumes of smoke. Or maybe it was multi-colored, leather Mardi Gras masks, cut, formed, fringed, dyed, hardened into shape, grinning, sneering, frowning, aghast, horrified, leering. Or poems. Poems about horses and angst, tempests and sex, sex and earthquakes, ennui and sex, lust and horses, stallions and flowers, petals and stamen, pistil and pollination. *Finally-finally-finally*, the garden you'd tilled since the scent of its verdant soil first caressed your nostrils in college would *have* to bear fruit, pay in the breakthrough dividends of continued flowering-to-fruit-bearing metaphors. It had to because ... *you'd* also put in the hours and had taken the lessons. And when it happened, someday, the most important dividend would be that no longer would you be spending any chilly hours answering phones and directing calls to auto salesmen and mechanics at the Ford dealership on El Cajon Boulevard that really couldn't claim to be part of Normal Heights. You'd walk away singing the jingle for the final time — *See Pearson Ford, We Stand Alone at Fairmount and El Cajon* — and the next house, in Mission Hills or Hillcrest or even Kensington, might have a full extra bedroom, maybe two, and a second bathroom, and a two-car garage that could become an even more invigorating workshop; you'd no longer be walking to the post office or laundromat, and there'd be no smaller house in the backyard sheltering another musician waiting for his turn to earn a living wage in a symphony. It shouldn't have been the fire — nor the house in the backyard, nor the less-successful musician in that house in the backyard — but success that impelled you away from Normal Heights.

It started long before the baseball game, on the side of the long, meandering road called *Camino del Rio South* that ran almost the length of the valley, just slightly up the rise of the southern canyon wall. The freeway in the river bottom was north of and also lower than Camino del Rio, and the former pastures and shopping centers and golf course and stadium were north of the freeway, then the river itself on the far northern side of the valley, was at least two, maybe four miles away from the road named road-of-the-river. Offices and restaurants and hotels had collected along Camino del Rio, but sometimes, between parking lots, the wild hillside still extended all the way from Normal Heights at the top to the sidewalk that snaked beside Camino del Rio where the maids who cleaned the hotel rooms, and the gardeners and cooks and janitors walked from the bus stops to work.

A cigarette thrown from a passing car. It was during a July Santa Ana wind, blowing in off the desert. July could easily be hot, but usually it was September when you felt the wind named for the Santa Ana Canyon, itself named by the settlers of Santa Ana California after Saint Anne, *not* Antonio Lopez de Santa Ana Perez de Lebron, the opium addict who'd defeated the Texans at the Alamo. Canyons like the Santa Ana help channel the hot dry desert winds toward the coast, thus accelerated their speed. But Santa Ana wasn't the only canyon. The big wide river valley with the freeway and the stadium, called Mission Valley, was a canyon, a shallow, smooth canyon, but on its eastern end it connected to the more severe Mission Gorge, and Mission Gorge was the real canyon that conveyed the winds that dried the grasses and brush on the side of the roads, like Camino del Rio South, where a cigarette was thrown from a passing car.

The wild oats — having shed their seeds and dried to paper

husks — the sage and brown tumbleweeds, the sumac and Father Serra's mustard crackled briefly in flame then crumbled to ashes as the snaky line of flame edged up the wall of the valley. Up there, in Normal Heights, the numbered streets, 30th, 31st, 32nd, 33rd, 34th, 35th, 36th, and the named streets in between, were all flat on a level plane, and they crossed the east-west business district of Adams Avenue then ended in cul-de-sacs north of the thrift shops and laundromats and natural grocery, above the south rim of Mission Valley. Those fortunate few houses on the cul-de-sacs had yards that extended into the canyon, mostly left to the indigenous flora to flourish right up to the border landscape bushes surrounding their lawns, and the masses of eucalyptus that made their shade.

The eucalyptus trees were brought to Southern California to grow as a crop for railroad ties, but the wood proved too soft for that purpose. So the trees grew tall and thick on the property lines of ranchos, and the former crop groves became shady parks. The trees thrived in the dry climate and were a way to turn Southern California green, leafy, and forested. Planted everywhere, a new sapling in every new yard, they quickly grew huge, and those in Normal Heights were easily thirty or forty years old or more. They're drought-resistant because their tough leaves are full of oil instead of water. In the Santa Ana winds they flutter like aspens, and rattle like bones. The lick of one flame, and — *boom* — the tree is a blazing oil-soaked torch. As the brush fire rippled up the side of Mission Valley . . . *boom* . . . *boom, boom* . . . *boom* . . . the eucalyptus trees making shady yards at the ends of the cul-de-sacs in Normal Heights exploded.

Not only did the fire trucks in Normal Heights have no ladders, the fire hydrants in Normal Heights had little or no water pressure. This could have been because the original lots were deep, and the houses small. During the postwar boom years, a lot of people built another, smaller house at the back of their property (thus the abode in your backyard). Then parents of the 1940s and '50s who'd raised their families in Normal Heights died or moved to retirement homes, and the houses had become too small for contemporary families, the neighborhood too multihued — the same people who would be mowing their lawns in La Jolla might live next door in Normal Heights. And who wanted to raise a family with a musician living in the little house in the back yard? But someone would still buy the lot and either rent the house, or both houses; or sometimes remove the house, or both houses, and build a low-rise apartment. The same amount of water that used to fill and re-fill one toilet, or two, now filled twelve or eighteen.

Water conservation was constant, as were the reminders. Use a car wash that recycles its water ... don't sweep with a hose ... water lawns at dusk or overnight, every other day at most ... *If it's yellow let it mellow* ... But still, the number of residents had easily quintupled since the grid of streets and sewer lines and water pipes and single-family homes had first been sketched on blue tissue paper. Firemen jumped from trucks and attached hoses to hydrants only to be met with a thin trickle oozing from the nozzle they aimed at the next fully engulfed house.

It was still before the baseball game. If you stood in your front yard, ash and cinders blew past, hitting you like fleeing insects. A wall of smoke rose from the northern side of Normal Heights. Helicopters dove, zigzagged and hovered. Tanker airplanes droned. The radio had news every half hour, and every broadcast began with the fire. Twelve houses gone, then twenty, then twenty-three. Threatening to advance south, leap over Adams Avenue, and continue to incinerate the numbered streets, hopping from the dry top of one palm tree to the next, from one brittle shake roof to the next, from one incendiary eucalyptus to the next.

But it was time to go, if you were going to the baseball game before the concert. The concert was not optional, it was his opportune job, but attending the baseball game was not mandatory. If you lived south of Adams Avenue, especially between Adams and Madison, what were the chances, really, of the fire cremating everything between the gorge and Madison Street, including everything inside that little house in the middle of the block on 36th Street with another smaller quarters housing another musician in the backyard. And if you stayed, what could you do, really, to stop it? On the radio, they were begging residents to not turn on their hoses, stop flushing toilets, resist taking a cooling shower, don't wash your clothes or cars or dogs today, not today!

There was a box game you'd had for a while, a municipal management game, where each player ran a small city and had to make decisions about things like how much police and fire protection to maintain, water supplies and landfill capacity, sewer water treatment and recycling — or choose to pipe it elsewhere; determine regulations for factory and car emissions, for suburban development, for curbside trash hauling, or just wait for the wind to blow your smog to the next player's town. It had been almost impossible to understand the game, then to win it, and you might've thought of revamping it, if you hadn't realized it was geared that way on purpose: Any player who tried to prioritize ecology would lose. But still, if you'd kept the game, you might've learned enough, over the years, through the water shortages and recycling programs and fires, to fix it.

That was the kind of game you liked best, though. *Not* two-person-only games, but games combining both skill and chance, where you had to make decisions and also deal with sudden information, good or bad. Games with complication, even drama. What role could you play in checkers? Sometimes, on concert nights, the musician-in-the-backyard who hadn't been good and lucky enough to earn a living wage in the symphony, came over to play games. But with just the two of you, it was hard to make even the box games — Fortune 400 and The Bottom Line and that city management game — rousing enough, and Trivial Pursuit was okay, if you had enough grass, but that was usually for after concerts, at someone else's house, with the rest of the lucky earning-a-living-wage musicians. The ones who were playing the concert after the baseball game at the stadium the day of the fire.

What else could you do, that day, but lock your house as usual, and, through the back door notice the long eye-shaped crack in the backyard musician's blinds as he jealously watched your husband go to another concert for which he was paid a living wage, even though the paid musicians grumbled and moaned about having to play classical "pops," the uncomplicated stuff, in difficult places like a stadium where the string players had to use their second-best ax because the cheesy fireworks they had to include to make *that* kind of audience think they enjoyed a symphony concert might char their best ax.

The cars filed into the stadium in the valley as usual. Your seats, as usual, the cheap ones in the upper deck. (A living wage for doing the thing he loved was one thing, box seats quite another.) You wouldn't usually sit in the very top row of the upper deck, but today was different. From up there, from above the right field corner, if you stood and faced away from the playing field — out over the concrete wall behind the last seats, past the parking lot and the blur of freeway and the hazy low office buildings along Camino del Rio South, up the side of the hill to the crest — you could count the number of black smudges that used to be houses, and you could see those still burning, dozens of them, a skyline of flame where once the skyline of roofs had been enshrouded in dense shrubs and trees. Over seventy of them in all. Only the monastery had a wall, not previously visible through the brush on the outside. Only the monastery was not burning.

Was anyone who lived on the rim of the canyon in Normal Heights at the baseball game that day? And if so, if it were you, would you stay to hear the symphony play its summer classics: *William Tell, Boléro,* "The Stars and Stripes Forever," and the *1812 Overture?* Would you cringe at each pop and blast of fireworks in the newly darkened sky? Was the hillside still glowing in the distance? When you returned home, would you be astonished, or was it only the inevitable you came back to see?

Adams Avenue was gloomy with hanging smoke, with dirty water in the gutters, with closed shops and ashy sidewalks. No one would blame you for not looking to see if any cats had crawled to the curb today to die. You might have more selfish concerns, and anyway, no one was screaming. Not anymore. After everything is gone, you tend to just stand and stare, poke at sooty debris with one foot, smash the blind eye of the skeletal TV with a black brick.

Okay, forget renters insurance, which you would've never had. Forget about the Salvation Army and friends coming to the rescue with clothes and bedding. Forget about The Red Cross and group-camping in a high school auditorium and free government surplus food (those huge bricks of orange cheese). When everything is gone, it's gone.

Gone: the leather masks, the ceramic abstract equines with contorted bodies waiting to be transported to the gallery (the fire too hot, they would be black, blistered, cracked, and even more contorted, if not complete rubble). Gone: the poems about hot-house orchids and heavy-breathing stallions, mosaics made of the parts from old manual typewriters and rotary telephones, the play about a musician who lives in the backyard of another musician, or the long, hand-dyed cotton skirts with strings of prancing po-nies hand-stitched around the hem.

So what if you still had your job at Pearson Ford. It was only a job to work at while you waited for the other stuff to lift you out. You were supposed to quit, when you started to live off the fruits of your passion, at least by the time you turned thirty. But if the passion had burned up, had helped fuel the searing fire, had in fact made the fire more intense, had kept the blaze crackling as long as possible, maybe even longer than it would've burned otherwise, it (the zeal) was now not buried and waiting to be found in the residue of your former sneakers and leather hiking boots, in the black debris of your former crock-pot and electric wok you'd gotten as wedding gifts, in the ashes of your former bricks-n-boards and the books that sat on the shelves they made, in the stink of the black mud that used to be your second-hand sofa. *It* was not just damaged . . . it was gone.

Now what do you do? You think this is some kind of game? And when it's over, when you lose or figure out the game can't be won, you just go back to Normal Heights and walk to the grocery store for wheat germ bread, buy a carrot juice, then some stamps, pick up a lost kitten crying in the shrubs outside the laundromat and feed it Tender Vittles and give it a flea bath and let your hus-band name it *You-Little-Nudnik*?

No, now is the time to be practical. For solutions. For survival.

Remember, going to college in the late seventies, do you re-call any career advisors? If they existed, they were the loneliest desk-squatters in the university, because no one was thinking about careers, not in that way. It was do-what-you're-good-at, do-what-fulfills-you, do-what-makes-you-like-yourself. For some it was music, and that was a career, and could, for the lucky ones, pay a living wage (or if they failed, they would have to live in smaller houses behind the small houses in Normal Heights and give music lessons in the back rooms of piano stores). For the others it was sociology, theatre, recreation, dance, art, literature, design, or liberal arts. No, there weren't any underwater basket weaving classes — a popular yuppie myth when the next generation came to school in these Reagan-'80s and deluged then saturated the business colleges and prelaw. By the time these Reaganites arrived on campus, you and your husband were out, *doing* it, living in Normal Heights.

Who said only the musicians could go out and *do* the indulgent thing you studied in college? So you get a job to help make money for rent and food, and keep doing the real thing in your *spare* time, which was your *real* time. And your husband the musician — one of those fortunate ones — even though they'd made him take ROTC in that conformist southern state college he'd gone to before coming West for graduate school where you met him, he would never have to fall back on that or anything else. He had his living wage from the symphony, enough to rent a one-and-a-half bedroom house on 36th Street in Normal Heights that came with another one-bedroom cottage in the backyard on the alley housing another musician — but this one not doing as well in the Practical-Life-of-a-Musician Game, no living wage, just the lessons he gave in a piano store. And that extra half bedroom in your street-facing house — a perfect studio, for you, wasn't it? It was where those poems or those masks or those flamboyant ceramic horses had been shaped. (Maybe the detached shed that used to be a one-car garage would be better for the masks and ceramics. The washer and dryer that no longer worked were a perfect workbench, despite the grooves in the metal made by the lids, but there was a utility sink with running water, and electricity. It could've also been a darkroom, a hothouse, a woodworking shop, or a drafting room for the design of board games. It could've also been another shack to house another musician.)

So you came of age after the draft ended, lived the you-can-do-anything life of a middle-class babyboomer for twenty years, then it was a day job and living paycheck-to-paycheck without mom-and-dad's subsidy in the proletarian-meets-bohemian enclave of Normal Heights. But *survival*?

Before Normal Heights and the former normal school university, in more childish days in the bedroom you were loaned in your parents' house, you'd once thought, with some puerile comfort, that if you found no one to marry you, and if you were unable to find work traveling with the Lipizzaner stallions or tending botanic gardens at the zoo, there was always the military as a safety net. (You had this thought even though your more up-to-the-minute, used-to-be-a-normal-school state university in California wouldn't dare force anyone to join ROTC. Even your husband's out-of-touch southern state college that mandated ROTC didn't require it for *girls*.) But if you found yourself unemployed and unattached, this was a military town and there it was: It could give you a job and pay you. But that was between Vietnam and the Gulf War, years of some modicum of peace — if you didn't count Africa and the Middle East and Afghanistan — and it didn't sound *too* bad, as long as you didn't say it out loud or admit it to anyone. The ads on TV had made it look sublime. Like you could maneuver the signal flags as jets came in at sunset to land on carriers in silent slow motion. You could be a nurse in scrub suit and surgical mask side-by-side with a doctor under glaring lights — no uniform, no *yessir, nosir* when the doctor asked for the next instrument, only his respectful eyes appreciating your skill. (How was it obvious the ad wasn't offering the doctor's job as a military option?) You could even twirl a white rifle — it wouldn't be a *real* rifle — in a parade, or be a pastry chef, or play in a band or orchestra. They made it sound like you wouldn't be crawling under barbed wire in the mud, and certainly like you wouldn't find yourself in South Korea or Libya. By 1985, though, you'd be almost thirty. Your secret military backup ship had sailed.

If you were going to be sensible, your first thought might have been teaching. But no, not that. Not because those who can't *do*, teach; but because those who teach don't *do*. Don't have time to, if they're worth a damn. Even if the fire meant you would no longer *do*, you wanted to have *time* to do, if you ever decided to *do* again. But still, you could've considered substitute teaching or parochial schools, or substitute teaching at parochial schools; maybe the monastery had a school tied to it? After all, you had gone to the university that had grown out of the old normal school. But had taken nothing practical, except maybe the letterpress printing class in the graphic arts department, even though offset was long established as the industry norm.

There probably aren't any letterpress printers looking for help from burned out, poetic, orchid-growing, stallion sculptors who took one letterpress class as an elective (you still had the business cards you'd made for yourself there). What are the other things you thought about?

Real horses. You never got to have one. Really, so few kids ever got that pony that's supposed to guarantee childhood is sweet. Wished for one every Christmas, but you always knew a shaggy little Shetland wouldn't show up in a paddock built overnight in your dad's backyard. Someone up the street had a mule her parents rented for six months. To be a jockey now, you would've had to earn your way in as an exercise rider. (Never mind that there hadn't at this point been any female jockeys yet, there had probably been female exercise riders). To be an exercise rider you would probably have to earn your way in as a stable hand. And plodding up the street on that girl's mule once or twice, or going to see the Lipizzaner stallions when you were six, or writing a few flabby poems about arching necks and flaring nostrils, then standing at the rail once or twice a year at the Del Mar track eating cheese puffs and yelling go-go-go didn't count.

Okay: then, cats. *You-Little-Nudnik* had been contentedly leaving his hair on any horizontal surface and his claw marks on any vertical one, when he might've ended up coyote-chow or a grease spot in the gutter. That's because of you. So your good deed could be expanded into a cat-rescue organization. Lost or abandoned or born wild: lure them in with Tender Vittles, de-flea them and introduce them to a litter box, then out the door to happy homes or adoptive businesses who might cover your cost of food and flea-foam, or the occasional vet bill when you find one who can't defend himself in a screech-and-slash because his last owner had his claws removed. Plus collect donations from the community, from the shops along Adams Avenue who would be grateful for your twice daily roadkill patrols, who knew a live cat in a storefront window might bring in customers, but a dead one in the gutter was nothing but repulsion (especially if someone couldn't stop screaming). And you could do it all from home, from the half-bedroom-converted-into-a-studio converted again into an office.

But wait. You're only doing this because of the fire — the fire that burned over seventy houses in Normal Heights one June day in 1985, and if yours was among them, there'd be no back half bedroom from which to run your grassroots cat rescue operation. Same goes for the orchid hothouse, or the craft shop making detailed miniature leather saddles for plastic horse statues that little girls get for Christmas instead of real ponies, or the come-watch-TV-with-me service for lonelyhearts in the evenings while your musician husband is playing a concert and other musicians who don't make a living wage are not.

So take a look for a minute at the musician in the hut in the backyard, and what would *he* do if it had all incinerated. He was already balding in his twenties, on the portly side, pear-shaped with a large reddish nose. He just couldn't draw a winning card. And even though nothing of any real value would have burned, when he looked for a new place to live, it couldn't be an apartment, *had* to be a little shack-like house — like the one with termite weakened frame and paint-peeling siding that would have made no more than a black smudge in the ashy lawn of your backyard — because he practiced that brass instrument hours a day (collecting practice hours in the Practical-Life-of-a-Musician Game so he could go to auditions and try to earn a living wage someday) and neighbors in apartments tended to complain about the noise. In fact, neighbors in neighborhoods with cracker box houses built before World War II also tended to complain, but if your closest neighbor was the brass-playing earning-a-living-wage musician in the house in front of yours, who would say anything? *That's* what had been razed for the musician in the backyard, because he couldn't move with you and your husband and Nudnik the rescued cat when you found yourself a livingroom-kitchen-bedroom converted chicken coop in someone else's backyard elsewhere on the fringes of Normal Heights. Or maybe outside those fringes. Way over close to El Cajon Boulevard, in the nebulous sprawl of other neighborhoods with less evocative personality, but you could still walk to the post office on Adams Avenue where you would keep a PO box with a Normal Heights zip code. And where you could walk to work singing *At Pearson Ford, we stand alone, at Fairrrr-mount and El Cajon.*

OK you're back here again. Games go round-and-round in circles (or squares). And if that's what you're going to do, maybe that's where you should look. *That's* the solution. What if you put the Practical-Life-of-a-Musician Game into the car before you went to the baseball game? What if you were going to take it to someone's house after the concert after the baseball game? Maybe the Practical-Life-of-a-Musician Game had undergone some recent tweaking and needed another play-through to check the pacing. Maybe the musician from the house in the backyard would even be there. Maybe you needed the opinion of one of those who never did get to earn a living wage playing concerts, even tacky concerts after baseball games, and instead had to force-feed music lessons to bratty monsters in the back room of a piano-and-organ store. Of course the test run-through of the game (not the baseball game) would be called off — that poor musician-in-the-backyard was never going to learn this game. But when you finished kicking the black bricks and trying to dust the soot from your palms onto the sooty thighs of your jeans; when you finished staring at the blob of black goo that used to be your record albums and was still a little warm and malleable — perhaps it could've been shaped into a thoroughbred's arrogant head or the thrashing figure of a stallion, but you didn't touch it — when you finished digging cinders out of your eyes looking for a tear, you would realize what's important: that in the car you still had your husband's ax. And the game.

You saved the game. The game isn't gone. You could set up a game-maker studio and go on improving it, developing it. Devote all your time to it. And now, this whole experience makes you realize what you had devised before is only the basis for a bigger game: The Living-a-Practical-Life-in-Normal-Heights Game. A little bit of Monopoly, a little bit of that impossible-to-win city-planning game, and not just the practical lives of musicians but of all who subsist in Normal Heights.

Like Monopoly, there will be properties, but of course, you'll be renting, not buying. There won't be any railroads or utility companies available. Buying residential property could be the eventual goal, except that as soon as someone owns real estate in Normal Heights, they usually leave Normal Heights then rent their property to someone else (you), or knock down a house and build a set of eight apartments, or add a cottage to the backyard and collect two rents. All that could come later, if the game gets that far. Suffice it to say, how you make your money to pay your rent is not from collecting rents from other players, even if you have a musician living in a shack in your backyard.

But you'll have to decide where your money is coming from. This means — how would they say it at the career counseling center at the normal-school-turned-university? — your livelihood, your profession, your vocation, your calling, your way of being yourself. The Practical-Life-in-Normal-Heights Game lets you choose from a whole plethora of pursuits besides classical musician: from the janitors, maids, cooks, and busboys in the offices, hotels and restaurants on Camino del Rio South, just down the canyon wall from Normal Heights ... to the antenna repairman, pizza delivery driver, the midwife palm-reader, the possibly brainwashed young men who run the vegetarian restaurant. You could mow the lawns in the courtyards of the Spanish-style cottages, or be one of the girls who make the juice assortments, a bartender at Elbow Inn, a monk at the monastery ... or live the practical life of an artiste who paints unicorns on black velvet and sells them on weekends at the gas station on the corner diagonally across from Pearson Ford (singing, . . . *we stand alone, at Fairrr-mount and El Cajon*).

But, at least at first, you can't choose to be anyone who *owns* the juice store or natural grocery, nor an antique shop, and you can't choose to be any of the real estate agents, or lawyers, or the gay bookstore owner . . . they probably don't live in Normal Heights. People who don't live there shouldn't be making all the decisions. That's why you're adding the city-planning aspect to this game. Not a mayor and city council — Normal Heights is a neighborhood, not a self-sufficient city — but just some practical decisions. When the neighborhood meeting card is picked, you have to all get together to determine things like: how much you'll each kick in for how many police officers and firefighters? How much will everyone have to pay for electricity and water and garbage removal? (The musician in the house in the backyard liked to say that maybe there's no need for sanctioned trash removal because Vietnamese refugees go up and down the alley, scavenging from the useless things people pile out there — it's how you got rid of that already-second-hand green sofa where you and the musician-in-the-backyard got bored playing Trivial Pursuit.) The game will have to have a mechanism to make these decisions have an impact on other aspects of the practical life of the player, even though you never really got to decide how many firehouses to maintain in Normal Heights, or the density of residential development in ratio to the decades-old sewer and water and streets-and-sanitation infrastructure. The first and obvious impact of these decisions is less money at each player's payday, but also maybe you'll have to miss your turn, miss one out of every five turns, if water is rationed or if you decide to go with Neighborhood Watch and volunteer paramedics and firehouse.

Meanwhile, for whatever occupation you choose, on your turn you go about the board collecting the things you'll need to do better at it . . . and collecting more things to do even better . . . like the practice hours and auditions for musicians. It would be broken antenna customers (who might also need their cats rescued from palm trees), or brainwashed vegetarian converts, or newly-invented juice combinations, or successful at-home natural births (the unsuccessful ones are going to cost you), or horse-loving art buyers. You're trying to land on the important squares that provide these rewards, and avoid the annoying *phone call* and *mail* squares, where you have to draw a card and do what it says, even though sometimes the phone will bring a musician an extra freelance gig, providing money for another lesson; or the mail might bring an acceptance from an art magazine that's using your sixth grade rendition of a kicking steed on its cover.

And then, maybe someday, when you're doing real well — one of those blessed scant minority who win an audition and are paid a living wage, or you're exhibited or published or promoted to housekeeping-supervisor or head-brainwashed-waiter, or recruited to run the orchid hothouse at the zoo — instead of moving out of Normal Heights, you'll be buying property and staying (this is one objective of the game), and it's always better if *you* own the house with another house in the backyard with an unsuccessful musician living in it. Unless you make the mistake of sleeping with him because you feel sorry for him — that'll be a card some hapless street-facing resident will draw, because it could wreak havoc, unless, first, the fire card is drawn.

Yes, at some point during the game — you don't know when, and you don't know who — someone will draw the fire card. And then . . . Literalists may want to actually strike a match and the game will easily burn. See who saves what. See what's imperative to whom. It's a one-of-a-kind game, maybe the best thing you ever made, but maybe you should give it up, let it go up in flames: tit for tat. Because you're experienced, you've already done this, you've actually felt the wall of heat, the rain of ashes, heard the explosion of ignition, the roar of combustion, the pop of fire meeting glass. You know, everything can blow: your provisions of clay, your hot-house lights, your antenna-repairing tools, your juice-concoction recipes, your Monopoly and Trivial Pursuit games, your midwife accessories (what might they be?), your flea-foam-bath and Tender Vittles, your pizza delivery truck, the stained green sofa you left in the alley for a scavenger. To ashes: tarot cards you could've read, vegetables you could've served while brainwashing a new customer, lawns you could've mowed, journals you could've burned yourself in the kitchen sink, business cards you printed on a letterpress in a graphic arts class in college and could've distributed when you started a business, poems you could've painted in calligraphy on velvet unicorn paintings. But anyone who's a musician in this game, especially a gifted musician who was out earning a living wage on the day the fire card is drawn, their ax doesn't burn. They still have everything they need. They win. The others might learn their lesson. They might win too, next time. They might learn what's important.

PROPORTION

If I was ever going to see him again, of course it would be in San Francisco. We'd been in San Francisco together once another time, at the onset of the eighties, on a chartered bus with an amateur chorus, and he'd said, "When you leave home like this, all you have to do is go 100 miles up the freeway and your life doesn't seem real anymore, everything's out of phase, out of proportion, like worrying late at night."

He was the choir director. I was a mezzo soprano. His marriage was falling apart. I was a virgin. It didn't seem to faze him.

And my life didn't seem real anymore, and I left the singing group soon after that. And heard he and his wife had gotten turned around, had a child, bought a house.

In San Francisco ten years later, at a coffee bar near Davies Hall, I watched him carry his espresso and a newspaper to a table in the corner, fold the paper over, sip from the tiny espresso cup, smooth a crease in the paper with one finger, touch his upper lip with the tip of his tongue.

I stood there long enough, eventually he looked up, must've seen me, didn't smile, stood, waited, holding the silly little espresso mug in his big hand.

The last time we'd been in San Francisco, in the morning, in the hotel cafe, he'd said, "That donut looks so huge. Know what a donut looks like to the rest of us? Trim an inch off your donut, all around the outside. That's what a donut looks like to me."

I got regular coffee, large, cream and sugar, felt him watch me make my way around tables and chairs, but I didn't look up until I had already set my big cup on his table.

I said, "Now my life feels real everywhere I go. Or else it isn't real anywhere. I no longer worry late at night." But I don't know if I said it aloud.

Maybe I said, "Exchange cups with me, then nothing will seem out of proportion to you."

If he did touch my face, his fingers were hot from the espresso.

TRICKLE-DOWN TIMELINE

Pac-Man became the first computer game hero. He was originally supposed to be Puck-Man (he was, after all, shaped like a hockey puck), but with the threat that rampaging youth might scratch out the loop of the P to form an F on arcade machines, Pac-Man was born, a name with literally no meaning.

Median household income: $17,710
Median cost of a house: $76,400
These things hardly mattered, or even meant anything to anyone who was just moving out of his or her parents' house and had found an apartment for $200/month which could be afforded on a $100 a week part-time minimum-wage paycheck while finishing a fifth and sixth year of college.

Ted Bundy was sentenced to death by electrocution.

Brook Shields purred in her Calvin Klein advertisement: *You know what comes between me and my Calvins? Nothing!* Shields also showed off what she had to offer as an actress in *The Blue Lagoon*. Anyone who went on their first date with the person he or she eventually married will remember this film, especially if either of them had to go see it twice because in the middle of the first time, one of their brand new bought-with-birthday-money soft contact lenses came out, and for some reason they still wanted to see how the movie ended.

Ronald Reagan visited the White House to get his job briefing from President Carter. Carter would subsequently disclose that the President-elect asked hardly any questions and did not take notes.

John Lennon was shot, ostensibly for being a phony, by a fan carrying *The Catcher in the Rye*. Doctors at the emergency room that received Lennon's dying body later said they could not have recognized him.

In fact there were few people less phony. As an emblematic death, it was the end of rebellion. Some people, though, were in the throes of being engaged, pawning high school rings to buy silver wedding bands.

1981

The hostages held in Iran for over a year were released on the day of
Ronald Reagan's Presidential inauguration. In his inaugural speech,
Reagan took credit for the release.

The public heard the first news report about a gay man's
mysterious death from an immune-deficiency disease. Later
when the media continued reports of the endemic, the
disease was defined as one that affected "homosexual men,
intravenous drug users, and Haitian men." The inclusion of
Haitian men in this early description was eventually dropped
without explanation.

Striking air traffic controllers were fired by President Reagan.

The Army suggested, *Be All You Can Be.*

The Reagan administration tried to count ketchup as a vegetable in
subsidized school lunches.

The minimum wage was raised to $3.35. At forty hours a week,
for fifty-two weeks a year, this would net $6,968, no taxes. The
poverty threshold for 1981, for a single person, was $4,620.
Two-thousand three-hundred forty-eight dollars of breathing
room for the year. Some people, however, went to college and
could now make $10,000 a year working behind a desk at a
hospital, or as a salesman (person) for a cement company, or as
a first year elementary school teacher, or even earn a little more
than that as a grocery checker.

Reagan Budget Director David Stockman said in an interview for *Atlantic Monthly*, "None of us really understands what's going on with all these numbers." He then conceded that trickle-down economics "was always a Trojan horse to bring down the top [tax] rate." And then, regarding the tax bill, "Do you realize the greed that came to the forefront? The hogs were really feeding."

Britain's Prince Charles married Princess Diana on live TV, and Americans began a(nother) immersion into Royal-watching. Some other people got married this same year. Some of them did so without the Diana-style wedding dress and hundred-yards-of-lace train. A few of them opted for a minister's office on a Thursday night, the bride wearing a brown corduroy skirt, the groom in white jeans (his best pants).

"Honey I forgot to duck," Ronald Reagan supposedly said to Nancy after he was shot by John Hinkley Jr. It was immediately assumed that John Hinkley was crazy.

1982

Bob Jones University, which did not allow admission of non-white students, was granted a tax-exempt status by the Reagan administration. A few months later, Reagan told Chicago high school students that the plan was not designed to assist segregated schools because "I didn't know there were any. Maybe I should have, but I didn't."

The poverty rate rose to 15 percent and the national unemployment rate reached 10.8 percent. There was a new plan, under consideration by the Reagan administration, to tax unemployment benefits. According to a spokesman, it would "make unemployment less attractive."

President Reagan did not like the media constantly reporting about economic distress. "Is it news that some fellow out in South Succotash someplace has just been laid off, that he should be interviewed nationwide?" He would have been pleased to hear that after six years of college, some people considered themselves fortunate, almost blessed, to be allowed to teach college composition for $250 per month per class; or rewarded to have started at box boy as an undergraduate and in six short years had become night manager.

An ad from Mattel for children's computers said, *Now you can get a smarter kid than Mom did.* Did college composition teachers discuss the ungrammatical awkwardness of this sentence? And why was Mattel advertising computers for children when some people, even those who taught college composition, were still using electronic typewriters with "correctable" lift-off letters?

Responding to the buzz regarding Nancy Reagan's appetite for fancy gowns, a White House spokesman said that the First Lady's only intention was to help the national fashion industry. Some people, especially those who rode bikes to work — without making a connection or considering it a protest — stopped wearing skirts entirely (even that brown corduroy wedding skirt).

Bottles of Tylenol were laced with cyanide in Chicago area stores and pharmacies. Seven people with headaches died of poisoning.

The Equal Rights Amendment also died.

In a mass ceremony in Madison Square Garden, 4,150 followers of the Rev Sun Myung Moon (2,075 of them women), were married.

"You know," Ronald Reagan reportedly said to the Lebanese foreign minister, "your nose looks just like Danny Thomas's."

1983

The Navy thought maybe it should eliminate expenses such as $780 screwdrivers, $640 toilet seats, and $9,606 Allen wrenches.

HIV was identified. By this time Haitian men were no longer blamed for carrying the disease. Fashion prognosticators predicted ultra thin would soon not be considered stylish, since those suffering with AIDS were ravaged by weight loss. Plumpness, however, did not find its way into contemporary style. Anyone who was still a virgin in 1980 when they met their future husband, then got married in 1981, was probably not ever going to experience uninhibited sexual experimentation or promiscuity.

Just Say No (also) became the (only) official anti drug-slogan.

The same year Karen Carpenter died of anorexia at the age of thirty-two (which would not do anything to help chubbiness come into fashion), a new pop star named Madonna released her first album. Her voice was compared to Minnie Mouse on helium. Some people, however, weren't buying new albums at the same rate they had when they lived with their parents. So they might own several Carpenters, but no Madonna. One of the Beach Boys also died this year, but no one remembers where they were when they heard Dennis Wilson drowned. This might have meant something, but nobody wondered what.

A White House spokesman said "preposterous" to conjecture about an invasion of Grenada. The following day, because the media was not permitted to cover the mission, the press received, from the White House PR office, photos of Reagan in his pajamas being briefed on the invasion of Grenada.

"I think some people are going to soup kitchens voluntarily," said Ed Meese (who, it turned out, was the same guy who came up with the plan to tax unemployment benefits). "I know we've had considerable information that people go to soup kitchens because the food is free and that that's easier than paying for it . . . I think that they have money."

$3.35 was still the minimum hourly wage.

Ed Meese (whatever his official position, he seemed to do and say a lot), gave a Christmas speech at the National Press Club: "Ebenezer Scrooge suffered from bad press in his time. If you really look at the facts, he didn't exploit Bob Cratchit. Bob Cratchit was paid ten shillings a week, which was a very good wage at the time . . . Bob, in fact, had good cause to be happy with his situation. His wife didn't have to work . . . He was able to afford the traditional Christmas dinner of roast goose and plum pudding . . . So let's be fair to Scrooge. He had his faults, but he wasn't unfair to anyone."

|984

Ronald Reagan, preparing for a speech, was asked to test the microphone. He said, "My fellow Americans, I've signed legislation that will outlaw Russia forever. We begin bombing in five minutes."

Penthouse produced its first issue with a man on the cover (George Burns). Inside, the nude centerfold was an underage Traci Lords. In most countries, including the United States, it is (still) illegal to own or view this issue. The same edition includes photos of the first Black Miss America, Vanessa Williams, a few years younger, and nude. Although it was not illegal to look at her photos, Miss America was asked to resign.

Advertisement for Softsoap: *Ever wonder what you might pick up in the Shower?*
Advertisement for Sure: *Raise Your Arm if You're Sure.*
Advertisement for Wendy's: *Where's the Beef?*
(Still an) advertisement for the Army: *Be all you can be.*

Despite complaining that it cost too much to administer, Reagan signed The CIA Information Act of 1984, an amendment to the 1966 Freedom of Information Act. At the time, the cost of administering the act was less than the Pentagon spent each year on marching bands.

Replacement umpires worked the playoff baseball games when umpires went on strike.

In a Presidential election debate, the former actor pointed out that much of the defense budget was for "food and wardrobe." The Great Communicator went blank in the middle of another answer, then said,

"I'm all confused now," before giving his closing statement. Afterwards Nancy beseeched Reagan's aides: "What have you done to Ronnie?" Reagan later claimed that if he'd worn as much make-up as Mondale, he would have looked better in the debate.

The Census Bureau reported that 35.3 million Americans were living in poverty and that it was an eighteen-year high rate of 15.2 percent of the population. On a televised interview, Reagan said, "You can't help those who simply will not be helped. One problem that we've had, even in the best of times, is people who are sleeping on the grates, the homeless who are homeless, you might say, by choice."

Median household income: $22,415, up 20 percent since 1980; median cost of a house: $97,600, up 27 percent since 1980. Minimum wage: still $3.35 / hour; still $6,968 for forty hours of work, fifty-two weeks a year. Some people say this was the best year of their lives. Even some who were right at the median, or even a little below. Especially if things like that didn't matter. Especially since they'd just left home in 1980 and doing their own laundry and grocery shopping — even laundry and grocery shopping for two — was still fun.

1985

In its 100th year, Coca-Cola introduced "New Coke." Three months later, after consumer objection, it reinstated Coca-Cola Classic. Some wondered whether the whole snafu was a planned promotional gimmick.

While most of the American public will only remember The Great Communicator demanding, "Mr. Gorbachev, take down this wall," President Reagan also said, prior his visit to West Germany, that he would not be visiting any site of a former concentration camp because it would inflict too much shame on a country where "very few alive remember even the war." (Whereas American veterans were in their sixties and many of them quite alive.) But the White House pronounced that Reagan *would* lay a wreath at the Bitburg military cemetery, "an integrated home to the tombs of American and Nazi soldiers" (although there are no Americans graves there). President Reagan defended his West Germany itinerary: "I know all the bad things that happened in that war. I was in uniform for four years myself." (His uniform, more aptly called *wardrobe*, was in training films he starred in).

The number of Barbie dolls sold surpassed the American population. Some people had contributed more Barbie dolls than they would children (as in two dolls to zero children). This helped, because that median income figure was for *two* people, not three (or four, or five...). Even though that wasn't some people's reason for not procreating.

A congresswoman, discussing Ronald Reagan's response to the balanced-budget bill, said, "We tried to tell him what was in the bill but he doesn't understand. Everyone, including Republicans, was just shaking their heads."

A *San Francisco Chronicle* reporter filed suit, under the new Freedom of Information Act, to obtain FBI files that would prove that then-California Gov. Ronald Reagan spent years trying to launch an illicit "psychological warfare campaign" against "subversive" students and faculty. The *Chronicle*'s questions were referred to Ed Meese (this guy again?), Reagan's chief of staff while he was governor (then too?). Meese said he did not remember planning any such activities. While it would take seventeen years for the *Chronicle* to win the challenge and get documents that in fact proved these things true, in 1985 the FBI only released documents that appeared to have altered Reagan's part as a mole for the FBI in the McCarthy era. Some people, if they'd watched the news more often than ESPN or reruns of *Kung-Fu*, might have wondered if their own activities in the seventies, including visiting a "known commune" (which has the same root word as communism) might have resulted in their *own* FBI file. But maybe some people knew, without knowing, that it was better to only know now as much as you knew then, when you visited the known-commune not knowing anything except you were there to get some grass.

|986

In thorny contract negotiations with musicians, management of the San Diego Symphony cancelled the season and locked out orchestra members. But even before negotiations officially broke down, management (anticipating the cancellation of the season) — to help pay for the newly refurbished former vaudevillian concert hall — booked shows by East Coast ballet companies, East Coast orchestras, a few comedians, and Barry Manilow.

The first postal killing happened in Oklahoma, netting fourteen postal workers.

Ed Meese (who now, apparently, had a different job) suggested that employers should begin covertly watching their workers in "locker rooms, parking lots, shipping and mail room areas and even the nearby taverns" to apprehend them with drugs. (*Just say no* may not have been working. This was plan B.)

On November 25, as the Iran-Contra scandal simmered, Ed Meese said, "The President knew nothing about it." On November 26, on national television, Meese said, "The President knows what's going on." A month later Meese suggested maybe Reagan did give his approval to the deal, while he was under sedation after surgery.

California Highway Patrol Officer Craig Peyer — who, it turned out, had a history of stopping young women driving alone and talking to them for lengthy periods — pulled college student Cara Knott off the freeway and directed her down a dark, unused off-ramp. Their encounter ended when Peyer strangled

Knott and threw her body off a bridge. The day after Knott's disappearance, local TV news chose Officer Peyer to do a safety-on-the-road segment.

An advertisement for Nike said, *Improve your husband's sex life.* The Army reiterated, *Be All You Can Be.*

The space shuttle Challenger exploded, live on national television. Decades later, a new generation will be defined as those who weren't alive when Kennedy was shot, but who knew exactly where they were when the Challenger blew up. This simplistic division ignores those who not only recall clearly when they heard the Kennedy news (recess cancelled in first grade), *and* when they heard about John Lennon (the afternoon of their last final exam of the fall semester of their senior year of college) but now also remember when the Challenger exploded (while doing sit-ups on the living room floor with the TV on before going back to the laundromat to pick up the white load so there'd be clean underwear for work that evening).

1987

"I hope I'm finally going to hear some of the things I'm still waiting to learn," President Reagan said as the Iran-Contra hearings began. In his January Tower Commission interview about the affair, Reagan conceded that he authorized the arms sale to Iran. In February, Reagan told the Tower Commission that now he remembered that he did *not* sanction the arms sale. While narrating his (re)recollection from a memorandum, Reagan also read aloud his stage instruction (which some remember said "be earnest" but they may be confusing it with the time George Bush Sr. read aloud his stage instruction, "message: I care").

President Reagan, in a *Washington Times* interview, reminisced wistfully about the time when Joseph McCarthy and the House Un-American Activities Committee exposed subversives.

The acronym AIDS — first used in 1982 when more than 1,500 Americans were diagnosed with the disease — was not said by Ronald Reagan in public until 1987, by which time 60,000 cases had been diagnosed, and half of those people had died. (Perhaps he was hoping it was still a mysterious disease among Haitian men, and maybe medical research money could go to beefing up immigration laws.) During a rally to protest the administration's (lack of) AIDS policies, Washington police wore large yellow rubber kitchen gloves when they arrested sixty-four demonstrators.

Playtex became the first to use live lingerie models in TV ads for the Cross Your Heart Bra. One might say they tested the waters for pantyshield companies who would, in the future, use live actresses to rave about a product that's "not for your period, just those other little leaks."

Gary Hart withdrew from the Presidential race when a sexual misdemeanor was exposed. One might propose that his candidacy died to save the future President Clinton.

> At the Iran-Contra hearings, no one, including the President, ever definitively found out what he knew or when he knew it.

Prozac was approved by the FDA. Some people needed it right away. Even anyone who had used audacity, cunning, and acumen to successfully fake a psychological exam and earn a 4F draft deferment in 1969 — that same someone might come home from an hour on the grocery workers picket line and cry, and be curled up in a fetal ball by the time anyone else came home, and not be able to afford Prozac without health insurance.

1988

The Bureau of Labor Statistics said that more than six million persons who worked, or looked for work at least half of the year, had family incomes below the official poverty level in 1987.

President Reagan on Michael Dukakis's campaign for the presidency: "You know, if I listened to him long enough, I would be convinced that we're in an economic downturn, and that people are homeless, and people are going without food and medical attention, and that we've got to do something about the unemployed."

A (new) Nike advertisement said, *Just Do It.*
Visa said, *It's Everywhere You Want to Be.*
The Army continued to say, *Be All You Can Be.*

A General Motors advertisement said, *This is not your father's Oldsmobile.* This campaign was credited with helping hasten the eventual demise of Oldsmobile, as the message confirmed for babyboomers the notion that Oldsmobile had been a make preferred by their fathers.

One and a half million acres of Yellowstone National Forest burned. For the fortunate who actually had that archetypal fifties and early sixties babyboomer upbringing, where the family station wagon, festooned with tourist decals, was certain to pull into Yellowstone at least once, this might have signaled the final death of childhood. Just to be certain biological clocks had been completely distorted, Old Faithful began to change its schedule.

Other factors contributing to early midlife-crises might have included the incursion of the first college-educated Gen-Xers into the job market the previous year. College composition teachers had already noticed the attitude change in their students, and the number of business majors who wore Bush campaign pins. Then the morning of the election, when the pedestrian overpass spanning the freeway beside the university was adorned with Dukakis posters, some people actually thought "maybe all is not lost."

In his last television interview as President, when asked to comment on his Presidency overlapping with a sizable upsurge in the number of homeless people, Ronald Reagan wondered if many of these were homeless by "their own choice." He extended this analysis to people without jobs. For the second time he clarified his point by referencing the number of newspaper classified job listings.

1989

A new East German government prepared a law to lift travel restrictions for East German citizens. On November 9, a government spokesman was asked at a press conference when the updated East German travel law would come into force. His answer seemed flustered: "Well, as far as I can see, . . . straightaway, immediately." Within hours, tens of thousands of people had gathered at the wall, on both sides. When the crowd demanded the entry be opened, the guards stood back, and the wall was disengaged, peacefully. It's possible the East German plan to allow "private trips abroad," never intended the complete and total opening and then destruction of the wall. Did Ronald Regan, almost one year out of office, try to take credit? (Yes.)

Pro-democracy demonstrators in Tiananmen Square were fired on by Chinese soldiers. Between 400 and 800 people were killed. (Reagan did not take the blame.)

Although he denied betting on baseball games, Pete Rose was banned for life from Major League Baseball. Why does it seem that Tiananmen Square and the Berlin Wall faded from the news quicker than Rose's fall from fame?

Ted Bundy was executed in Florida's electric chair. This event did not muster much outcry. There is still more debate over whether Rose should be allowed back into baseball than the efficacy of the death penalty, although, admittedly, Rose is a slightly better example for debating baseball's betting rules than Ted Bundy is for a discussion of capital punishment. However, while Bundy simply solidified for the Right their belief in society's moral right to kill undesirables, it only caused

shades of grey for the Left, some of whom were distracted
further by the realization that even mating with someone of the
same political persuasion didn't guarantee a sublime unison,
and some kinds of disillusionment could not be fixed, even
with Prozac.

Since 1980, the median income went up $11,196 or 63 percent.
The median cost of house went up $72,400 or 94 percent. The
overall cost of living rose 48 percent while minimum wage was
still $3.35/hour. If you went to college, but didn't major in
business or engineering, medicine or law, you could probably
hover right near the median two-person household income
of $28,906, provided you sustained the two people in the
household.

Some people got married this year; actually two million four-
hundred-three thousand two-hundred-sixty-eight. A nearly
as impressive number, one million one-hundred-fifty-seven
thousand, were divorced.

Although, later, the eighties would be called — usually by
patronizing college students who'd grown up in soft middle-
class homes — the era of superficiality and decadence, some
people never got to become yuppies or conspicuous consumers
or marital swingers or weekend cokeheads. Maybe they already
were all they were going to be.

OUR TIME IS UP

1987

The word, that year, was *codependent*. Barb was in a co-dependency group. Too young for a *midlife crisis* (that, believe it or not, was from 1965), but was exactly where she should be to begin probing the concerns of *adult children* (1983). *Yuppies*, identified in 1984, had already discovered if their families had been *dysfunctional* (1981), and were ready to become *empowered* (1986) but first would need co-dependency therapy. They wouldn't *reinvent themselves* until 1989 and couldn't find their *inner children* until 1990.

Barb was only half-listening when the counselor began her opening speech at the first meeting. Besides Barb there were three other women. Somehow Barb had already learned: MaryPat was a waitress who used to be something else. Gloria was loud and flamboyant, newly divorced, and Barb didn't know what she did. Belinda did something in an insurance office and had two pet rabbits and a husband who

. . . you may deplore the behavior — it may hurt you, terrify you, drive a wedge between you and your spouse or child or parent; it might make you feel hopeless, helpless, frustrated, angry. But are you helping to keep, to maintain the trouble in your relationship? Are you addicted to the addiction? If you

traveled a lot. The counselor had been seeing at least two of the other women alone, and had recently decided to have group sessions. So when Barb had been calling the numbers listed in the phonebook under counseling, this was the first one who'd said she had an opening in a new group she was starting for women. How was Barb to know the counselor held sessions in a small bedroom converted into an office in her apartment in one of those old neighborhoods near the park where a jet had crashed a few

do anything to assist the addicted person to get through his or her day, you are co-dependent, and you are ENABLING. You're assisting them to continue their dependence — that is, allowing the condition to continue and even to get worse. If you grew up this way, being co-dependent to an addictive parent, your dysfunctional family experience trained you that this is the only way to subsist, to co-exist in a relationship, and so you will likely be co-dependent in your adult relationships. It is only by breaking the cycle that you can experience a healthy, supportive relationship.

years after they'd moved here, the type of place where everyone was a vegetarian and still wore their graying hair long and parted in the middle and didn't shave their legs and let their horny toenails show through leather sandals while they were holding group counseling. And it took over an hour to get to San Diego from their condo in Del Mar, so she'd had to miss her afternoon aerobics class and sit in Friday afternoon gridlock to get here. Who had group therapy on Friday?

After she had found the group, but before the first meeting, last Saturday morning, Bobby found her where she was reading on the pool deck. He was holding a folded newspaper and said, "I know you like dance movies. There's a new one, let's go see it."

She'd looked at him and almost said, "Don't try so hard. It hurts." But she went to the movie with him. It was *Dirty Dancing*.

Near the beginning, Bobby leaned over and whispered, "They can't be serious, a character named *Baby*?" Afterwards he said the movie had reached new levels of cheesiness.

Barb bought the soundtrack, the next day after work. Bought it on LP even though

There are other expressions of co-dependency besides enabling an addict. Much of it stems from low self-esteem. You may have been abused or neglected as a child. You may be someone who will decide what to do based on how much it will please others.

they were trying to switch, but the album had a larger picture of Patrick Swayze than the cassette or CD. Before Bobby came home, she made a cassette and put it in her car, unmarked. Bobby would never notice the album, slipped in between *Flashdance* and *Fame*, to the right of WHAM ("Wake Me Up Before You Go-Go"). Tuesday afternoon, she asked the aerobics coach to use her *Dirty Dancing* tape, even though she knew exercise tapes had to be custom mixed so all the tunes were the proper speed: warm-up, build-up, aerobic peak and maintenance, through warm-down. *Dirty Dancing* had all different tempos, and they came in movie-plot order. Growing up, learning about sex, falling in love, then profoundly changing someone's life didn't necessarily happen in the same progression as heart rate during aerobics class. So she listened to the cassette going to and from work, Wednesday and Thursday, and going to work this morning, and on her way to group an hour ago.

Barb was on a sofa with compressed cushions, the brown plaid fabric pilled and scratchy. Belinda was beside her. The counselor was in a scratched dining-table chair to

You may only be able to feel good about yourself when you are helping someone or listening to a friend describe her problems. Then if you're in a situation where you need help, you may turn away from help, feel

Barb's left. This put the counselor's bare toes closest to Barb. Gloria sat in another dining chair facing the counselor, and MaryPat, on a vinyl avocado green ottoman, faced the sofa.

uncomfortable receiving that kind of attention. You may appear to all the world as a competent adult, but you're so focused on what others need and how you can please them, you know very little about how to direct your own life.

Barb's husband didn't drink, smoke, gamble, or do drugs. Both sets of their parents were still married, hadn't ever beat them or their siblings, hadn't tried to have sex with them, hadn't neglected them at Christmas or birthdays, came to their school plays and band concerts, likewise didn't drink, smoke, gamble, over-eat, or do drugs. Couldn't you have all that and still be unhappy?

Now Gloria was talking: *. . . to be for the first time only responsible for mySELF, and I'll tell you, it's so empowering. I even enjoy doing my laundry and cooking my dinner. I'm the one deciding when to go to bed and when to get up — at least on weekends. Weekdays I still have to be at work at 7:00 a.m. But I'm going to start applying this whole concept to my boss too.*

Barb was deciding what she should say when it was her turn. How much would be enough? Start where she and Bobby moved here from Terre Haute in 1976 the day after he graduated from ISU with his engineering degree? Neither of them even had a job, and within four days of arriving, amid the unemployment of the late seventies, she'd started making appointments and checking patients

I've enabled him to be disorganized because he knows I'll keep track of everything, I'll never let him miss an appointment or lose a file or forget to pay a bill. I guess it's made me feel important that he needs me so much, so now I understand: I'm co-dependent to the scatterbrained contractor, and believe me, he is addicted to his own organizational incompetence because it makes him feel more important. He does the in at Dr. Easly's old office in Santee. Bobby found his job a few weeks later, a civilian company with contracts from the Navy, but he'd moved from that job, and had moved several other times before finding the one he stayed with, designing recycling machines for a local company that sells them to municipalities and waste management companies (commonly called dumps) all over the world ... But that was really getting off the point, even though Bobby's cutting-edge work would make the rest of these women's husbands or exes look like redneck meatballs, but that wasn't really the point either.

Someone else had started talking ...

creative or important thinking and decision making, I'm just the dull administrative assistant who can only think in daily details. But as soon as I stop enabling, I'll be out of that cycle and can empower myself with other kinds of value. That book just absolutely changed my LIFE. Like when my ex tried to come in the house last night, claiming he needed to get his tools and it was part of the agreement — I wouldn't let him in. I'd changed the locks. When I'd made this so-called agreement, I was still being co-dependent, allowing him to bully me into getting his own way just because it was easier than fighting. So in my mind it's invalid.

It was MaryPat: "But ... if you didn't make appointments and file ... I mean, isn't that your job?"

"It doesn't have to be who I *am*."

"So I serve drinks to drunks. It isn't who I am, and it doesn't mean they've forced me to be a waitress. I chose to be a waitress because I make a hell of a lot more money than when I was a junior high band teacher."

"MaryPat," said the counselor, drawing her sandaled toes back underneath her dining-table chair, "is there some subtext you'd like to share?"

Yeah, we were both music majors, and we both wanted to be band directors, but all along, now that I look back, they were aiming me toward junior high while it was always understood he would have a high school. And that's exactly how it turned out. Bruce was Mr. Important field-tour-nament-band-director, busing to Los Angeles, to Phoenix, to Santa Barbara for tournaments with his entourage of equipment trucks and band parents wearing some kind of their own uniform, horning in on their kids' high school life, coming home with trophies, blah, blah, blah, while there I was teaching Mary's Little Lamb to eleven year olds spitting into trumpets for half the pay. Well, not half, but not

Barb is trying to listen to this one, but she honestly can't imagine how anyone could care if their husband's dumb band got some trophy and yours didn't. Bobby makes model cars and little radio-controlled airplanes and sometimes comes home from his weekend shindigs with a plaque or a ribbon, and Barb didn't start complaining it was a chauvinistic plot. She could give a flying flip about his little cars and airplanes, really, even though he tries to show her the minutest details on them (sometimes she has to just pretend to be seeing what he's talking about).

even three-quarters. So I quit and went back to waitressing and now I make more than him, but obviously I work nights and we barely ever see each other, especially week-ends when his buses have to leave the school at around 5:00 a.m. to get to whatever tournament they're doing. And when he gets home, he expects me to have waited all day just to find out how well his band did. If I don't gasp with enough awe, he gets cranky, and there's another evening we barely speak.

"So you're enabling him to out-do you by quitting and letting him be the star," Gloria said, shifting her butt and re-crossing her legs as she spoke. Like Barb, she hadn't changed from her skirt and pumps before coming to the group, but Gloria's nylons looked too glossy. "You're actually addicted to being second chair."

"I just said I make more money than he does. I just can't

always be saying oh-you're-such-a-wonderful-high-school-band-director-honey with any real enthusiasm."

"Maybe you're greeting him with other kinds of you-messages," the counselor said. "You should concentrate on using only I-messages. Do you know what that means?"

MaryPat shook her head, so the counselor started explaining. Barb felt like she was falling into the crushed sofa, like her butt suddenly weighed twice as much. Which is often what happened when she missed aerobics. Friday there was jazzercise after aerobics, and Bobby always stayed at his office Friday afternoon, having a beer with his partner and waiting for the rush-to-weekend traffic to pass. There was never any reason to believe it wasn't what he was doing. Until he surprised her a few months ago. But she's not going to start there. Is it important to say that they met while Bobby was in college, but she wasn't a student, she just happened to grow up in Terre Haute? After she graduated from

You-messages can easily be, and often are, accusatory, even hostile. Why did you do that? You're making me feel worthless. You were late. You're being insensitive. You're not being fair. You're spending too much. You're the one who thought we should buy this. Most people will get defensive when receiving you-messages, and then a useful communication will be impossible. Try I-messages instead: I feel sad that this is happening. I'm trying to understand why you're upset. I'm sorry you feel that way. I'm worried about our money. I-messages invite the other person to communicate, rather than shut the doors to communication.

high school, she started right away as a key punch operator at Fieldcrest Industries. She'd been working there three years when she met Bobby, and went on working there after they (secretly) moved in together before they got married. She'd cried the night of their wedding, but not the tears-of-joy weeping girls did in the novels Barb read; she'd never done that kind of crying and didn't know why — what was wrong with her? That night Bobby had asked her why she was crying and all she could think of was, "I just never thought I'd get married." Was that an I-message? They were all practicing their I-messages.

"I feel I'm ready to participate more in the business," Gloria said to her contractor boss.

As if any contractor was going to ask his secretary for construction advice — like how many nails he would need, how much cement?

"I'm sad that my plans to be a band director got wrecked," MaryPat said to her band directing husband, "and yours didn't."

"Should he apologize for that?" the counselor asked.

"Okay — I'm sorry that you think I should be happy that my plans got wrecked and yours didn't?"

"You don't *sound* like you *chose* to be a waitress," Gloria said.

What a ball-bender, that's what Bobby called women like that one.

"That's a you-message," MaryPat returned. "Besides, a waitress is almost a self-sufficient private contractor. It's one of the few things women have if they want to be independent."

Another would be prostitution.

"I don't like spending so much time without you," Belinda said to her traveling husband.

"Have you said that to him?" the counselor asked.

"Yes. I think so. I don't know."

"Or did you say, 'Why do you have to leave me alone so often?'" Gloria asked.

Who's the counselor here anyway?

"Maybe. I don't know."

"What does he say?" the counselor asked.

"If I say anything about it,
How about GET A LIFE? he gets real quiet and goes to watch TV or sits in his study. He says traveling is what makes him like his job so much. He bought me the rabbits so I wouldn't be alone."

"Long-eared rats are no substitute for a husband," Gloria said.

"Why not a dog?" MaryPat asked.

"They don't allow dogs in our apartment."

"I'm going to get a dog,"
Are there enough I-messages in MaryPat said. "I think I want
that one? a dog with papers. I want to show it."

"I think that would be good for you," the counselor approved. She turned toward Barb. "We haven't heard from you yet, Barb."

While Barb is talking in group therapy, Bobby is still in his office at the recycling machine company, with Carl, the other engineer, having a few beers and waiting for Friday rush traffic to dissipate. It's September, so they talk about football. The Chargers haven't lost enough games to be out of contention yet, but the baseball team was a lost cause months ago and aren't worth an exchange of two sentences, except to bemoan how the Chargers have to play with a dirt infield outline on their football field grass until the baseball season mercifully ends at the end of the month.

One Friday Carl had brought Wild Turkey and they'd done shots, and Carl had the brilliant idea to call a guy he knew in the manufacturing unit who knew how to contact a girl who would come over and give blow jobs for fifty bucks. They did, one at a time, in the engineering office, while the other sat just outside. Bobby had never had a blow job before, but he didn't admit it to Carl. Barb said asking a woman to do it was demeaning to her, not just because you're asking her to put his body's waste-empty-ing conduit into her mouth, but because he could experience the whole thing without once touching her, and, in fact, it was like he could be alone, watching TV while he got it. He didn't know how it was much different than the hand jobs she gave him to "take care of him" when he was horny and she wanted to go to sleep. She didn't use the word *conduit*; she probably made up some medi-cal-sounding word, which she was prone to do at parties when she made pronouncements about vitamins or nutrition and he saw people exchange glances. He took a long time to come because he did feel weird about it, coming in the girl's mouth, but she wasn't being paid by the hour, and Carl didn't say anything about how long he'd sat outside the door; he'd already had his turn.

About a month later, Carl brought up calling the girl again, and he still sometimes suggested it, maybe once a month, but Bobby always said, "We don't have anything stronger than beer," and Carl let it drop. Bobby had already told Carl about his worry that something was going on between Barb and someone at the doctor's office she worked at — not the doctor, but someone like a doctor. Barb had said it would take too long to explain what a PA was, more than a nurse and less than a doctor, she'd said. As though he was some geek with his head up his butt.

Since they do this almost every Friday, Bobby doesn't bother to tell Carl that Barb is at her first group therapy meeting. It had been her idea to go. While she'd been deciding, and vacillating, he'd tried to be encouraging toward whichever way she chose, indi-vidual, group, or none at all. She'd been dramatically listless — at least when he saw her, at home — since that night three months ago. He didn't know what she was like at work. He couldn't imagine how she would describe that night, or what else she might be saying tonight, like what was going on inside the house in Tierrasanta that he had waited outside for over an hour. After Barb had come out of the house and walked past him — giving him only a startled look, and maybe even saying "hi," (*hi*? as though they were meeting on a campus between classes?) — he'd gone straight to his office, this office. Another time that he sat in his office, long after working hours were over, except without Carl, and without a girl giving him a blowjob. He'd already had Kathy's phone number in his wallet. He'd had it for a few weeks, since he'd called information in Terre Haute. He sat for a while before calling. Kept hearing Barb saying "hi," but not really sure if she'd really said it, or maybe he said it. Maybe *he* was the one who said it, from the darkness under the tree he stood beside, and that's when he'd seen her surprised look.

While everybody looked at her, listening, Barb said, *I don't know how it happened . . . it just . . . I don't know . . . happened. I met someone who . . . listened to me, thought I was funny and . . . I don't know . . . smart . . . He understood the things that worry and bother me, and . . . talked to me about what worried and bothered him. With him, I felt so . . . I don't know . . . more myself . . . like I was myself for the first time in my life. And I . . . But I . . . couldn't*

She wasn't looking at them anymore. *be with him because . . . I don't* She picked at a little loose ball of *know . . . he was engaged . . . He'd* nylon on her knee. *been engaged for so long, but wasn't married . . . He'd been married before, but . . . I don't know . . . that doesn't matter . . . He lived alone. Lives alone. He . . . Sometimes I . . . need to talk to someone . . . about things . . . Just things that . . . I don't know. It had been three months. One . . . or two days a week . . . I went home with him, instead of to my aerobics class. I needed it. It was something I . . . I don't know . . . had never had. Then . . . it wasn't right for him, for Bobby to . . . follow me like I was a criminal . . . and spy on me . . . I don't check on him when he stays after work and drinks with his buddy. He told me what they do and I believe him. I don't remember what I told him . . . I told him something . . . he should've believed me . . . I might have said I need to do something . . . that I needed to . . . It was something I needed . . . to do. To do for me. If I didn't . . . take care of myself . . . like my aerobics . . . I . . . I don't know . . . But anyway, he followed me . . . I don't know how long he was there. He was standing outside when I left. Just standing there in the dark like a secret agent. When I told Hal, the next day at work, he . . . later he said we needed to . . . stop. The shit hit the fan for*

She wasn't going to tell them what she and Hal did. It would desecrate it to reduce it to words. They were the most beautiful, sheer, breathtaking, alive moments of her life — that's what drug addicts probably said, but she didn't need drugs — but she wasn't going to give it away by trying to explain.

him too, he said. Just like that. His fiancé was getting uncomfortable and asking questions, he said. It was . . . so easy for him . . . to say it. So easy for both of them to just . . . I don't know . . . tell me I can't have . . . what I need.

From where he stood in the dark outside the PA's house in Tierrasanta, Bobby had gone directly to his office in Chula Vista, which was the opposite direction from the condo in Del Mar. But while he'd stood outside that house in the dark, on the parkway beside the sidewalk, under a tree that rained some kind of pollen or seed shit he later found in his hair, what had he thought about? Sometimes Barb asked what he was thinking, and she didn't like his answer: that he was hungry, that his football team was lousy, that he was too tired to get up. That night, if she'd asked instead of walking past, he could've said he was thinking about how they periodically found old World War II munitions buried in back-yards or empty lots in Tierrasanta, because during the War it had been an empty Navy testing ground, far from any populated areas, and now it was in the middle of a city, a whole community with a name that meant Sacred Ground. Bobby had learned some Spanish before moving to California because he'd heard it could help you get a job. He'd learned from tapes, listening to them over and over during the drive from Indiana — he drove the U-Haul and Barb the Datsun — and also had practiced by looking up in a dictionary the English translation for all the town and community names. *Of the Sea ... Hidden Valley ... View of the Ocean ... View of the Plateau ... Beautiful View ...* and just plain *Beautiful.* So he'd gotten curious and wondered what Terre Haute meant. It was French and meant High Ground. So, standing there in Tierrasanta, he'd thought about coming from high ground to sacred ground.

He made the call from his office in Chula Vista, which he hadn't been able to translate with his little dictionary. A view of something. His dictionary, still on his desk, said Chulo meant pimp. That was weird. He hadn't thought about that for a long time, not even when they'd called the girl to give blow jobs. She had been a Mexican girl, and that had troubled him. He'd become the Ugly American. With Kathy, he had only kissed her and touched her large breasts through her sweater or blouse, and yet it had been far more exciting than his first blow job.

It was almost nine o'clock in Terre Haute. It would be ten o'clock if it weren't daylight savings time, but Indiana didn't use daylight savings.

Kathy answered. A simple, uncomplicated "Hello?"

"Hi," he'd said. "It's ... Bobby."

"Pardon me?"

"Bobby. Bobby Winston."

"I'm sorry?"

"Remember ... from high school?"

"Oh."

"I'm calling from California."

"Oh ... ?"

"I moved here after college. I guess I haven't talked to you since before that. I don't remember the last time we ... "

"Oh, *Bobby*."

"Yeah, it's me." His voice almost a whisper.

"I'm sorry, I guess I haven't thought about high school for so long."

"Yeah, me neither. I got married and graduated and moved ... Or graduated and married and moved ... I don't remember. So, how are you? You didn't get married? I mean, your number is listed with your last name, I remembered it — "

"I'm divorced."

"That's good." He swallowed, blinked hard. "I mean, maybe you can tell me, what *that's* like ... I mean ... it's hard, being married. Isn't it?"

"Why are you calling, Bobby?"

"No reason. Just to say hi. I just thought I'd see what you were up to."

"Why? That was high school. I've been married, divorced. Then I made a clean break from that part of my life. I'm born again. I can't be taking calls from another woman's husband."

"I didn't mean ... "

"Goodbye, Bobby."

There was a moment of silence. Barb wiped her last tears. She was holding a Kleenex she doesn't remember taking from a box beside her. She looked up, and then they started:

Oh, wow, been-there-done-THAT . . . I've been the one picking up the phone and hearing it disconnect. I've been the one wondering why it takes so long for him to drive home from his job fifteen minutes away. I've been the one finding the Virginia Slims cigarette box in

Not looking at them anymore, again. The loose ball of nylon was now the start of a run from her knee to her thigh. Not sure she's still breathing.

his car, the one wondering why his court shoes are still at home but he said he was playing basketball after work, the one crying myself to sleep because of that bastard and his current floozy. Who's the co-dependent here? Maybe your husband needs co-dependency therapy, he's the one not divorcing you after finding out you're cheating. HE'S enabling YOU . . .

I would never do that. I could just never do that. Randy's away from home so much, but . . . I could just never do that. That's . . . just something I could never do.

How could I expect you to understand. Rabbits really are the perfect pet for you.

Are you sure you're in the right group? I mean, maybe it is my fault I gave up, and it galls me that Bruce's band is winning all the time, but . . . to go behind his back, to have an AFFAIR? That wouldn't be my answer. And believe me, it wouldn't be difficult to find someone, in my line of work. But that's just tacky. It sounds like a

You're right, this is obviously the wrong place, the wrong group, the wrong . . . oh God, why did I come here?

soap opera. It sounds like the drama is what you're after. Like coming here and crying is part of the whole deal, and you like it as much as the sneaking around and cheating. Is that it? Didn't you ever ask yourself IS THIS ALL THERE IS? You yuppies — isn't that a Beemer you drove here in? — what's the UP for you anyway, what do you want?

Barb, maybe we need to hear about your feelings in a different way. What did you want from the group when you shared?

She could hear herself answering, and the questions came from everywhere, the know-it-all, the surly ex-band director, the rabbit girl, the hairy-legged counselor. She didn't remember the kleenex box moving to her lap. She kept hearing herself answering, but she was thinking about getting into that BMW which seemed to have made the band director so angry—or even *more* angry—and start driving and keep driving, all the way back to Terre Haute. She'd had such a cute studio apartment there, near the campus, near the football stadium—she should tell MaryPat how she could hear the drums and knew when it was halftime—until she'd meet Bobby, a student living across the hall with two other guys, then somehow her cute apartment was gone and she was living beside the train tracks with Bobby, in a building filled with college kids, a place she'd been glad to leave for the adventure of moving to California. And now ...

"I don't know."

No, I think MaryPat meant what were her upwardly-mobile goals?

"To be ... To not have to work someday. For my husband to ... "

What — did you want to have children and stay at home and have no financial independence? Why didn't you go to college?

"I don't know."

Why don't you have children?

"I don't know."

You say that a lot.

Did you ever ask your husband about it, Barb?

"I don't know. I think so."

What did he say?

"That I never said anything so he never said anything."

Didn't he want children?

"I don't know. We liked the way things were."

Then why are you unhappy now?

What *had* she wanted, ever, once upon a time or even a year ago? And why had she moved here? Because Bobby had been preparing for four years and had decided, before he met her, to get out of Indiana and go somewhere where the things an engineer did could matter to the world. The day after graduation, that's what he did, and by then she was beside him, packing a U-haul long into the night. That had been ten years ago. Did she ever wonder, that night, if she were single, would she have chosen this? But what *else* would she have done? Before she met Bobby, what did she think she'd be doing in a year, in ten years? Had she ever given it a single thought, or was the naive pleasure of paying her own rent and arranging her own things in her single room and buying her own bag of groceries once a week too much of a giddy drug? But once here, she'd become comfortable, immediately, with things she enjoyed: walking on the beach, especially in the winter when the threat of burning into blistered, peeling red paint was past; or her jazzercise classes with other women who tore the neckbands out of their sweatshirts; or the condo's pool where she read a book every week and could

And why did you cheat with someone else's man?

"I don't know. It just happened."

That's what addicts say, they don't take responsibility. You could've just-said-no.

Is there an AA for soap opera addicts who try to live like they're in one?

I read they have CoDA organizations, a twelve-step group, I guess we're not a big enough group for that kind of thing?

Twelve-steps are religiously based, but here we can support each —

CoDA is a music term, a passage at the end of a piece or movement that brings it to a close.

It's for Codependents Anonymous. So let's bring our co-dependency to a close. Your band can play a symphony when my boss realizes I'm not a doormat.

I don't have a band. Doing your job isn't being a doormat.

Not getting credit for it is. Isn't that why you quit?

I changed jobs.

Tomato tow-ma-to. You should

casually say to people at the office, I read a book a week, even though Bobby called them *rescue-me-fuck-me* books. Hal liked her to read to him.

at least tell him the real reason you did it. You should get the book, really, it changed my life.

Girls, I think our time is up.

Girl, as a pejorative, never earned the horrific level of *boy*. In fact, just the opposite. It even became *girl power* (1986), while *boy*, racist undertones notwithstanding, at best was limited to its *toy* rhyme-ability or connotation, as in *game boy* (1989). An adult male did not want to be a *boy*, but could be a *New Man* (1982) which, near the end of the decade had disintegrated into a wimp or *wuss* (1984). Being a *girl* was better than being *wimmin* (1983, a spelling to remove the word *man*). While *girl* hadn't yet become *grrl* (1994, but not an attempt to remove the *I* from girl) the pretty, gentle word may have helped women feel younger, even pleasantly vulnerable. Or less alone, as in *girlfriend*.

Barb never went back to the group, and she quit her job at Dr. Easly's office, even though she might have become office manager someday. Bobby either didn't notice or didn't comment, until she told him she found a better job at a hospital doing outpatient and emergency room billing. He said, "That's good, you'll probably get some additional computer training." Doctors never came into the office where her desk was, where she kept a picture of Bobby beside her telephone, and a magazine cover of Patrick Swayze in her drawer.

One day, when Bobby didn't want to figure out how to use the coffee maker, he was going to boil some water for instant coffee and found a video tape hidden in a pot in the cupboard. Of course he played it and found an interview with Patrick Swayze on *Entertainment Tonight*.

Meanwhile, there were always new words. For example: The *virtual reality* (1987) of rush hour traffic is that *road rage* (1988) is like a dance movie *from hell* (1987) where you can't tell *moshing* (1987) from *wilding* (1989).

Bobby came home one day and went directly to where Barb was reading on the pool deck and told her he was moving out. Barb cried for what seemed like three days straight. There was no one to ask her why. She had to pretend Bobby was dead, like Patrick Swayze in *Ghost*, and had told her he'd love and protect her forever, and was hovering near her every moment, watching over her. When Bobby started seeing someone, Barb told him she was dating a doctor named Patrick. But eventually Patrick had to leave to open a clinic in . . . Paris. Of all places, Paris needed a free clinic with a handsome American doctor named Patrick. Barb could've started a Patrick-Swayze-anonymous group — PSA, like the airline that had fallen from the sky, just a few years after they'd moved here from Terre Haute, and exploded not far from where the fading hippie counselor held co-dependency therapy.

TWISTER PARTY

He'd gotten a postcard six months or so after she got married, which was six months or so after the one night he'd had with her. Which wasn't even a whole night, and they hadn't "had" everything, just the parts that could have told her how he felt, if she'd wanted to hear him. Tone deaf to his caress, his quivering need held in abeyance, his fingertips pleading, six months later she was married, to someone else. Six months after that the postcard:

February 2, 1981
Dang, Cal [he could hear her hard, squeaky laugh] *we were such kids, such babies. Someday you'll see and we'll be able to be great friends. I needed stability so I could go after what I always wanted. Found out I need psychology and animal behavior classes if I'm going to be an animal trainer for the movies, and then a pro who'll take me on as an apprentice. Learning and watching and always practicing, like you did with your sax. Don't abandon it, Cal.*
X

It. What she didn't want him to abandon. Of course clearly she meant the sax. Otherwise, if *it* was something else — the *it* containing everything he felt about her — she would have provided her new address. That *it*, the real *it* refused to be abandoned.

In 1981, when he got the card, he didn't feel like a kid. He didn't even feel young, although he hadn't yet acted out of wretched acquiescence. (*Wretched* in 1981 was jargon for *horny*, but eventually it returned to its original meaning.) By 1982 a woman with two kids who was supposed to be a one-nighter, a *road gig* as they said in the band, was living with him in the equally wretched desert where he found work in a music store, taught lessons and fixed band instruments.

One night in 1995, when the cops got there, they found the living room furniture a little askew, the TV trays totally upended, dishes from dinner on the carpet. But in the kitchen there was a carnage of the watermelon on the floor, more dishes — broken ones — and the knife meant to split the melon standing upright, its point buried in the cutting board. They also found Cal on the front lawn, locked out of the house. The cops, male and female, took turns, one inside, one outside, asking the same questions. "Are you okay? Are you hurt anywhere? Do you want her arrested?"

Yes, no, and no. Sticks and stones . . .

Worthless piece of shit.

"How'd she get a 200-pound man out the door against his will?"

"I didn't fight back."

"Good idea."

"Yeah, I just went the direction she was pushing me. I knew she'd calm down."

"What was the fight about, sir?"

"I won't send any more money to the . . . kids."

"Your kids?"

"Actually . . . hers."

"You could decide not to press charges, but if it got worse, you couldn't stop us from arresting her."

"It was just dishes, and ... I moved my horns down to the shop."

The cops, of course, didn't understand that.

He walked around the block, 8:00 p.m., temperature still in the nineties. When he got home, the kitchen was cleaned, the garbage taken out to the cans at the side of the house. She was, by this time, his wife, and was making ice cream sundaes with root beer. He wrote a check for $150 to the twenty-five-year-old burnout.

The stepdaughter's name was Trinity. In September of 1983, she was having a birthday party, the first one to have boys. September, like June, July, and August before it, still damn hot. But she wanted a piñata out in the yard, and Twister in the living room, with music. No other baby games and *good* candy in the piñata. She nixed Cal's idea of including small school items like new pencils or pens.

"Hey Trin, how about some movie tickets, or McDonald's gift certificates?" Her mother called her *Trin*. Her girlfriends called her *T*. Cal could guess where the boys would take that.

"Why not just put a whole stereo and a couple of records inside?" he asked.

"You can butt out," the girl said.

"We'll need you to swing the piñata," the woman said. Her name was Virginia. *Her* girlfriends called her *Virge* or *Virgie*. Cal didn't. He used the whole thing, to emphasize something he was trying to get her to understand, or if there was any reason he needed to get her attention during dueling idiocy with the girl instead of (what he usually did) just butting out.

When he'd first learned the girl's name — at some point after the supposed-to-be-a-one-nighter with her mother but before moving together out to the desert, maybe even when Virginia was introducing her daughter to him (on a so-called date arranged by Virginia after the supposed-to-be-a-one-nighter when she kept calling him because she'd gotten his number from the band's female singer, and he figured *what the hell* . . .) — he'd said, "Trinity. That's interesting." He wasn't sure if maybe there was a church reason, but didn't know if he cared enough to ask.

"It's because when she arrived, we became a Trinity, a threesome."

"I thought there's an older brother," he'd said.

"Yes, Angel, so with Trinity we became three."

"What about . . . " Then he'd decided not to ask. And by the time he knew about the man, Merle, who sent the child support checks for the girl, it was no longer in his head to ask about the trio thing. At least Merle was the same man who the boy went to visit in Las Vegas every weekend. Cal wasn't sure where the bus fare came from. But he wasn't looking too closely at the bank statement in those days.

Virginia had had a job. He'd thought she'd had one when she was hanging around his gigs, but it turned out that was an assumption based on, well, people had jobs. She said she'd been a casino cocktail waitress in Las Vegas. At first, living with him in the Imperial Valley, she'd worked at Kmart for about a month. They let her go, she said, because the other women talked about her in Spanish behind her back and she wasn't going to take it. Did that mean she quit? He didn't ask. But he did inquire, "How do you know they were talking about you if they were speaking Spanish?"

"That's how they are," she said. "They also run into me with grocery carts in the store. On purpose, I know it."

Cal's friend who owned the music store where he worked once got his brother's catering company to hire Virginia as a freelance party waitress. She was too slow, Cal's friend said, and she tried to tell the bartender he was making the drinks wrong. When she applied to be a teacher's aide at Trinity's school, Cal discovered she hadn't quite finished high school. But in those days school districts actually paid parents or retired people as the crosswalk guards or playground proctors. Then she suddenly stopped doing that after a few weeks. "Trinity didn't want me there," she'd said.

At her party, Trinity wore the tight designer jeans she'd requested for her birthday. Neither Trinity or Virginia responded to his inquiry: had she sat down in a bathtub of blue paint? Trinity had a two-page magazine spread of Brooke Shields, wearing those same jeans, taped to the wall of her room. But instead of the flowing silk-looking blouse Shields wore — buttoned only between her smallish breasts, falling away to show her flat suntanned stomach — Trinity chose to wear a halter top. Some of the other girls wore tanks or sleeveless tops, one of them with leg warmers and a miniskirt, but none of them were as physically developed as Trinity.

"Are you letting her wear that?" he'd whispered to Virginia in the kitchen.

Virginia shrugged. "She's old enough to dress herself."

Virginia had fixed Trinity's long hair so her face looked small in the middle of a big ratty mess. It was one of Virginia's styles, except she wore a wig. That was probably why Virginia's hair didn't change much, but Trinity had hers in a messy, sweaty ponytail after the piñata. Cal had executed his assignment manning the rope, raising, lowering, and swinging the smiling black-and-red bull-shaped piñata while each blindfolded kid took three or four swings with the souvenir bat Cal had gotten as a kid on bat-night at the ballpark but had never used. All three boys, Black, Latino, and white, were skinny shrimps compared to Trinity, but as quick as her with cliché kid talk, *awesome* and *radical, killer* and *badass*. They each wore a T-shirt with some big words or nasty-looking cartoon. One of them — the Black one, or maybe Latino/Black — had a cap like a cab driver mashed onto wet-looking curls and big aviator sunglasses he had to take off when he was blindfolded. While the kid whaled away, Cal could smell whatever goop had been used to make those wet-looking curls. No one touched the piñata (a few almost clobbered Cal or each other).

"Let them *hit* it," Virginia shouted. So they all had another turn without the blindfold, and in five or six swings, the bull was tufts all over the yard, the kids scrambling together on the ground on hands and knees, greedy bastards trying to get the most for themselves. One seemingly younger little girl with short dark hair who'd come in a dress with a sailor collar — maybe someone's little sister or one who hadn't kept up with her classmates — stood to the side of the jumble of arms and legs, hair and feet and hands. So Cal went inside (taking his now scuffed bat), grabbed the last box of the chocolate bars he'd hidden away after loading the piñata, and dropped it whole and unopened into the dark haired girl's sack.

When Twister started, Trinity said, "We don't need you for this," then turned the stereo up. Kool and the Gang. Now Trinity was wearing the cab driver cap. Cal went to the kitchen for a beer. At some point, when four or five kids were snarled up on the Twister mat, Cal happened to look through the kitchen's pass-through window and saw a boy sink his teeth into the bulge of Trinity's halter top.

Cal went down the hall to his bedroom. The bedroom he shared with Virginia. In a ritual he used to do at gigs, he peed, holding his dick with one hand while his other hand held the beer bottle to his mouth, trying to pee as long as it took to swallow the rest of the beer. What a boor he'd been then. A dirtball. And yet in some ways not dirtball enough, since he'd had to be stoned in order to finally fuck one of the women who hung around at gigs and then ended up living with her, raising her children. A spineless dirtball jellyfish with a dick, and now probably just a jellyfish.

He was almost back down the hall bringing the beer bottle to the kitchen when the Twister game broke up, apparently because the cabbie hat fell off Trinity's upside-down head so another girl picked it up and put it on her own head. Some names were called. *Bitch* and *ho*. Hands slapping at each other's faces in girl fight posture he'd seen too many times at club gigs, bodies so far apart only their upper arms can reach each other. "Where's Trinity's mom?" he asked the dark-haired girl with the sailor collar, sitting at the kitchen table with the eviscerated store-bought decorated cake and four or five plates of smashed cake pieces.

"She said she was getting something she forgot from the car."

In a junk tray on the pass-through windowsill, Cal kept an old sax mouthpiece still holding a frayed reed, specifically for times like this, although usually for bouts between Trinity and Angel, or Trinity and her mother. (Virginia and He's-My-Angel never fought.) Cal tongued five pig-squeal bleats. A burst of laughter, hoots, and exclamations. Maybe the fight was already over anyway. Someone turned the music up. Hall and Oates. Two of the boys came into the kitchen for more cake. The bathroom door slammed. One of the boys said, "She tweakin'," then slid his eyes sideways toward Cal, ducked his head. The dark-haired girl was no longer at the table. When Cal went back to the bedroom to get away from the thumping funk, one of the other girls was in there, looking at the dresser, the top of it where boxes and bottles sat. Not his shit.

"You lost?" Cal asked.

"Uh, where's T at?"

From the living room Virginia called, "Girls, Cal brought some new records from the store."

Like hell he had.

But Virginia had six or eight albums fanned out on the floor, the Twister mat kicked aside. Journey, Foreigner, Styx, Genesis, The Go-Gos, Duran Duran, Mötley Crüe, Black Sabbath . . . Maybe the whole top sellers rack. Four or five of the kids were on hands-and-knees sliding the albums around on the carpet, flipping them over to see the photos and songs listed on the backs. Cal couldn't see Trinity out there. "Let's have a dance, I can still shake it up," Virginia said, over the top of the Hall and Oates still playing. She ripped the cellophane off an album and stopped Private Eyes with a screech of the needle across the grooves.

The dancing started, Virginia bumping hips with some of the girls, and Trinity literally leaped back into the room — from her bedroom? The bathroom? — the cabbie hat perched on her back-to-big-and-loose ratty hair, and now also the aviator glasses screening her eyes. The wet-curled boy, who'd arrived wearing both, danced tentatively, while Trinity boogied in a circle around him. Maybe if he had his hat and glasses back he'd start to get down, but was an undressed Superman without them.

In the kitchen, Cal started throwing away paper plates, plastic cups, and spoons. The plates and cups had pictures of E.T. riding a bike, thick and waxed, used once and piling up in the trashcan. He looked through cupboards to put the rest of the unused ones away and found two different drawers plus a cupboard crammed with paper plates and cups, from a stack of a thousand plain white ones, to Valentine, Christmas, Easter, and Halloween themed plates, plus sets with pictures of balloons or stars, some not opened. While looking, he also found a cupboard with no less than ten boxes of prepared cake mix.

A car passing in the street rattled the manhole cover. On reflex Cal looked out the window and saw the dark-haired girl sitting on the raised brick garden box that separated the front porch from the driveway. The garden box had one Bird of Paradise plant, most of its fronds dead or broken. Cal was only renting this house and had asked the owner to pay half the water bill if he took care of the lawn. He hadn't had a chance to do anything with the gardens, but maybe fixing them up would be another way to stay out of the house an extra hour or two in the mornings before he went to the music store.

The dark haired girl was picking tiny weeds out of the garden box, making a little pile of them on the brick edge where she also sat, her bag from the piñata beside her. Cal had bundled the trash and come out the front door. "Dancing not your thing?" He put the trash bag down on the porch, on a bench that was there with two other trash bags waiting for a trip to the container around the side of the house. The porch area, tucked between the house and the garden box, also collected blowing trash from the sidewalk and street.

"I guess not," the girl said, not looking up from plucking the spindly weeds. From the house, either thumping of the bass or feet on the floor. The screeching, whooping voices inside were all female-pitched, but then again, these boys hadn't started changing.

Cal cleared his throat. "You're a friend of Trinity's?"

"I guess."

"Well, she invited you, didn't she?"

"I guess so."

"How do you know Trinity?"

"I help her with math."

"That's nice, how's she doing?"

"Okay I guess."

A breeze hit Cal's face, cooling his sweat. Over his head, a sign Virginia had hung there squeaked a little. The sign said *Cal & Virgie*. In script, cut into wood, then varnished. When the dark-haired girl turned and looked at him, for the first time since he'd come onto the porch, she likely wasn't looking at that fucking sign, but said, "You're not her dad."

"No, I'm not." Then he wondered if she'd said that to mean he shouldn't be asking questions about Trinity. But she's all of what, eleven years old? He picked up the trash again, then picked up the other two bags. "Guess I'll get these where they belong." And who was he explaining his actions to?

When he came back, the girl was just sitting there, as though waiting for him. She smiled a little. Didn't she? Cal said, "Trinity's copying your math homework, isn't she?" The girl's smile faded. Cal almost touched the top of her head with his index finger as he passed to go back into the house, but stopped his hand at the last second. He paused in the doorway, then turned back, went back. Cleared his throat again. "Did she say she'd hurt you if you didn't let her use your homework?" He noticed the girl was holding the little heap of weeds in one cupped hand. She didn't close her fist. She also didn't answer and wasn't really looking at him, although she'd turned to face him when he'd spoken. "If she did," he said, "tell your parents, or the principal. Tell someone." He waited, but she didn't move. "Do you need a ride home?"

"My mom's coming. I called from inside."

"Here," he said, extending his hand beneath hers. She tipped her palm and dumped the snarl of wilting weeds into his.

By the time the last kid was gone, the indestructible Twister mat was torn and three records were in five or more pieces. "We didn't want to dance to them so we danced *on* them," Trinity gasped. She'd seemed to be laughing or hiccuping for an hour, still wearing the wet-curled boy's hat.

Cal got his car keys from the kitchen so he could go to the music store. "Can you take these back and say they were broken when we opened them?" Virginia asked. He pretended he hadn't heard and kept going into the garage, glad for the excuse to spend a Saturday evening in the repair shop, because he'd given up the daytime hours for the party. He'd more than once told Virginia (usually when she asked why they didn't go out dancing *anymore*, as if they ever had, unless she counted hanging around at his gigs) that, since he worked day hours in the music store, nights and weekends were when he had time to devote to his repair business. Even if he was really just sitting there listening to his records (most of which he kept there) on the music store's stereo system. And thinking. He took care of himself there. It was nice if he didn't have too much of a backlog of instruments to repair, so could focus on just the right image. He didn't keep a picture of X. It wasn't *that* private. But sometimes, just seeing a girl of about that age, the age she'd been when he saw her every day, scratching her bare shoulder while she looked at something in the display case. Or if he'd spotted a couple dancing at one of his (fewer lately) gigs, and the girl was a lot shorter than the guy, and sort of draped against him like a ribbon. Even, rarely, one of the models they used in *Playboy* might appear more vigorous than languid, have a wry smile, austere eyes that impaled him, short dark hair. It was not necessarily if a woman or model looked similar, but the way she looked *at* whatever she was looking at, some glint of expression, a sharpness that hid something deeper and heavier, and, admittedly, in *Hustler* a girl might be looking with layers of deep meditation at a guy's cock, or over her shoulder with smoky complexity, locking eyes as he fucked her. But, really, once Cal closed his eyes, he didn't need the staged bare genitals.

Sometimes he did both, fixed a few instruments, then had his "alone-time." And was able to not be back home until Virginia was already in bed, on her side against the wall. He could steal in and lie still, and sometimes even have another session of alone-time when he woke, somewhere after midnight, and began the wake-doze slide toward 5:00 a.m. Daytime was much too busy, even if he was home, the kids were usually around, phone ringing, music playing. Hell yeah, he made thin excuses — the kids would hear, he was tired, he didn't feel well — until the thinness was on the verge of transparency and he had to give it a go, often faking a finale if he knew he was losing it, or after he'd figured it had been long enough to be enough.

No he didn't pretend Virginia was someone else. How would that even be possible? The basic ingredients weren't just a wet place to put it. He knew other guys really got off fucking any-thing who would fuck, the anonymity or the variety putting the fencepost in their dicks. Maybe he'd already had the biggest hard-on he would ever have — how many years ago now, almost three? — one he hadn't used that night, and it wasn't novelty or big tits or contortionist positions that caused it.

Now it was only this: Turrentine or Coltrane or Brecker on the stereo in his shop. An oscillating fan passed by his face in slow rhythm, cooling sweat that prickled between passes, until later, when the sweat would run crooked rivulets through his chest hair. Not a reverie just to see himself with the saxophone, himself on the stage or in the spotlight, himself speaking the mood with his reed, his horn, his breath, and body. If it's him playing, he plays for her. She comes into the club. She feels it in the way the horn phrases the tune into emptiness and longing. In subtone or with a hard core, burbling runs or sharp tonguing, vibrato growing wider, slower, or a deathcry scream. She would stop, framed for a moment in the open door, only a silhouette, except the sax player can't see, plays with his eyes closed. The door gently shuts, like an eyelid dropping before sleep. In darkness, she can see the sax player in the low floods on the tiny stage. Stars occasionally glint from the sax's bell. Dark backs of heads between her and him. Sometimes someone gets up, a black human shape blocking the sax player from her for a moment. But laughing, talking, glasses clinking don't cover what his horn is saying. She's still there by the door during the last two or three block chord changes, when his playout utters his ultimate plea. His last note is held, throbbing, and he opens his eyes and meets hers.

So he took care of himself.

Afterwards, *I'm sorry, I'm sorry, I'm going to have to,* pounded in his temples like a tune entrenched in his head. He said it to her postcard, which he kept in a drawer under scraps of cork sheets. He didn't have a photograph. He didn't need one. He said it to the sideways look she might give him, and the way she would probably say *Dang, Cal, who are you apologizing to . . . or for?*"

It feels like cheating.

Isn't it what happens when people are married? You must obviously know I'm not a virgin.

You don't love me, so it's not cheating for you . . . even though . . . even if you're . . . even when you're . . . somewhere else.

The sad smile, the dull glaze in her eyes before her gaze dropped away from his, the heartbeat of silence before her eyes returned, the almost imperceptible shrug. He finished before he'd slid the straps of her tank top down over her shoulders.

But felt he should apologize, again, remembering he would have to do it, next time Virginia brought it up. He tried to explain, while he had a cigarette, outside the closed-and-locked music store:

Sometimes I can tell it's coming because she's been crying. Or if she's still up when I get home. She might have a story about one of her friends dissing her, not being invited somewhere, her sister receiving a surprise delivery of flowers while at work. She wants to be hugged. I know it. Sometimes I manage it beside her, sideways, one arm across her shoulders for a few seconds, the usual EVERYTHING'LL-BE-OKAY bullshit. If that doesn't snuff it, the next thing will be her hand on the back of my neck when she takes my plate after dinner or my coffee mug after some TV show is over, then comes back from the kitchen and uses both hands, starts to massage my shoulders. Even though it does feel good, I don't let it go on too long. I usually get up and go outside for a cigarette. I know I should quit. But, really, WHY? Maybe it'll all be over sooner if I don't. When I go back inside, she'll be done with the dishes, if I was on a dinnertime break. I can either go back to the shop, or find some work outside. I'll be so sweaty and tired when I come back inside, instant sleep will be more honest, and defensible. But I know I can't hold off forever. Things are getting too hot. Not in a good way. It might defuse some of the poison. Some of the rage. Some of the fear. No, I'm not afraid. Not of her. Not really. The money . . . the kids . . . what does it really matter? So why do I have to appease if I'm not afraid? Just so it's all peaceful or at least neutral . . . until it's over. That's all. To do the thing required. Believe me, though, I don't want to. I have to.

Every time the next time loomed, the sick anticipation was what probably made him remember the last time. Virginia had used a different signal, a new one. It had been a Saturday evening before Cal went back for a stint at the shop, she told him she was making huevos rancheros Sunday morning, so plan to sleep in and let the aroma awaken him. But it hadn't been an aroma that woke him. Virginia put his *Stan Getz with Oscar Peterson* tape on a portable player and had come into the bedroom with it playing. When he'd opened his eyes, the tape player was on the floor by his nightstand, Stan was still playing the head of "I Want to Be Happy." He didn't see Virginia. But almost immediately had felt the bed jiggle as she'd gotten on from the other side, then moved up against him.

"No one's home but us," she'd whispered. He was on his side. Her hand crept under his top arm and onto his stomach. Just muscles and nerves reacting, like an anemone, the curl of his body closed tighter, his knees tucked up higher. She'd started kissing the back of his neck. Two choices were: squirming sideways and falling off the bed, or turning backwards and flailing to knock her away with an elbow. He'd remained static. The mantra became *get it over with, get it over with*. Her hand was pushing its way down below his stomach. His tight fetal position blocked access. But how long could that last? It could have easily ended in a completely differ-ent kind of exchange if she'd gotten her hand on him, found him flaccid, and then it stayed that way even after she started fondling. It had been imminently obvious what he had to do.

He'd rolled slowly, dislodging her arm and hand. Then, face to face, she could move her kissing to his mouth. He opened his lips enough but didn't use his tongue — he never had with her, he knew what she would consider his M.O. in that department. Likewise there was never any touching breasts, sucking nipples, he hadn't ever even encouraged complete undressing. Probably the first time, the time that was supposed to be the only time, he'd been so horny he was raging and ready simply because of the unexpected opportunity, the shots he'd downed, the weed, the whole stranger-sex mystique.

His own hand had pushed down to his crotch to do what was needed to get hard. And tried to do it without her knowing what he was doing. In fact, it seemed the rhythm, the motion wasn't familiar to her. Apparently she really did sleep through it, those times he'd been too lazy to get up and go into some other dark room at three a.m. to have an alone-time session. Even odder, (or maybe fortunate but he hadn't felt very lucky at the moment) the position of her pelvis was such that the back of his hand was coming in contact, and she'd grinded herself there, perhaps assuming that was his goal.

She'd started vocalizing softly. He was taking longer to get it up than he was accustomed. He needed an image, a story to follow. But it seemed so wrong to bring X into it. Wrong to X . . . and wouldn't anyone agree also wrong to Virginia?

That kind of thought stream naturally hadn't helped. But his dick knew his hand, and something was happening. In his bathroom drawer he'd stashed some condoms when he'd starting knowing the time was coming. Not just to prevent pregnancy but to prevent evidence that he wouldn't finish. He had to get a condom on without her realizing what he was doing. He gasped, "Just a sec, my bladder's bursting" and surged out of the bed, into the bathroom. He did pee, because she would hear if he didn't, then worked a little while longer with an image of X when they were sixteen that he hadn't brought up in this kind of situation for a while. That worked to get to the point where the condom went on. When he'd returned to the bed, thankfully, Virginia had rolled to her back, so moving to the final stage was not only accessible, but it would've been too weird if he hadn't.

Propped up on his arms, eyes shut, he'd realized he'd been

counting his thrusts when numbers in the thirties were pounding in his head. Then he'd consciously counted into the forties and decided it was enough. Breathing a little more rough, he'd stopped moving, tensed his body, let his head drop and hang. He stayed still, again had found himself counting, and this time when he got to twelve, he withdrew. He'd removed himself from the bed as well, returning to the bathroom to wad the condom in some toilet paper and discard it. She had no reason to paw through the trash, but still, he'd been in his underwear out in the garage emptying the bathroom trash into the big container, even tying off the bag, when Virginia had come to the kitchen to start huevos rancheros, which turned out pretty damn good.

Usually, coming home late, he didn't have an urgent unease. But that night, after the party, after midnight when he got home, Virginia was awake.

It was dark, but he could tell Virginia was sitting up. He turned away, pretended to be feeling for the light just inside the bathroom door. The dim bathroom light was the only one he used, mornings getting up before dawn and coming to bed after her in darkness. If she was asleep, he didn't even worry about how loud his pee hit the water or the toilet's flush, but tonight tried to do both more softly. Just before he turned out the bathroom light, he saw Virginia still had her wig on.

Cal sat on the side of the bed, his body in the shape of a question mark. From behind him, Virginia asked, "What're you doing?"

"Taking off my socks." His socks still on his feet, his feet on the floor, his hands on either side of his legs on the mattress.

Virginia shifted, maybe getting closer to him. "Didn't today make you think?"

Cal couldn't think of an answer.

"Babes, what's wrong?"

"Nothing. Six or seven horns came into the shop today."

"Oh. But didn't today just make you *think*?"

"Okay, what was today supposed to make me think?"

She was closer behind him. "Birthday parties! I wish we could have a birthday party every week, but that would mean Trin is growing up too fast."

"What is she, eleven going on eighteen?"

"I know, girls are such sweet wild things."

His sudden intake of breath might have sounded like a sigh. He cleared his throat to cover.

"Babes... don't you think... I think you need a child of your own."

Cal hadn't moved, and she hadn't touched him yet. He swallowed, clutched the edge of the mattress a little harder. When she shifted even closer, the old box-spring groaned and the mattress noticeably sank in the spot where he sat, which would help her to slide against him. He could stabilize it by lying down on his back, but didn't think there was room now.

All the furniture had been Virginia's, taken when she'd moved out of her husband's house. She'd wanted new stuff and said, "You shouldn't have to use that asshole Merle's dresser, Merle's sofa, even Merle's *bed*." Cal had said if they still worked, then why throw them away? He didn't say that whatever Merle had done in this bed meant nothing to him, but Virginia seemed to believe it should, because she'd said, "I'm a different person now, I'm not the woman who slept in this bed before, I'm like that goose who's been born into a whole new world." Earlier that day Cal had told her about a music lesson he'd been giving where the kid came in using the same bad embouchure every week, and

Cal taught him how to do it right, and every week he came back doing it wrong again, "like a goose who learns where the food is and every day can't find it again because he's born into a whole new world."

He realized her bizarre suggestion was still hanging in the air, as though he were considering it. "Let's just raise the two you have."

"No, Cal, you really need a child of your own. Every man needs his own child."

"Can't every man decide for himself what he needs?" Cal tapped his socks on the shabby shag carpet. Virginia also wanted new carpet, and he knew it wasn't unreasonable. Every room was a different disheveled color, with stains and decades of dirt.

"Sometimes you don't know until you have it. It's what you need. Let's start trying. Let's — "

Cal stood before she could drape herself over his shoulders. "I think Trinity needs your full attention. Did you know she makes other girls — "

"Cal, this would be for us."

He propped himself against the wall with one hand and stripped his socks off his feet. "I don't think anything needs to be changed. We've got enough to deal with as it is."

"I just feel it's right, Babes, I just know it's what you need, I just...do."

He held his socks in one hand. The clothes hamper was at the foot of the bed, beside the dresser. He thought his walking over there, lifting the lid, placing the socks in the hamper, and taking the four steps back to where he'd been standing probably seemed like acting. But when he got back to where he'd started, he said, "I'm not sure you're able to be objective about this kind of decision."

"It's easy for me to be objectionable."

Cal was standing in the dark beside his bed, still wearing jeans and a t-shirt. He felt himself nodding. He imagined a burst of brittle laughter. *Dang, Cal.*

Virginia was half reclining on her hip just about where he would have to lie down if he were going to sleep tonight. "Really, trust me, a child in your hand is worth . . . Well, you don't know because you haven't . . . you *need* your own, Cal, you just do." Virginia rolled a little more to her back, one knee still bent. She lifted the wig's longish curly hair out from under her shoulder and lay it on the pillow. "C'mon, Babes, c'mon, trust me, come here with me, let's . . . tonight."

"I'm not . . ." Cal muttered.

"What, Babes?"

"I'm tired, Virginia. Horns have stacked up at the shop while I was playing around here today. Move over."

He was lying down, covered up, open eyes staring at the closed bedroom door, with Virginia back on her side of the bed. He could feel the telltale vibration, hear the occasional sniffle. He realized he was still dressed in jeans and t-shirt. A piece of shit, still fully dressed, lying in bed beside a woman he'd asked to come live here with him.

Some years later, in the spring — February in the south-central California wasteland — a bird pecked at the windows of his house, sitting on the sill, tap-tap-tapping, painting the sill with purple shit. Two, three, four different windows, all day, rat-a-tatting. One morning, Cal was cleaning window screens, because the major form of precipitation here was dust. He also washed the sills, a job not tacitly included in the screen cleaning task that had been not-so-tacitly requested of him. But it would have been difficult to ignore the plum-and-black splats of shit and pretend the chore was complete. The screens were drying propped against the garage door, the windows cranked open, so the bird achieved its life's wish. It was finally in the house. And, inside, realized this was not what it wanted at all.

Cal caught the bird in a sheet, put it in a cardboard box. He drove it twenty miles away, into a state park in the desert. When he opened the box, the bird, wings somewhat tattered from its hours up against the window glass, flew instantly, gone in a fluttering second, the force of its departure knocking the box out of Cal's hand. Gone so fast he barely could follow the directional line of flight. But thought, perhaps, it was — by accident, just fluke — the route back to town.

Later, the screens back in place, the windows shut, the bird returned, tapping, not knowing why it so fixatedly wanted this thing it wanted, this thing that has frayed its feathers and bewildered its instinct, this thing that upon achieving led to imprisonment, darkness, and miles of flight, only to return and want it again.

He looked it up. It was a male brown-headed cowbird. Instead of spending its time with a mate, building a nest and making hundreds of daily trips back and forth with bugs to stuff down the pre-fledglings' throats, the male cowbird had time to spend pecking at windows because the female, producing up to a dozen eggs a season, laid them into the nests of other, usually smaller, birds. Industrious sparrows, dove, towhees, catbirds. The cowbird hatchlings grew faster, frequently crowded the bio-kids out of the nest and occupied the step parents' time and resources. Why wasn't it the duped, dutiful sparrow or dove pecking with aberrant wretchedness at his window?

In the room where Trinity used to sleep, Cal got his saxophone out, sat on the bed fingering the keys, but didn't put the mouthpiece between his lips.

ACKNOWLEDGMENTS

Acknowledgments and thanks made to the following publishers who first published these stories in books:

Fiction Collective Two for
"From Hunger," "Animal Acts," "Dead Dog," and "The Family Bed" which appeared in *Animal Acts* (1989)

Fiction Collective Two for
"Second Person," "Is It Sexual Harassment Yet?" and "His Crazy Former Assistant and His Sweet Old Mother," which appeared in *Is It Sexual Harassment Yet?* (1991)

FC2 Black Ice Books for
"Revelation Countdown," "Not Here," and "Between Signs," which appeared in *Revelation Countdown* (1993)

FC2 for
"Former Virgin," "Let's Play Doctor," "Hesitation," and "Dog & Girlfriend," which appeared in *Former Virgin* (1997)

Chiasmus Press for
"Her First Bra," which appeared in *Many Ways to Get It, Many Ways to Say It* (2005)

Red Hen Press for
"What If," "Proportion," "My Husband's Best Friend," "Trickle-Down Timeline," and "Our Time is Up," which appeared in *Trickle-Down Timeline* (2009)

The Coachella Review for
"Twister Party" (2016)

CRIS MAZZA's last title was a real-time memoir titled *Something Wrong With Her* chronicling the 25-year journey to reunite with a boy from her past. She then became co-producer, writer, and lead actress for a feature film, *Anorgasmia*, a fictional sequel to that memoir, a groundbreaking blend of memoir, documentary and fiction. Mazza has seventeen other titles including her first novel, *How to Leave a Country*, which won the PEN/Nelson Algren Award for book-length fiction, and the critically acclaimed *Is It Sexual Harassment Yet?* She is a professor in the Program for Writers at the University of Illinois at Chicago.